The
Lazarus
✦ Heart

Voyager

POPPY Z. BRITE

The Crow™
The Lazarus Heart

*Inspired by the series
created by James O'Barr*

HarperCollins*Publishers*

Voyager
An Imprint of HarperCollins*Publishers*
77–85 Fulham Palace Road,
Hammersmith, London W6 8JB

A Paperback Original 1998
1 3 5 7 9 8 6 4 2

A catalogue record for this book
is available from the British Library

ISBN 0 00 648365 8

Printed and bound in Great Britain by
Caledonian International Book Manufacturing Ltd, Glasgow

for Caitlín

Poppy Z. Brite was born in 1967 in New Orleans. She has worked as an artist's model, a stripper and (since 1991) a full-time writer. She has published three novels, a short story collection and has edited the anthologies *Love in Vein I* and *II*. She recently published the biography *Courtney Love: The Real Story*. She is currently working on her new novel and her second collection of short stories.

When I have sex with someone I forget who I am. For a minute I even forget I'm human. It's the same thing when I'm behind a camera. I forget I exist.

—Robert Mapplethorpe

There is a dark side to the human soul that is filled with conflict and torment. It is a side of the human soul that few people are brave enough to explore.

—The priest who said mass
at Mapplethorpe's funeral

acknowledgments

Thanks to John Edward Ames, Jennifer Caudle,
Jeff Conner, Richard Curtis, Christopher DeBarr,
O'Neil DeNoux, John Douglas, Christa Faust,
Neil Gaiman, Caitlín R. Kiernan, Rich Miller,
James O'Barr, Jeanne O'Brien, Edward R. Pressman,
David J. Schow, John Silbersack, Jimmy Vines,
and Leilah Wendell.

one

DOWN THROUGH THAT PART OF THE EVENING THAT IS NEITHER night nor day, the big black bird comes, finally, to the old cemetery in the old city on the river. Such a long flight back from the places where the dead wait, marking time until they've forgotten what time is, until they've forgotten even themselves and nothing remains but these earthly stones and the moldering skeletons they signify, and even these will pass in time.

The crow descends through the low, thin clouds that have lingered behind an afternoon thunderstorm, fading blue sky traded for gray. A woman walking along Prytania Street hears the bird's grating cry, looks up to see a violent smudge of ebony against the summer twilight, crosses herself, and walks a little faster past the crumbling walls of Lafayette No. 1 Cemetery.

Maneuvering between magnolia branches, brushing against stiff dark leaves like dripping dragon scales, the crow follows instinct and duty. With nothing that could be called thought, but with something more than the simplest bird impressions, the crow understands the immediate and undeniable task before her. She understands the terrible things that must be done before she can return to the clarity of her carrion life.

And so the crow finds the smallish mausoleum near the center of the cemetery. The pale gray marble is fresh and polished, not yet blasted by the delta sun and angry Gulf storms, a modest jewel tucked between its ancient, weathered neighbors. Around it are monuments placed over the course of more than a hundred and fifty sweltering years, fallen crosses and angels with broken wings, inscriptions worn smooth as silk. And then this newcomer, at once tasteful and decadent: a tomb that speaks of the wealth of its dead, but speaks also of their otherness.

The crow lights upon the vaulted roof, her talons gripping the slippery bronze acroterion above the sealed door. The acroterion is cast in the reclining form of a pretty young man, hands bound above his head, ankles bound as well, and a gag tied tightly across his mouth. His head is bowed, his eyes closed in perfect supplication. The crow shifts nervously, impatiently, from one ebony claw to the other. Standing on the bronze boy's shoulder, the metal still years away from the streaking stigmata of verdigris, she caws once more: for herself, for the dim uncertainty she feels. Then she folds her wings, and the resurrection begins.

So much damage to a corpse after death, the slicing ministrations of pathologists and undertakers. Because this man died violently there was an autopsy, organs removed, divined, dumped back into their cold cradle of meat and bone. The application of glue to seal eyelids and hold fingers together, lips sewn neatly shut, caustic chemicals painted on or pumped into this body sealed beneath the crow. All these things she must undo before the soul can be returned, and the bird carries the knowledge of these tasks in her skull, knows them now as she knows the sweet, greasy smell of roadkill on summer asphalt miles away, as she knows the simple routine of her life.

A silent flash of lightning far away, toward the swamps where the storm has retreated. The crow blinks her weary eyes and pecks once at the bronze sculpture. The sound echoes softly through the necropolis around her. There's a faint scratch where her sharp beak struck the burnished metal, and she pecks at the boy's shoulder again.

2

It makes a sound she can feel through her feet, a sound that reverberates within the marble confines of the mausoleum, growing louder in the dark spaces along the walls, louder still inside the newest coffin on its granite pedestal, amplified instead of dulled by passage through stone and steel.

Selective, though, this magic. She has come for one man, and one man only. The man who sleeps beside him will hear nothing, his ill-used, pieced-together body remaining in stasis, indifferent to what has begun. The crow's dagger beak strikes the acroterion a third and final time, and now there is movement inside the mausoleum, inside the newest coffin.

The thread that holds the dead man's thin lips closed tugs itself free, drawn out through needlepoint incisions, and falls away. The cyanoacrylate that holds his eyelids closed, that holds his fingers together across his chest, becomes brittle and then becomes no more than dust. These things are simple though, and the crow shudders, captured now in the dark and irreversible process she has started.

The long incisions in the abdomen reject their stitches also and begin to heal, flesh knitting as if in time-lapse photography. The crow cries out again, giving up parts of herself to the accelerating restoration of the body below, life chasing death. Even the bird's mind understands the wrongness in these actions, the violation of an order more primal and sacred than all the religions of mankind, but she is helpless to withdraw. She huddles on the mausoleum roof and feels her life borrowed, the measured draining of her life for the working of these magics.

There are escape clauses built into the fabric of the universe, undeniable rules that have brought her here. The crow knows none of this, only that she should be moving, flying swiftly and high and far, far away from this soulless place where the memory of life lies pinned beneath heavy stone.

Still more stitches ravel, and the body bleeds not blood but an acrid hemorrhage of embalming fluid, milky spray from opened arteries. The heart is shocked rudely back to life, pumping alien liquid through desiccated veins, and this time the crow does not caw, she *screams* as the body beneath her expels four gallons of embalming fluid into its coffin. A pulsing stream from

3

the carotid, from an incision in the upper arm and another in the groin, until the circulatory system is completely empty, purged, and the Lazarus heart pumps only formaldehyde-stinking air.

As the open arteries knit themselves closed again, another trick is turned and the crow trembles on her perch, sick and maybe dying; she would believe herself dying if she understood death as such. Blood from the genetic memory of pickled cells, water from wine, pours from the heart to fill the parched pathways of arteries, veins, and capillaries. The crow spreads her wings in sudden panic and pain, black feathers against the growing night, as the lips of the dead man part. Collapsed lungs heave, then expand and contract, forcing more bitter fluid out past his rouged lips, fighting to draw precious breath for the first time in five days, coughing, vomiting death. The crow folds her wings again, hurting, but this part is done, at least; this part is over.

The bird crouches on the immaculate bronze victim and listens and waits for whatever has to happen next. Far away, toward Lake Pontchartrain and restless waters the color of bad coffee, there is the gentle, threatening sound of thunder.

He has no memory of waking, only the sudden, jolting knowledge that he *is* awake, the impossible pain of the first breath. There's something filling his mouth, and his cold tongue struggles to push it aside, to spit out the sodden, cottony mass. His eyes are on fire, like when he was a child and caught pinkeye and his mother held a warm washcloth to his face to soften the crust that sealed his eyes shut. If she were here, she might do that for him now, might take away his confusion and pain.

But she is not here. Jared Poe, who knows little else, knows this much: that he is alone, beyond alone, somewhere more solitary than alone can ever be. Smothering in that certainty, he exhales, a jagged, rattling sound that could be final breath instead of rebirth, and he opens his eyes.

Even the diffuse light around him is blinding after so profound a night, after such complete and perfect darkness. Jared Poe shuts his eyes again, tightly, before the glare burns away his thin lids and leaves him helpless to stare into it forever.

I was dreaming, he thinks. *I dreamed I was flying*. A useless little thought mired in so much agony, the pain that soaks every inch of his body, coalescent with the stinking wetness around him. His chest heaves, a sudden, involuntary gasp, the contraction of too many unused muscles at once. His back arches as the air is forced out again. Something vile fills his throat, fluids driven from his lungs or stomach or both, now spilling out of his mouth.

I was flying above New Orleans with black wings, he thinks. The next gasp makes him bite his tongue, a little harder and he might have bitten it in half. His mouth fills with cleansing, living warmth, iron-water taste to wash away the bitter burn of chemicals. He rolls onto his side, coughing, reaching for the shreds of dream already fading, slipping from him before he can be sure they were even his. *Flying above New Orleans*, and then a clearer thought, like drawing that first breath again—*I was dead*.

Jared Poe screams inside his coffin, puts the oxygen forcing its way into his unwilling lungs to good use. He screams against the hateful flood of memory, the images that follow from what he cannot deny—*I was dead*. Flashpowder revelations as unwanted as the life flowing back into him and the death leaking out. The big Cuban motherfucker with the .35 Magnum tattooed on his right arm, the Virgin Mary on his left, and when Jared looked down, the hand shoving the sharpened spoon into his gut. Pushing it in, the metal going deeper and deeper, twisting. Another scream and the sound of steel bars sliding shut inside the carefully constructed hell of Angola. Lockdown. Jared's stiff hands clench. He pounds the padded satin walls of his new prison.

A little farther into himself and the stale library smell of the courthouse comes back, the condemning sound of the gavel and the vindicated mutter of the crowd as the verdict was read aloud, the doughy fat woman with ill-fitting dentures who read the words to the judge, all the faces he didn't know.

"That's far *enough*—" Jared Poe is making words with the screams, with his fury and the impact of his fists against the walls of the coffin. "That's fucking far enough! I don't want to see any more!"

But there is so much more to see, so many more little supernovas going off behind his eyes, and every explosion is another secret he wants to keep from himself, another piece of the almighty shitty puzzle he's trying not to solve.

The cigarette and sweat smell of the police car, the handcuffs biting into his wrists. "We ought to just drive over to Algiers," the cop in the passenger seat said. "You know that, Henry? We ought to just drive this faggot pervert son-of-a-bitch right over the river and let him suck on a gun. Blow his murdering brains out." The cop behind the wheel just laughed, is laughing still, like the frantic wings of black birds in burning cages, and Jared feels the metal of the coffin begin to buckle around him.

But not yet, for here comes the last and worst memory. He's climbing the stairs to their apartment on Ursulines, his and Benny's apartment, and he doesn't want to see but it's already out before there is any hope of denying the acid rush of images. His key wrestling with the stubborn lock, the door swinging open on so much red, red like lipstick and roses and carnations, oh, God just let it be *anything* but what he knows it is. The groceries he's carried from the French Market slipping through his arms, scattering across their foyer that smells like a slaughterhouse. The same smell as the time he did a shoot in a slaughterhouse, the red stench that had stayed in his nostrils for weeks afterward.

"I won't, I won't, I won't," he mutters, a helpless litany to gods he has never believed in. "*I will not see this again.*"

The coffin bursts, shatters like something made of Elmer's glue and Popsicle sticks, and Jared is falling. A very short fall to the stone floor as hard, as cold and senseless, as the sight of Benny scattered across their bed, his hands and feet still neatly trussed, thoughtful Boy Scout knots joining wrists and ankles that are divided from everything else, from the careless litter of limbs and organs . . .

6

"Oh, fuck, oh, fuck me," Jared whispers through ragged sobs and oily tears that drip from his face and pool on the marble floor. "Benjamin," he sighs, and there is more pain in those three syllables than his body could ever hope to contain. The coffin shrapnel raining down around him clatters like brittle bones or jackstraws.

He isn't sure how much time has passed since he opened his eyes, since he began to breathe again. The tiny stained-glass window set high above the mausoleum door has gone from the darkest shades of green and cobalt blue to black, so he knows only that it's night now. Another night in this little city of the dead, and night in the world of living men beyond. Jared sits with his back against the stone wall and stares at Benny's coffin. This is all he has done for all the minutes or hours he hasn't bothered to count. He hasn't been able to bring himself to touch it, the mahogany glinting faintly in the gloom, the brass and rotted spray of flowers on its lid. He doesn't need to touch it to know it's real.

There comes the faint, sharp sound of scratching overhead. Jared looks up, realizes he's been hearing the sound all along, ignoring it the way he has ignored the aching emptiness in his stomach, the dryness in his throat. The way he has ignored everything but Benny's coffin, still sitting undisturbed beside the ruin of splinters and twisted metal that was his own.

Jared closes his eyes again. There are no more tears left in him to cry, only the hurt that rolls over and through him in endless ebony waves, battering him as smooth as the stone at his back. There is only hurt and loss and the bottomless, churning anger.

As he sits listening to the restless sounds above, busy little claws like Morse code or impatiently drumming fingers, Jared begins to comprehend that it is precisely this anger he must embrace now. This anger that will get him up and moving, that might hold some purpose. There can be no response to the loss he has suffered, no sane answer but oblivion, and now that's been stolen from him too. But the rage is a thing beyond him, a thing that wants out, a hungry beast that can be fed and sated.

All these things he hears hidden in the scratching at the roof of the mausoleum. Now he remembers the dream of midnight wings, the dizzying dream of flight, and he rises on legs as stiff as scarecrow sticks. He stands in the dark and listens to his heart, to the faint rumble of traffic on damp streets, and the black bird calls to him.

If the door to the mausoleum was bolted, the crow has seen to that too, and as Jared pushes at the metal he feels the first hint of a physical strength he never knew in life. The tall door swings open as if it is made of plywood, disused hinges squealing loudly for a teeth-gritting instant. Then there is only the gentle sound of the light rain again, gathering on the roofs of the voiceless inhabitants of Lafayette Cemetery.

Jared looks back once, his eyes running over Benny's elegant coffin and the shattered mess where his own lay, before he steps out into the night. He pushes the door shut so he can't see anymore, so that nothing can get in. He lingers there a moment, his face pressed against the cold, wet metal, taking some vague comfort in the steady warmth of the raindrops. Then the bird caws, loud and harsh, and he turns around. The four steps leading up to the mausoleum are decorated with a scatter of votive candles and flowers in various stages of wilt and decay. *Someone still comes here*, he thinks. Lucrece, and maybe others—perhaps the core group of fans he retained after the incident, what the press called the "sicko contingent."

The bird lands on Jared's shoulder, damp feathers pressed against his neck as if there were some shelter there. The night stretches out before him, past the cemetery walls, stretches the way a great sable tomcat would stretch. Something out there is vaster and more confident than this fetid city and its infinite corruptions, perhaps even vaster than his loss.

Jared begins to listen to what the bird has to say.

8

• • •

Sometimes, like tonight, the man in the big house by the river calls himself Jordan. There is a river called Jordan in the Bible, and he likes the names of rivers. Sometimes he calls himself Joseph Lethe, for another river and what it means, and sometimes he's Stanley Hudson. But these are secret names that he never tells anyone—except those few he's chosen. Those he's sure will never be in a position to spread the word, to give away his names carelessly, like telephone numbers on filthy fag-bar rest room walls.

The newspapers do not know his names. To them he is the Bourbon Street Ripper, a flashy moniker earned for the first one the cops found, years and years ago. He is sure that name sells more papers than any of his real ones could. Lies always sell better than the truth. He always reads about what he has done in the papers, but he never saves the things he reads, the official police comments and the wild speculations of illiterate journalists. That, he thinks, would be like taking a trip to Manhattan and buying an I ♥ NY T-shirt.

Death is not cheap, despite what the world may believe or how it behaves. It is actually quite expensive; he has been able to finance his research only because his mother left him drilling rights to some land in Texas. Perverse to the end, she'd waited until after the oil bust to die, so there was not an enormous amount of money from the sale of the land. But it is enough. His needs are not great, except where his research is concerned. He will not cheapen death.

From his high window, the man who is Jordan tonight can see the river winding silent and powerful through the stormy night, a fat brown snake sliding between the levees. The most powerful thing in the world, a river like that.

He waits for another flash of lightning and closes the curtains before the thunderclap. There is unfinished work here, and he cannot remember what distracted him. Something at the window or down in the streets, but whatever it might have been, it's gone now and the one he brought home with him is waiting. He doesn't always bring Them home, only the very special ones, the ones who have gone all the way and so deserve more time, more attention. The ones that have the most to teach him about what They are, what abominations They have become.

Like *this* one: stretched out on the shiny steel operating table in the highest room of his house on the river. It watches him as he turns away from the window, watches him with wide eyes that are still very aware. He is always amazed at Their tolerance for physical and psychological pain. Another part of the mystery, another thing that excludes them from humanity and makes Them so dangerous.

But not half so dangerous as he. No, not even one quarter *that* dangerous.

This one, for example. This one with the Louisiana driver's license that claims its name is Marjory Marie West, that has an F recorded for its sex. This one that he's already started upon, but still it watches him, alert, aware, as if waiting for a chance to escape. As if there could ever be such a chance. Even though he sliced out its tongue before the Demerol wore off, cauterizing the slippery stump so it wouldn't bleed to death. Even though the tongue floats in its neat jar of formalin in plain sight. It's still hanging in there, this *thing*, and this is important.

The man runs bloody latex-gloved fingers through his oily black hair, pushes his straggly bangs from his flat blue-gray eyes. He selects a scalpel from his tray of surgical instruments. Some of the instruments he has ordered from medical supply houses or bought as sets in antique stores. Others he has made himself, the ones he couldn't buy because no one's ever needed them before.

On the table, it watches him, this sexless creature that would hide itself in the world of men and women, the black and white world of opposites and opposition. He knows it is not merely evil, knows that's the sort of shit a crazy man might think. There is no evil. Rather, it is *alien*, viral, and he must be careful in his campaign if he is to succeed. If the world is to be free of these monstrosities once and for all.

The man who is Jordan tonight checks the restraints, the

10

strong leather straps and steel buckles. Soon he will pull back the sheet, all that hides its impossible body now that he has removed the deceiving clothes. And it watches him, and the thunder growls its useless protest from somewhere above the house beside the river.

Just because the man keeps no scrapbook doesn't mean he has no memories. A scrapbook would be tawdry, tasteless. There is nothing tasteless about the records he keeps in his head.

It's been seven years, seven long red years like a bolt of scarlet lace, since the sweltering August morning when his work first made headlines. That one had been a cross-dressing hustler known on the streets of the Quarter only as Josie, barely nineteen, though "she" could have passed for twenty-five. Most of what he left was found stuffed into three garbage cans outside a tourist bar on Bourbon Street. *Most* of what he left, because it had taken a lot of blood to cover the walls of the filthy alley next to the bar. There had been no witnesses, but plenty of talk from the two garbagemen who found the dented cans crammed full of meat, and photographs of the parts he left hanging from a fire escape like strings of Christmas popcorn.

That wasn't his first, of course. Only the first that he'd wanted Them to see.

"There comes a point," he wrote in one of his yellow legal pads, "when you must show a little of yourself to the enemy in exchange for Their fear. Fear must surely weaken Them."

So four days later he left a second body in a hotel on Rampart, a fat transvestite named Petey, plump discard floating facedown in a tub of soapy water and blood, naked except for his precious lingerie and high heels. A hotel maid found this one. When the police were finally done with her, the man had read, she moved back to Chicago. Petey's real name turned out to be Ralph Larkin, a happily married father of three who ran a hardware store in Metairie and was a long-standing member of a local chapter of the transvestite "sorority," Tri Ess.

The man can still remember how Petey begged for his life,

11

how he swore he didn't know anything about the Invasion or the Cabal or even the Gay Mafia, but They all lie. Even the pretenders, the hetero pricks hiding hard-ons inside satin panties, the ones who only want to dress up in ladies' clothing and know they'll never be fit to cross over. Jordan suspects that they are all controlled by implants, nanites hidden in the sinus cavities or the rectums, miniscule robots that would look like BBs or bird shot, if he could ever find one. Jordan suspects that the nanites are programmed to teleport out of any body that is captured or killed . . . or perhaps they simply dissolve, leaving no trace.

It's almost midnight now, and the transsexual on the operating table has lost consciousness again. He has broken ammonia ampules beneath its nose three times already, shocking it back into the world, but this time it may be slipping away for good. He sighs, lays aside the speculum and the long probe with fish-hooks soldered along its length, and looks down at his notes. A dark smear of gore mars the close-ruled yellow paper, making it hard to read what he's written; Jordan knows he'll have to copy the page over again later.

Its chest abruptly expands, sucking air, revealing the faint crescent scars beneath the breasts. The scars no one is supposed to see. But *he* sees everything. When it exhales, there's an uneven, wet sound from its chest. Its eyes flutter weakly open to gaze at him one last time. This one is very, very pretty, but he quickly and expertly pushes aside anything like sympathy. He's done enough experiments to know that the compassion and regret he sometimes feels are just chemically induced reactions, triggered by genetically engineered pheromones excreted in Their sweat and tears.

"It's not too late," he says, although that's a lie, of course. It has been too late for this one since he bought it a drink just after sundown. "It's not too late to come clean. I can be merciful."

And then it's gone and Jordan is alone in the room, and

there's nothing for him to think about but the smell of its bladder emptying on the tabletop.

His memories are as clear as the words he puts on paper.

Sometimes, when the answers he seeks seem forever out of reach, the memories are his only comfort. Reassuring memories of his resolve and his boldness and the harvests of his dedication.

Hardly a week after the fat man in the tub, Joseph Lethe picked up one of the Quarter gutterpunks, a baby queen he lured into his car with a vial of crystal meth and drove all the way to Arabi before he pulled over and put a bullet in the kid's head. He never asked for a name and the boy never volunteered one. The boy was wearing tacky thrift store drag, '70s retro polyester and a black wig that fell off when Joseph pulled the body from the passenger seat. He chained the corpse to the rear bumper of his car and drove unpaved back roads through the bayou until nearly dawn, the lonely places between cypress and tall whispering grass, no one to see but the birds and alligators. He'd wrapped the raw and featureless thing in plastic and left it under an oak in Audubon Park.

After that, he decided to become Jordan again for a while, as he watched the city begin to draw the connections he'd left for it to make. As he watched the fear settle over the Quarter's gay populace like a theater curtain falling halfway through a film. He walked the streets and *smelled* the fear, like fresh pomegranates and old gardenias, as it ripened.

So there could be no mistaking his message, he did one more. A postoperative female-to-male transsexual, castrated, its surgically constructed genital abomination sewn up inside its mouth. That one had read his signs well enough, had even been interviewed by a local TV news crew investigating the Ripper slayings. That one had claimed there was someone preying on the city's transgendered community, a serial killer. Seeing that made Jordan proud: He hadn't been misunderstood by those that mattered. Never mind that the police were so fucking apathetic or incompetent they couldn't find their

13

reflection in a mirror. The point was that *They* understood. They would spread the word that They were no longer free to infiltrate the city unopposed.

He'd meant to stop then, to slip back into his old habits. Taking the occasional strays and freaks, the ones that would never be more than missing persons, missing but not *missed*.

But the fleshy, sweet smell of Their fear was intoxicating. Now, sometimes, he thinks that might have been a trick to lure him into the open: an actual chemical They secreted to addict him. Given enough time, after all, even the cops might come around. It had been like trying to put toothpaste back into the tube when he tried to stop the public displays. Instead, he hunted farther afield and less often. And the years rolled by and he has learned. Even if Their numbers have not diminished appreciably, at least They know that *he* knows.

And he knows that They are afraid of him, because if They weren't, he would be dead by now.

Jordan finishes cleaning up the vivisection table, runs all the instruments through the autoclave and puts away the new tissue samples, some floating in jars of formalin, others stored in Tupperware containers and stashed in the antique refrigerator rumbling noisily to itself in one corner of the room. After he has wrapped the transsexual's body in blue plastic garbage bags and duct tape, he returns to his seat by the window.

The man with river names opens the curtains again and looks down at the black crook of the Mississippi, the glittering lights of the city reflected in it. Later he will carry the body out to his car, but first he will allow himself time to reflect on what he has seen tonight. And the other things on his mind, the dreams he's started having: dreams of flying high above the infected city of New Orleans. Dreams of black feathers and a familiar face he can't quite seem to place.

A barge on its way to the Gulf of Mexico flashes a slow beacon, and he watches without blinking as it passes in the rainy night.

• • •

When she has finished her small dinner, the olives and French bread and dry bit of tuna fish, Lucrece clears the table, puts her dirty dishes in the sink, and sits down again, very still in the straight-backed wooden chair, watching the clock above the stove until the sun goes down. There's been rain off and on all afternoon, and now it's on again, spitting against the roof of the apartment. The sound makes her sleepy, so she listens a little harder to the music from the stereo in the next room, Nick Cave like worn velvet wrapped around rusty gears growling "Do You Love Me?" So much sadness in that voice and those words, but so much courage too.

When the shadows have grown big enough and dark enough to fill the courtyard outside the window, Lucrece leaves the kitchen. Her bare feet are almost silent on the hardwood floors as she walks along the short hall leading to the big front room that looks out onto Ursulines. The persistent dark has found its way in here too. She takes a book of matches from the glass-block coffee table and lights a sandalwood-scented candle. The warm pool of light pushes the night back to the dusty corners of the room, and Lucrece pauses at her gaunt reflection in a mirror, the huge mirror in its ornate cherry frame, something Benny found in an antique store on Magazine Street and gave to Jared for his thirtieth birthday.

Lucrece cautiously touches her pale face, traces the hard lines of her high cheekbones, her full lips painted the same kohl black as her eyelids. She can see that the circles under her eyes have gotten a lot deeper since the last time she noticed, or maybe it's the way she's holding the candle. In this light she looks so much like him, the same pallor that Benny spent years cultivating. Lucrece wears it honestly, the dues of so many months spent away from the sun, of near-fasting. She has to close her eyes and turn away from the image in the mirror, the ghost-reflection of the woman her brother wore like a change of clothes: she cannot bear to see that reflection alive and breathing while he lies so cold and alone.

"Jesus," she whispers, standing motionless for a moment as

15

the sickening blend of déjà vu and vertigo slowly fades. She concentrates on the sound of the rain, on the words Nick Cave is singing in the dark apartment.

Benjamin and Lucas DuBois were born in Pike County, Mississippi, in a town so small and ugly it was usually left off the maps. Identical twin boys born to a girl too young and frightened to care for them, and so when she finally ran off to Pensacola with a traveling evangelist, they went to live with their Great-aunt Isolde. She owned a rambling derelict of a mansion just off what passed for the town square, a house built twenty years before the Civil War and showing every sun-bleached decade of its age. Their mother never returned for them, though sometimes she sent postcards. These were almost always gaudy religious scenes: their favorite was a 3-D picture of the burning of Sodom and Gomorrah. Hold it one way, and you could see a pair of wicked-looking spire-topped cities crumbling beneath angry skies; turn it the other way and the Hand of God hovered over a fiery orange mushroom cloud.

When she was a girl, Aunt Isolde had gone away to college in Starkville, and she taught the twins how to read and write before they turned four. She read aloud to them from the books that filled her house—*Treasure Island* and *Wuthering Heights*, all of Dickens, *Dracula* and *Ivanhoe* and Mark Twain. She taught them history and the lives of the saints, geography and a little French. In return, they wrote plays and acted them out for the old woman, raiding trunks for costumes, improvising their sets from the musty Victorian furniture.

One Christmas, the year they turned twelve and Aunt Isolde turned sixty-three, the twins performed two scenes from *Antony and Cleopatra*. They learned all their lines by heart and even made costumes on an old Singer sewing machine they'd found in the attic. Lucas played Cleopatra, and for the death scene they used a live rat snake they'd caught hibernating in the cellar. Aunt Isolde was delighted, shouting, "Bravo! Bravo!" until she was hoarse.

More Christmases passed, and the pretty boys grew into prettier, disturbingly perfect teenagers, their hair dark as anthracite coal and their eyes the muted green of dogwood leaves at midsummer. They hardly ever left the house and its vast, overgrown yard except to run errands for Isolde, and they knew the rumors the people in town whispered behind their backs. How unnatural it was for two boys to be raised by an old spinster lady in her creepy old house, not even attending a public school, much less church. The townspeople had never liked Isolde anyway, because she'd kept herself apart from them even as a young girl, had spent too much time with books and not enough with boys.

Sometimes, as the twins were walking quickly along the red-dust road that connected their house with the rest of town, other children would hide in the bushes and throw rocks or dried-up cow pies at them, calling them sissies and weirdos. Lucas always wanted to run, would tug at his brother's shirt sleeve and beg him not to stop, not to listen. But Benjamin did listen, and sometimes he stopped on the path and hurled the rocks back. Once he hit a boy named Jesse Aderholdt in the head and Jesse and his friend Waylon Dillard chased them all the way back to the house. When they reached the rickety old front gate, Lucas crying and screaming for help and Benjamin yelling at him to shut the hell up, Isolde was waiting with a baseball bat. Jesse and Waylon stopped in the road, stood safely out of reach shouting profanities while the old woman led the twins inside.

"You dried-up old cunt," they yelled. "You goddamned old witch! You *better* protect those little queers or we'll kill 'em." Then Waylon Dillard shouted that his daddy was in the Klan and, if he wanted, could have their house burned to the ground. Eventually they went away, skulking back toward town. But Lucas lay awake that night, thinking about fire. When he did drift off to an uneasy sleep just before dawn, he dreamed of men in white sheets on horses, and crosses burning.

• • •

The summer the twins turned sixteen, Isolde died of a heart attack in her sleep. After the funeral, which no one else attended but the priest, some women came to the house with a sheriff's deputy and said the twins couldn't stay there alone. They were still minors, and they would have to go to foster homes—maybe two different foster homes, because it would be hard to find a family who'd take two teenage boys.

"We're gonna let you boys stay here until we talk to the social worker in McComb. Give you time to get your things together and all," the deputy said. That night the boys took a few clothes and books and all the money Isolde had kept in a mason jar beneath the kitchen sink. Benjamin used kerosene from the toolshed to start the fire. They left the suicide notes Lucas had written nailed to a pecan tree.

They hid for a while in a blackberry thicket atop a hill half a mile south of town, held each other and watched the red glow of the burning house rage against the midnight sky, wiping out the stars. There were sirens, and Lucas imagined he heard men shouting. Neither of them said a word.

After a while they crawled out of the briars and walked away, through the woods to the highway. The twins hitched a ride as far south as Bogalusa, where they bought bus tickets all the way to New Orleans.

The bedroom that was her brother's, and her brother's lover's, has become Lucrece's church. After their grave, this is her holiest of shrines, and one by one she lights the dozens of candles until the room is bathed in soft golden light. Then she sits in her corner beside the canopy bed: another uncomfortable chair. She folds her arms about her chest, hugs herself tightly. She's put everything here right again, everything just exactly the way it was before the long nightmare began, the one she still hasn't woken from. The black-and-white photographs on the wall are the portraits Jared took of Benny in his latex and lace wedding gown, the corset underneath pulled so tight that Benny looks like an insect, so fragile, so easy to break.

18

These were the centerpieces in Jared's first big gallery show, the one that snagged him a write-up in the *Village Voice*, that caught the attention of collectors as far away as Amsterdam and Berlin: people with money to spend on art.

There were photographs of Lucrece in that show too, of her and Benny together, but she couldn't look at those anymore. Jared had posed them together, the twins as inverted mirrors, dressed in restraining costumes that recklessly, elegantly swapped their genders back and forth, that rendered them even more inter-changeable than the work of their genes. By the end of the first shoot, eight hours on nothing but cigarettes and bottled water, Lucrece was nauseous, dizzy, and less certain of her tenuous iden-tity than she'd been in years. She started crying and Benny held her until the world bled slowly into focus again.

Now she's staring at the photograph above Benny's dressing table, the steel frame shining dully in the candlelight. Benny stretched out on a rough and crumbling concrete floor, his head turned so sharply to the side his neck might be broken, a satin blind-fold hiding his eyes, his blackened lips parted ever so slightly. Sometimes Lucrece wishes for the strength to tear the photographs from the walls of the room, to burn them and this whole god-damned building with her inside. Set a cleansing, erasing fire, as she and Benny had done so long ago. In the life before, two lives before, when she was still a frightened teenage boy called Lucas on the run, with the future stretching out endlessly in front of them. Now the future is a cinder-block wall that she could touch if she had the nerve, a cold dead end to the ever-narrowing avenue of her life.

But Lucrece knows she doesn't have the nerve, the strength to make that final gesture, to close the distance dividing her from her brother and put an end to the loneliness. She has the strength to bear this pain forever if necessary, and the strength to hold these memories, and she will ask nothing more of herself.

The clock on the chiffonier ticks off the last minute before midnight. Lucrece sits up straight and continues to pretend that she's only waiting for Benny to come home.

• • •

The setting sun was a hazy fireball sinking into the vast expanse of Lake Pontchartrain as the bus carrying Benjamin and Lucas crossed the causeway they thought would never end. It was like something from a fairy tale, something from one of the books gone to ash in Isolde's library, a bridge spanning the gap between their childhood and the dangerous, wonderful city that lay ahead.

At that moment Lucas leaned close to whisper into his brother's ear the only thing he'd ever kept from his twin, the one secret so heavy he'd never imagined it would ever become words and cross his lips. But he understood that there was a wild magic in this crossing, and if he didn't speak it then, it might stay locked inside him forever. And after it was out, Benjamin only smiled his easy smile and kissed his brother on the cheek.

"Did you think we didn't *know?*" he said, and Lucas was too shocked to answer, too overwhelmed by his confession and Benjamin's casual response, by the world slipping past so fast outside the window of the bus. "Well, we knew. We thought you *knew* we knew."

Lucas managed to shake his head.

"Jesus," his brother sighed, an exasperated sound, but he was still smiling. "You can be a dense little thing, can't you?"

"Then you don't hate me for it?" Something slipped across Benjamin's face so fast Lucas almost missed it, anger put back in its black box before it could do him harm. Benjamin shook his head. "We're both freaks, Lucas. We're nothing like these others . . ." he whispered, motioning at the people in the seats around them. "And that's our power."

Lucas closed his eyes. As the bus rolled off the causeway and into New Orleans Benjamin whispered an old story, one they had invented together years ago, about two identical fairy brothers, changelings left for human children and taken to be raised by a kindly old woman in a house full of riddles and dust and fat scuttling spiders.

● ● ●

Lucrece is almost dozing in her chair when the tapping at the window begins, the French windows behind the bed and all its black linen drapings. At first she thinks that the sound must be coming from the door in the other room, someone knocking at the door to the apartment, someone wanting in, and she whispers his name before she can stop herself.

"Benny?"

Then the sound begins again, sharp, like small stones hurled against the glass, almost hard enough to shatter it. Lucrece stands up. Her legs are weak and the small hairs on the back of her neck are prickling, a cold sweat blooming wetly beneath her dress, across her forehead and upper lip.

There comes a rumbling sound like thunder, except Lucrece knows it *isn't* thunder; it is much too contained and close for thunder. It rolls slowly across the roof, and she looks up at the ceiling as the windows are blown open by a sudden violent gust. The candle flames flicker, and the room fills with the smells of rain and hot wax and ozone.

"Benjamin?" she says, louder this time. The storm seems to draw its breath, and for a moment there is only the sound of the rain coming in the window, falling on the bed and floor, peppering her face.

And then the sound of wings, and she almost screams as the huge crow lights on the headboard and the windows slam themselves shut behind it.

"Jesus Christ," she gulps. The bird caws loudly as if in reply, puffs out its black feathers and shakes tiny beads of water all over the damp bedspread. As it cocks its head to one side, beak like an assassin's dagger, Lucrece wonders what her sorrow has conjured from this haunted city, what dark spirit might have come to wonder at her vigil.

She takes one step toward it, leaning forward. The crow blinks and caws again, spreads its ebony wings. Lucrece steps back and crouches at the edge of the bed.

"Who sent you?" she asks. "Who sent you to me?"

"Lucrece," a voice behind her says, a voice as familiar and as alien as anything she could ever imagine, a voice that carries everything it's felt and everything it's seen wedged fiercely

21

between every word. She's too afraid to turn and see, her heart going mad inside her chest, but she knows that despite her fear she will *have* to turn around sooner or later. Like Orpheus or Lot's wife, never mind the penalty of seeing. The not-seeing is a thousand times more horrible.

"Jared," she says, whispers more quietly than a whisper. "Is it . . . ?"

"Yes, Lucrece," he says. "Yes," and she turns to see.

Jared has been following the bird for what seems like miles, down the wet streets of leering, suspicious faces and cars that honked when he didn't get out of their way. He thinks that the bird has put something inside him, a burning thread so bright it could blind him and blot out the rest of the world, a hungry cutting thing that has dragged him through the storm to this place he never would have come on his own.

When the crow led him to the Quarter, he'd stood for a while across the street from the apartment, silently watching the bedroom window through the rain. He wondered at the dim flickering light visible through the lace curtains, at who might live there now that he was dead. Then the bird leaped into the air from its perch on the lamp post and the wire coiled inside Jared pulled taut again, and he followed the black wings.

Downstairs the security door was standing open, so that anyone might walk in off the street, any crackhead with a gun, or thief, or killer. He'd pulled it shut behind him and the iron bars clanged hard and hollow like the door to a prison cell.

And now he stands in the doorway of the bedroom where Benny died, and Lucrece is on her knees in front of him. The crow is watching him from the bed. He feels the wire in his soul slacken and he swallows, still tastes the chemicals, still tastes stale death like a hangover, an aftertaste like old vomit and alcohol and cigarettes.

"Why?" he says. The voice seems to come from somewhere nearby, but not really from his throat or his tongue. Jared can think of nothing else worth asking, nothing else that could possibly matter except that one word, "Why?" and so he says it again.

Lucrece seems incapable of answering him, stares unbelieving and speechless. She looks so much like Benny it hurts to see her there, Benny's impossible, identical female twin. Jared feels as if he's falling, holds on to the door frame for some support, but there's nothing to combat the vertigo sucking at his bare feet. The apartment, this fucking room, kept like an altar because she's too weak to let go. The bird seems to smile, and he wishes his hands were around its neck.

"*Why*, Lucrece?" he says in a mean growl that he can feel as well as hear. Jared closes his eyes, presses his forehead hard against the wall. He marvels that he feels the pressure of the hard wood against his brow. "What have you done to me?"

"Jared," she says again, repeats his name like something holy. When he opens his eyes, she's rising very slowly to her feet, moving as slowly as a dancer underwater. She extends one hand tentatively toward him and he feels his knees begin to buckle, so he grips the wall more tightly.

"You should have left me *dead*," he moans, the rage rising from his guts like puke, rage almost smothering his words. He slams his head into the door frame and Lucrece screams.

"You should have left me dead. I *am* dead and you should have left me dead."

"Jared, I didn't *do* this," she says. He knows all her courage comes from the fear that he might hurt himself again, might damage her precious voodoo prize from the grave, so he smacks his face against the wall. Something cracks and he leaves a dark smear of blood on the white paint.

"Yes, *you did!* You and your fucking magic games, Lucrece . . . you sent that fucking bird to dig me up."

"Jesus, *no*, I swear . . ." She's coming toward him as if her fear doesn't matter, as if there's simply no alternative left for her. Jared almost feels sorry for her, almost ashamed, if there was any way for him to reach those feelings through the suffocating anger. The candlelight glints off the tears running down her cheeks, off her bright, wet eyes. Then he is falling, finally,

23

but he falls very, very slowly. Sinking, so that by the time she crosses the room, he's huddled with his broken nose squashed against the wall, tasting his own blood.

"God, Jared." Lucrece puts her arms around him, pulls him close to her. He can smell her, tea rose and spice, her clean dress, her sweat, her fear crackling around him like an electric current. She holds him very tightly and when she speaks her voice sounds as weak as an old and dying woman's.

"I've *never* lied to you, Jared. You *know* I've never fucking lied to you . . ."

"But why, Lucrece? Jesus Christ, *why?*" Then there's a sudden, stabbing pain between his eyes, a raw and grating sound, and the flesh on Jared's face feels more than alive. It has begun to move and shift, and he thinks of maggots first, that maybe his skull's full of maggots where his brain used to be, and now they're eating their way out through his face. There's an audible *pop* as skin and bone and cartilage writhe. He sees that Lucrece has covered her mouth with one hand.

"Oh, Jared," she whispers, her voice swollen with terror and awe. He reaches up, expecting to find a thousand tiny larval bodies spilling from his nostrils, a cold gush of rancid fluid. Instead there's only his nose, his perfect, unbroken nose. Not even a drop of blood, and Jared stares at his fingertips as if they've betrayed him too, as if this is just another lie.

"What's happening?" she asks, her voice as brittle and jagged as a broken light bulb. He can only answer by pushing her away, shoving her so hard she loses her balance and sprawls over backward as he fights his way back to the solid, incontestable wall.

The crow is still watching him from the bed. Jared imagines that he can *see* its hold on him, the shining wire running from its livid breast to his heart, strung like fishing line, the hook buried so deeply inside him he can never dig it out.

"*You*, you black motherfucker!" he screams. The bird blinks at him. "*You* did this, didn't you?" Jared's hands grab frantically at empty air, grappling for a link as intangible and undeniable as memory. "Let me *go!*" he screams, struggling to his feet. "Send me back where I belong!"

The crow only caws once, an annoyed, impatient sound, and hops a few inches farther out of his reach.

"Jared, please, stop." Lucrece is reaching for his ankles, sobbing as he kicks her unwelcome hands away. "Can't you *hear* what it's telling you? For God's sake, stop and *listen* to it, Jared."

But something inside him has burst, something ripe and festering, and the dark, acidic fury is out before he knows it's found a way. It pours from him in a wild and mindless flood and he tears a picture from the wall, only dimly aware of what he's holding, and hurls it at the black bird. The frame crashes against the footboard and explodes in a shower of glass and splinters.

Now he *is* staring into Benny's eyes, at the face in the ruined black-and-white photograph staring back at him. The shot that was printed in the *Voice*, Benny with his hands bound behind his back, out of sight, and the softest hint of a snarl on his lips. The figure against a shadowy backdrop, blazing wings stretched wide behind him, stark projected wings that seem to grow from Benny's bare shoulders. Jared named the photograph *The Raven*, and Benny complained how obvious that was, and that it was a very dumb joke.

"Oh." His voice is just another bit of flotsam thrown out in the scalding cascade. "Oh, fuck you."

"Please," Lucrece says, begging now. Begging him to please stop as he seizes the Tiffany torchère by the door and throws it like a spear made of bronze and stained glass, driving it through the center of the photograph. And he smiles for the crow now, a vicious razor smile so wide he thinks it might split his head in half, will surely slice open the corners of his mouth. The bird squawks and retreats to the safety of the headboard.

"You think that's funny? Huh, you think that's fucking funny?"

Then Lucrece is standing in front of him, putting herself between him and the crow, and his anger switches focus in the space between heartbeats.

"Get out of my way, bitch."

"No," she says, her voice low and firm and sounding male now, the way it sounded when Jared first met her and Benny at a gallery opening uptown. "No, I won't. Whatever's happening here is happening for a *reason*, Jared."

"No, *Lucas*," he says, all the emphasis he can find loaded on top of that discarded name, such a simple, easy weapon lying there conveniently. Lucrece flinches but doesn't move. "It's just a *fucking joke*. Just a goddamned sick joke on all of us, by a sick-ass, twisted universe. Don't you get it, *Lucas*?"

"You know it's not," she says, glaring, and the heat gathering behind her eyes is almost a match for his anger.

"Jesus, you never did have a sense of humor." Jared turns away from her and rips another of his photographs from the wall, smashes it against the floor. The glass and steel cut his hands and they heal immediately, like flesh in a time-lapse film. He turns around again slowly, raising his palms so that she can see the gashes sealing themselves closed. So that he can see the look on her face.

"Then please, darling, by all means let me refresh your memory." Jared moves so fast he knows Lucrece doesn't see it coming, shoves her stumbling back into the bed. He drives words at her like nails, each one sharper and harder than the last, as if his voice alone could crucify.

"'But the Raven, sitting lonely on that placid bust, spoke only . . . that *one word*, as if his soul in that one word did out-pour. Nothing *farther* then he uttered; not a *feather* then he fluttered—'"

Lucrece slaps him, the sound of her palm loud against his cheek, and Jared pauses in his recitation long enough to laugh at her, long enough to savor the stinging sensation her hand has left behind.

"Leave me alone," she growls. Jared slaps her back, hits her hard and she trips over the lamp and falls onto the bed. And he remembers now how good the violence can feel, the cleaning release, and he leans low over her like a movie vampire.

"'Till I scarcely more than *muttered:* Other friends have flown before—'"

Lucrece drives her knee into his crotch and uses her other foot to push him off of her.

"I said to *leave me alone*, you son of a bitch!"

Jared releases her, falls in a heap at the foot of the bed, crumples next to what's left of the lamp and *The Raven*. Lucrece rolls off the bed, breathless, expecting another attack and ready for it this time. But Jared doesn't move, just stares blankly at the photograph, at the torn ghost of Benny still trapped inside the remains of the frame. The crow silently watches them both from its perch on the headboard.

"I didn't kill Benny," Jared says, speaking to Lucrece or to no one at all, his anger spent for the moment. The sound of his voice makes her shiver despite the adrenaline hammering through her veins, such a flat and hollow sound, like someone speaking from the bottom of a deep, dry well.

When she answers him, she speaks as carefully, as soothingly, as she can manage.

"I know that, Jared."

"Yeah," Jared says, "I know you do." He starts pulling the photograph out of the broken frame, brushing away powdered glass from the image of his murdered lover, her murdered brother. The crow caws again, flaps its wings loudly, but Jared doesn't look. Instead he stares down at beautiful, lost Benny.

"Jared, you *can* understand what it's saying, can't you?"

His head turns very slowly toward her, as if he's reluctant to look away from the photograph for even a moment, as if he's afraid it might dissolve. His eyes are as far away and empty as the sound of his voice, and she wants to hold him again, wants release from all these months she's spent alone, no company but her own selfish, devouring sorrow. But Lucrece does not move, glances instead at the bird.

"It's brought you back," she says, "to find out who did do it, and stop them from ever doing it again."

The crow seems to regard her warily, maybe a glimmer of mistrust in its small and golden eyes, and so she says to it, "Am I wrong?"

"No, Lucrece," Jared says, answering before the bird has the chance. "You're not wrong. I can hear it too. I don't want to, but I can hear it just fine."

"I can help you," she says, still watching the crow, the mistrust mutual now. "If I can understand what it's saying, then I can help you. I know things about what happened to Benny, things they wouldn't let me say in court."

The crow flies the short distance to the foot of the bed and perches on the footboard above Jared, looks from him to Lucrece and back to him again, its eyes as sharp as its beak, somehow nervous and confident at the same time.

"I can't let you get involved in this, Lucrece," Jared says, hugging the photograph to his chest now, stroking its smooth surface as if there is something there more precious than mere paper.

"Bullshit," she answers. "I'm *already* involved."

He can't think of anything to say to that, nothing that would convince her, but he knows well enough that she can't follow where he has to go. So Jared Poe sits quietly on the floor of the room and listens to the rain falling outside on Ursulines and the less comforting rhythm of his Lazarus heart.

two

Detective Frank Gray has been watching the Weather Channel for the last half hour, too drunk to give a shit that he's seen the same local weather report three times already, too drunk to bother changing it over to something else. He takes another long swallow of Jim Beam directly from the pint bottle and returns it to the safe cradle between his legs. At least the bourbon still feels the way it should, the only thing left in his life that hasn't found some way to betray his trust. It burns reassuringly in his belly, adds its part to the mist he keeps between himself and the world.

There's a tropical storm somewhere in the Gulf, a great spinning swirl of white against blue on the satellite photographs. He's managed to understand that much. But the storm and any threat it might represent are far away from him, like everything else, like the rain drumming steadily against the window of his shitty apartment. Frank takes another drink from his bottle, sweet fire in his mouth, blazing down his throat. He closes his eyes when it reaches his stomach, and in the drunken darkness the hustler is there waiting for him.

The kid *said* he was twenty-one, and Frank knew it was a lie but didn't push the issue. He'd gone into the bar after his shift for a beer, the first drink on his way down into the long drunk of the weekend. It was a nameless place on Magazine

Street, just a sign that read BAR and a neon four-leaf clover over the door, neon beer signs in the dark windows, Patsy Cline on the jukebox. Frank ordered a Bud and was sipping it at the bar when he noticed the kid watching him from a corner booth, sitting there alone, an army surplus duffel bag occupying the seat across from him. When he looked back a few minutes later the kid was still there, still watching him. There was a bottle on the table, though he didn't seem to be actually drinking from it.

And then the kid smiled at him, a practiced shy smile, and looked back down at the table, picked at the label of his beer bottle.

The pushy, nervous voice in his head said, *No, Frank. We don't shit where we eat, man,* but he'd learned a long time ago how to keep that voice in its place. It was only another minute or two before he went over to the kid's booth.

Up close the kid looked a little bit older than he had from the bar. Blond hair shaved down to his scalp, Huck Finn freckles under his eyes and across the bridge of his nose. His eyes were the vacant blue of an October sky.

"Hi," Frank said. The boy said hi back to him, looked up for just a second, a quick smile for Frank before he went back to picking the label off the half-empty bottle of PBR. Frank pointed at the duffel bag and asked, "Coming or going?"

"Coming," the kid answered. "I just got in from Memphis this afternoon. On the bus."

"Memphis, huh," Frank said, and before he could say anything else the kid whispered, "So, you want a blow job, mister? I'll blow you for twenty bucks."

Frank glanced over his shoulder, automatic caution. The place was empty except for the two of them and an old woman sipping a Bloody Mary at the far end of the bar. The bartender was on the phone and had his back to them.

"Jesus, kid, you don't waste any time, do you?"

The kid shrugged, pulled the rest of the label off the brown beer bottle. "What's the point in beating around the bush?"

"I might be a cop," Frank said.

The boy smiled, smoothed the ragged label on the tabletop.

"Oh, you're not a cop. You don't even look like a cop. I've given cops head before, and you don't look like a cop to me."

"Really?" Frank sipped at his own beer, glanced over his shoulder again. The old woman was saying something he couldn't understand to the bartender, who was still on the phone and ignoring her. "Maybe you should be a little more cautious."

The boy sighed then, looked up at Frank, and all the flirt and pretense was gone from his face, a hint of annoyed impatience at the corners of his mouth.

"Look, man. I gotta take a piss. If you want a blow, I'll be waiting for you in the john, okay?"

As the boy stood up and pushed past him Frank stammered, "Yeah, uh, sure," but the kid was already halfway to the rest room door.

If asked, Frank Gray would be hard put to think of anything he had ever wanted but to be a cop. He spent his childhood on a steady diet of television police dramas, everything from syndicated episodes of *Hawaii Five-O* and *Dragnet* to *Starsky and Hutch* and *Baretta*, *Police Story*, *Mod Squad*. These were his cowboys, his heroes, his models of what was good and what was masculine.

And, if asked, he would also be hard put to remember a time when he was not attracted to men: these men in particular, with their navy blue uniforms and shining badges and forceful self-assurance. He never passed through a time of sexual confusion, the tentative courting of girls he wasn't actually attracted to, the belated discovery that men and only men were the proper object of his sexuality. Everything was clear from the beginning, and he never saw any conflict between the objects of his lust and his desire to be a cop.

But this naïveté did not even survive his academy training. He didn't need anybody to pull him aside and tell him, "Frank, faggots are not welcome on the force." He saw the hatred in his fellow cadets and recognized it for what it was, absorbed an acute awareness of the silence he would have to keep like priestly vows of celibacy if he was to have both these things, sex with other men *and* the badge, without having to endure any

31

lessons firsthand. He saw others who were not so sharp, and that was enough for Frank.

By the time he came on the New Orleans PD as a beat cop in the Fifth Ward he understood the fine line he would have to walk, and he kept his arms out straight, placed one foot carefully in front of the other. Shortly after he entered the force two officers were busted after trading leniency for sexual favors from male hustlers in the Quarter. Before their subsequent hearings and dismissal Frank saw the *other* things that happened to them—the threats and beatings and humiliation—and he took note.

Four years later he was promoted to the rank of homicide detective, four long years he'd spent walking the walk, talking the talk, and satisfying his hungers with his hands and pornography, and even the pornography was a big risk. He knew that, and he kept his magazines in a locked strongbox in the back of a closet and never bought anything from the local newsstands or porn shops. Everything arrived at a post office box he kept in Bridge City under a false name, sexual care packages in anonymous brown paper, the magazines and videocassettes that served as surrogates for anything like actual companionship or satisfaction.

He learned the masquerade, the smoke-and-mirrors game, and prided himself that no one suspected a thing. He dated fictitious women. Whenever the guys were going on about some woman or another, Frank was always right up front, his lines as well rehearsed as any actor's on opening night. "Oh, man, did you see the titties on that bitch?" somebody would say, and Frank would clutch at his crotch and grin on cue. He knew every queer slur and joke, excelled in the phony swish and lisp and limp-wristed pantomime. He had looked the other way on more than one occasion when he saw cops beating up on fags. The machismo was just another part of his uniform, after all, just as easy to put on and take off again as his hat and shoes, and if there were ever doubts, well, that's what confession was for.

It was all easy enough to rationalize. If they'd just show a little fucking self-restraint, if they'd act like *men*, nobody would know and this shit wouldn't happen to them.

But sometimes he would catch a glimpse of his thin face in the bathroom mirror or a store window and there would be only the mask, no vestige left of the man hiding underneath. He would have to stop then, would have to lean against a wall or sit down until the vertigo passed. There was a ballooning sense that he was somehow slipping out of himself, that the man he saw reflected had already consumed the *real* Frank Gray. And even this was something small enough to dismiss. Shit, it was a stressful fucking life and he couldn't expect *not* to feel it every now and then. He told himself it was just something else that came with the territory and if he had to have a few drinks before bed to keep the nightmares away, so be it.

The boy in the bathroom stall smelled like sweat and sunlight, and Frank tried hard to concentrate on those delicious smells instead of the sour stink of urine and deodorant cakes. He sat on the toilet seat, his hands savoring the soft bristle of the kid's scalp, holding back, wanting it to last, knowing it might be weeks before he allowed himself anything this wonderful again, weeks before he was desperate enough to risk it.

When he finally came, Frank leaned over and kissed the kid's scruffy hair, tasted salt and Vitalis. Tiny bursts of orgasm still lingered somewhere between his dick and his brain, and he didn't want to open his eyes, let in the ugly light of the rest room, the uglier reality of his situation.

"Jesus, I *knew* you were a fucking cop," the kid said, and when Frank did open his eyes the kid was holding his service revolver, had slipped it from his ankle holster and was pointing it at Frank's chest.

"So, since you went and *lied* to me, maybe I got a little bit more coming to me than just the twenty, huh?"

Frank swallowed, his mouth and throat gone suddenly dry, feeling like a goddamn fool, stupid enough to let this punk catch him off guard, his pants around his ankles and his shriveling dick dripping cum into the toilet bowl, the barrel of his own gun aimed straight at his heart.

"Just give that back to me before someone gets hurt, okay?" Like he really thought there was any chance of that happening.

33

The kid shook his head and smiled, used the back of his free hand to wipe his mouth, careful not to take his eyes off Frank.

"What?" Frank asked him, fear and exasperation fighting for control of his voice. "You think you're actually gonna shake down a policeman with his own fucking gun and get away with it?"

"Do all the other little piggies know you're a faggot?" the boy said. Frank punched him hard in the face, sent him crashing backward into the locked door of the stall. The revolver tumbled from his hand and clattered loudly on the filthy tiles. He grabbed the kid by the collar of his T-shirt, slammed his head hard against the door. The boy slumped into a whimpering heap. Frank moved slowly, reaching for the gun with one hand and pulling up his pants with the other. He shoved the .38 back into its holster before he stood up and kicked the kid once in the stomach, once in the face for good measure.

"You stupid little shit. If I ever see you again . . . if I ever so much as fuckin' *see* you again, motherfucker, they'll be dragging the river for the parts the alligators didn't want. Do you understand me?"

The kid coughed out a mouthful of blood and Frank Gray kicked him in the guts again.

"*Answer* me, fucker."

The boy managed a choked strangling sound and half a nod. Frank kneeled beside him and stuffed the twenty he'd earned into a back pocket.

"I'm going back out there, and I'm going to finish my beer. You're going to stay right here for a while." Without waiting for a response, he left the kid curled fetal and moaning beside the toilet.

Frank takes another drink from his bottle and watches the lazy counterclockwise spiral of the storm tracking across his television screen. The weatherman points to the tattered delta and barrier island coast of Louisiana and says something Frank can't hear because he's turned the sound down all the way. It's better to hear the rain, he thinks, better just to listen to the fucking incomprehensible rain.

He's always heard stories of hustlers robbing cops, stealing guns and badges when the cop wasn't looking, or trying to blackmail them later on. *Fuck that*, he thinks drunkenly, remembering the fear and surprise shining like a fever from the kid's eyes. *Fuck that to hell and back again.* But there's another voice in his head, the voice that tried to stop him from speaking to the boy in the first place. Sometimes the alcohol muffles it to a whisper, but now it's loud and it says, *Yeah, it's easy for you to talk that macho crap now, Frank Gray. But you were ready to shit yourself today, weren't you, buddy?*

Frank fumbles for the remote control and turns the volume back up until he can't hear anything above the meteorologist's nasal voice.

The heavy drinking began a couple of months before his promotion to detective, when Frank was still just a beat cop working the Iberville projects east of Canal Street. His partner was a young black woman named Linda Getty, a rookie he'd been working with only a few weeks when they got the call, what he would always remember as the Bad Call. It was a rainy Shrove Tuesday and for Frank that afternoon would mark the moment that his descent began, his piecemeal disintegration to this place of self-loathing and boozy rot.

"This domestic shit is the worst," Frank said. Linda nodded, flicking the butt of her cigarette out the window of the squad car as he answered dispatch.

"Yeah, we're only a couple of blocks from there now," he said into the radio handset, and turned the car around. Now, whenever he thinks back on the four or five minutes before they reached the maze of tenements bordering St. Louis No. 1 Cemetery, it always seems that there was some vague sense of foreboding, something more urgent than the usual dread of getting himself in between two people who hate each other as bad as married couples can. But that's probably bullshit and he

35

knows it, like someone seeing St. Paul in a bowl of gumbo just before they almost choked to death on a crab shell, making something out of nothing for the sake of consolation.

"I know you must have heard this a hundred times in training," he said to Linda, talking fast like he always did when he was nervous, "but this mundane shit is a hundred times more dangerous than, say, robbery calls or drug busts. At least you go into those *expecting* someone to take a shot at you or something. Shit like this, you just never fucking know what to expect."

"I hear you," said Linda, trying to sound tough and sure of herself. The way that Frank remembers it, he wished she really did.

A small crowd had already gathered by the time they pulled up outside the graffiti-covered red brick building, people in the muddy yard and a few standing in the street looking at something on the blacktop. Distrusting, resentful faces turned toward them as they got out of the car. Frank remembers thinking that at least the rain had stopped.

"What the hell you gonna do about this?" a woman said, a short woman almost as wide as she was tall, with mint-green curlers sprouting from her hair. Frank could hear a man's voice from one of the apartments, loud and crazy.

"You folks need to go on home," he started, and then he heard Linda gasp, the sound someone makes when they've just seen something a hundred times worse than they've ever imagined anything could possibly be.

"Don't you be tellin' me to hush up and go away," the fat woman scolded, strident, angry. "I done asked you what you gonna *do* about this!" But Frank had already turned his back on her, was staring at Linda standing on the other side of the car, one hand over her mouth and her voice filtered through her fingers.

"What is it?" he asked. "What's wrong?" But she was already pointing at the thing he'd noticed in the street as they'd pulled up to the curb. *A fucking dead cat*, he thought. *Jesus, she better not be pulling this scene on me over a goddamn dead cat in the fucking road*.

Linda fumbled for her cigarettes, lit one and inhaled frantically to keep from vomiting, a trick he knew well. "Frank," she mumbled, "Oh, God. Oh, *look* at it."

He stepped around the back of the patrol car, trying to keep his eyes on the restless onlookers and the general direction he'd heard the man's voice coming from, trying to get a better look at whatever his partner saw lying in the street.

It wasn't a cat. He saw that a second later, a glimpse of the small brown body between the figures huddled around it, naked skin and sticky red smeared across the blacktop. The baby was maybe six months old, and Frank didn't have to ask to know that a car had run over its head.

Linda was leaning against the car, coughing, repeating, "Oh, God, oh, God," over and over like a prayer between puffs, like maybe there was some way to forget what she'd just seen, a trick that would allow her to *unsee* it. Someone in the crowd laughed then, a dry, hard laugh that Frank remembers as clearly as the broken body. And then the first gunshot and he could move again, the spell broken. He remembers yelling at Linda to get her shit together, pull it together right *then* or he was going to kick her fucking ass.

"I'm sorry," she whispered, wiping her mouth and reaching toward her holster. "But Jesus, Frank . . ."

"There ain't nothin' you can do for that poor child," the fat woman shouted at them from the other side of the patrol car. "You best be worryin' about the ones he *ain't* killed yet." And Linda glared at the woman, squinted through the tears leaking from the corners of her eyes, spilling down her cheeks.

"Listen to the lady," Frank said. He leaned past his partner into the car, trying to sound calm as he grabbed the radio mike. "Hey, we need some fucking backup out here!" He paused before going on, took a deep breath, and wondered if the operator could hear his heart pounding away in his chest, could smell the blood and adrenaline straight through the radio.

The man who had fired the shots was waiting for them on the second floor, had barricaded himself inside with his girlfriend and her three children. One of the kids was the dead baby in the street—the fat woman had told them that when Frank had

37

finished radioing for backup. The guy's name was Roy and he'd been smoking crack all day. The fat woman had also told them that. They both drew their guns before starting up the iron-and-concrete stairs to the second floor, where they crouched just past the top of the stairway, Linda pressed flat against the wall, Frank a few feet closer to the door, a lot more exposed.

Almost five minutes had passed since he'd called for assistance and they still hadn't even heard so much as a siren. Frank's hands were sweating, slick around the grip of his pistol. They could clearly hear the man and woman inside, screaming at each other, and the terrified voices of the children, but there had been no further gunfire. On the way up Frank had glimpsed movement through a broken window. He'd guessed it was the same window from which the baby had been tossed.

"Shit," Linda hissed behind him. "Where the fuck *are* they, Frank? We shouldn't even be up here without backup."

"Just shut up a minute, okay?" he snarled at her, bracing himself against the iron railing, setting himself up for a clear shot if the door to the apartment opened and there was *anything* at all in that asshole's hands.

When he shouted to the people inside, he could hear the strain in his voice, the fear coiled there. It made him feel almost as sick as the sight of the dead kid had, the tire tread pattern pressed into the pulpy mess where its brain and skull had been.

"Roy? Roy, can you hear me in there? This is the police. Put down your weapon and open the door before anybody else gets hurt—"

"Hey, fuck *you*, motherfucker!" a male voice boomed from behind the door. The black paint was coming off the metal door in big, ugly flakes, and Frank could see a lighter, older shade of black revealed underneath. He remembered these details so clearly.

"I ain't doing *nothin'* for no goddamn City of New Orleans cops! You gonna get your lyin' cracker ass back into your police car and leave me the hell alone or I'll blow this bitch's brains out!" And then the woman screamed again.

"Jesus, Frank, where the hell *are* they? They shoulda fucking been here *twice* already."

He didn't have an answer for her, but he knew they were in over their heads.

"I don't know, *okay?*" he whispered, struggling to sound calm against the panic gathering in his belly, filling his insides like cold lead. "But we're going to have to back off and just wait . . ."

"Back off and wait for *what*, Frank? Nobody's coming, and he's ready to kill those people in there. There are *children* in there, for Christ's sake."

"Hey, motherfucker!" the man's voice boomed again, a ravening, mad-dog voice that Frank knew there could never be any reasoning with. No answer to that voice except force, force enough to kill before it would back down. "Are you deaf or what? I *said*, get the hell off the goddamn stairs or I'm gonna pop this bitch in the fuckin' head!"

"It doesn't matter," Frank said, speaking to Linda as loudly as he dared. "There's nothing we can do by ourselves." He called out to the man behind the door, "Okay, Roy, we're going to back off now and leave you alone just like you said. But I want you to do some—"

And then the shotgun made a sound like thunder trapped inside a metal box and wanting out, tearing its way free, and the black door was blown completely off its hinges. There was no time for them to get out of the way—Frank saw that at the same instant he saw Roy raising the Mag–10 Roadblocker for another shot. The woman was sprawled at his feet. Frank could see that she'd been caught between Roy and the door when the monster Ithaca semiautomatic had gone off, that the blast had cut her in half. Roy was covered in the woman's blood, and the air was thick with smoke and a settling crimson mist.

"*Stay down!*" he screamed at Linda, stealing precious seconds to aim before he fired his revolver twice, both shots catching Roy cleanly between the eyes. The huge man jerked backward and his spasming fingers squeezed the Roadblocker's trigger one last time, but the shot went wild, blowing a hole in the ceiling above his head, adding plaster dust and more smoke to the haze already billowing from the doorway of the project apartment. Roy stumbled backward, tripped over a coffee table, and fell dead to the floor.

"Mother Mary . . ." Frank whispered, but he couldn't even hear his own voice for the ringing in his head, the smothering echo of the shotgun.

"Are you okay back there? Linda, are you okay?" She didn't answer, but he was already up and moving, advancing on the doorway, the barrel of his .38 not moving from Roy's prostrate form. He'd fallen backward and both his feet were sticking up in the air, his expensive athletic shoes soaked in blood, his own blood and the woman's.

Frank stepped carefully past the buckled, broken door; the hole blown in the center was as big as his fist and he knew it was fucking amazing he wasn't a dead man. He stepped over the shredded mess slumped in the door, something that had been a human being hardly a minute before. The floor was slippery and he steadied himself by leaning against a wall. That was covered with blood as well, and his hand came away red and sticky. There was no sign of the other children. Frank guessed they were hiding somewhere in the apartment.

"Linda, I could really use your help up here," he shouted, leaning cautiously over Roy's corpse. "We gotta find these kids."

He noticed that there were two neat punctures just above the bridge of Roy's nose, a widening pool of blood and gray matter on the floor beneath his head. Both of his eyes were wide open, staring blankly up at the ceiling or God or his killer. The shotgun was still clutched in his hands.

"Linda? Did you *hear* me?"

When she finally answered him it was a weak, uncertain sound. He looked slowly over one shoulder, reluctant to turn his back on this crazy man even now, even when there was absolutely no way he would be getting up again. Frank stared out through the clearing fog of smoke and dust, the doorway of the apartment gaping like a ragged exit from some backwater recess of hell.

Linda was sitting at the top of the stairs, her back against the brick wall of the building, surrounded by a spreading puddle of her own blood.

"I think I got hit," she said, her words already mired in dulling shock. "Frank, I think the bastard shot me."

40

Frank almost slipped in the dead woman's intestines on the way out, barely managed to catch himself. Even from a distance he could see the blood jetting from the wound in Linda's thigh, bright red arterial gouts in time to her heartbeat, spilling her life out onto the dirty concrete. Linda was staring at the wound dumbstruck, as if it amazed her, as if it was the most incredible thing she'd ever seen but no *part* of her, nothing that could have happened *to* her.

When he reached her Frank dropped to his knees and looked at the hole, her brown skin and pink muscle chewed to hamburger. He had no idea how the blast could have missed him and caught her until he saw the jagged piece of shrapnel sticking up out of the wound, a piece of the door that must have sailed right by him.

"Listen, I've got to get you an ambulance," he said, stripping off his shirt for a pressure bandage. "And while I'm gone you're going to have to keep some weight on this." She nodded listlessly. *She's gonna fucking die right here*, Frank thought as he wrapped his shirt tightly around the hemorrhaging wound. *She's gonna bleed to death right here before I even get to the fucking car to call for help.*

"I think I'm okay," she slurred. "It doesn't hurt that bad. I think I can walk."

"Shut up, Linda," he said, tying the sleeves of the shirt, finishing the bandage. "If you don't sit still and keep pressure on this leg you're not gonna have to walk anywhere ever again. You'll have angels to carry you wherever you want to go."

She looked at him, blinked, and smiled, a stupid junkie kind of smile. Then she was pulling something off her finger, pressing it into his blood-smeared right palm.

"Please, Frank," she said, "tell Judy I'm sorry, okay? Tell her I still love her. You'll do that, right?"

He stared down at the ring, a simple white gold ring, trying to understand what she was saying to him.

"If something happens . . . if I don't make it . . . you tell Judy I said I was sorry." Linda folded his fingers closed around the wedding band.

Frank took a deep breath, knowing there was no time for his

surprise or the pampering of his own fears. The bandage was already soaked through. He put both her hands on it and pressed down hard, and she almost passed out. He slapped her cheeks until she was conscious enough to keep her own hands over the shotgun wound.

"You keep your hands right there, Linda, and you're gonna be just fine. Ain't nothing gonna happen to you if you do what I say. Do you *understand* me?"

"Yeah," she said, sounding very faint and far away from him. "Yeah, I know what you mean, Frank."

"I'll be right back, I *swear*. I'm only going as far as the patrol car, okay?"

"Yeah," she said, and he left her there and descended the steps to the crowd of people still milling about in front of the building. The fat woman with the green curlers looked at him and grinned, showing a bright silver tooth right up front.

"You leave anyone alive up there, young man?" she asked him as he stepped between their bodies. He didn't reply, ignored them all. It had started to rain again while he and Linda were upstairs and he felt the drops cold against his skin, washing him clean. He gripped the ring in his hand and walked toward the car, praying to no God he believed in that he could at least reach it before he puked, praying that he could get help before she died alone up there.

As he reached the curb there was the sound of thunder off toward the river, a rumble like muffled shotgun fire, and the urgent wail of approaching sirens.

Linda Getty didn't die, but she almost lost her leg and would walk with a limp for the rest of her life. Frank visited her only once in the hospital, when he returned the white gold ring to her. Linda accepted it as if she were taking back a confession. She was in fact doing something very much like that, Frank knew. Linda resigned from the force while she was still struggling through physical therapy, and Frank moved effortlessly up to homicide.

42

But not before he learned that there had been at least two squad cars within minutes of their location in the Iberville projects that afternoon. Both had reported engine trouble to dispatch when the call for assistance had come in over their radios. And when Frank got back to the station that day, he found that someone had spray-painted DYKE in fat red letters across the front of Linda's locker and taped used and bloody tampons to the locker's door.

He stood looking at it for a while, his old familiar fear of discovery wrestling an outrage he'd never felt before, not in all those times when he'd gone along with the idiot queer jokes or turned the other way when someone was roughing up a fag, all those times he'd played along for fear of arousing suspicion and drawing the bullies' wrath his way.

He stared at the desecrated locker and saw Linda Getty slumped limp against that wall, her life pumping out of her, the blood staining her blue cop pants black. She hadn't even fucking cried, had calmly slipped the ring off her finger.

Tell her I still love her.

The ring was still tucked in his shirt pocket, and the sticky blood staining its smooth metal surface was so much like the crimson graffiti slur splashed across the locker door. Later Frank would know that if each man is given only one moment when redemption is somewhere within his reach, that moment in the locker room had been his, his one chance to change the course of his life. A handful of seconds when everything was suddenly made so clear, as simple as the resigned tone of Linda's voice coming through the pain and shock.

And then Donovan said something behind him, "You gotta be careful who you ride with, Frank," just like that, and the anger rising inside him was drowned in the fear, the cold, watery fear that had put out so many fires before and would smother a thousand more. Frank turned and faced Joe Donovan, a heavyset man with acne scars, and the words were on his lips, the *right* words, but when he spoke they slipped away and all that came out was, "Yeah. Yeah, I guess you can't be too careful, can you?"

"No," Joe Donovan said, "you sure as hell can't, buddy." He

43

smiled with the reaffirmation that he was speaking to one of his own, someone who understood that sometimes sacrifices had to be made for the sake of maintaining a greater purity. "It wasn't nothing personal, Frank. You know that."

"Yeah," Frank replied, "yeah, sure."

So the next day, hung over and exhausted from long hours filled with drunken nightmares where he was forced to face down Roy the psycho crackhead again and again, Frank went to see her and return the ring. When he arrived there was another woman in the room, a skinny white girl with a jewel in her right nostril and tattoos on her arms. Linda whispered something to the girl and she left them alone, glancing suspiciously at Frank as she passed him on her way out to the hall.

Linda's eyes were as glazed with the painkillers as they had been with pain the day before, her voice flat and raw, sludgy. She blinked at him and attempted to smile. Frank fished the ring from his pocket. He'd washed the blood off it, and it shone dully in the white light of the hospital room.

"Thank you," she croaked.

Frank shrugged. "No problem. Hey, they treating you all right in here?"

"Everything a girl could ask for." She did smile then, a tired and honest smile that made him glance down at the scuffed toes of his shoes.

"Well, you let me know if you need anything. I gotta get back to the station. All the goddamn paperwork from yesterday. You know how that shit goes." She nodded, then reached out and touched his hand.

"Frank, you did know, didn't you?"

He didn't answer, looked nervously from his shoes to her to the door, just wanting to get the hell away.

"No," he said, and that part was the truth, he hadn't.

"Shit. I'm sorry. I thought everybody knew."

"You just rest and get better, okay?" he said. The girl came back then and stood in the doorway, silently announcing that his time was up.

"Thanks," Linda croaked again. "You saved my ass out there."

"Hey, just doing my job, right?"

"See you soon," she whispered as the drugs pulled her back down toward unconsciousness, releasing him, his duty done. Frank made it all the way to the elevator before he started shaking so badly that he had to sit down.

He often dreams about Roy the psycho crackhead these days. A very simple dream, a short-subject sort of dream where he's watching from somewhere outside himself but still close enough to smell the gunpowder and his own terrified sweat. The details are always so much clearer than anything was that afternoon in the projects, edited and retouched for his viewing pleasure. The loud, mechanical sound of the Roadblocker ejecting the spent shell and chambering the next, the one with his name on it. The parchment yellow nicotine stains on Roy's teeth. The blue-gray loops of the dead woman's exposed intestines.

Sometimes in the dreams it all goes down the same way it did the first time and Roy takes two in the head before he can get off another shot. But sometimes it goes other ways—Frank's revolver jams, or he's one second too slow, or his aim is just a few inches too far to the left or the right—and old Roy gets his second chance after all. The blast never hurts, or at least Frank never remembers the pain when he's finally awake and dripping cold sweat in the safety of his bed. There's only the impact, the mangling, bone-crushing force that takes his breath away, drives him backward and over the flimsy railing.

Sometimes he falls for a long, long time, like Alice dropping down the rabbit hole to Wonderland. And sometimes he only seems to fall for an instant before he jerks awake. But so far he's never hit bottom.

Frank Gray finally changes the channel on the cruddy thirteen-inch Zenith he got from St. Vincent de Paul's and finishes the

45

bottle of bourbon to an episode of *The Untouchables* he's seen at least a dozen times before. Through the sleepy alcoholic fog cushioning his brain the scratchy black-and-white violence is comforting, the screech of tires and ricochet of machine gun bullets as reassuring as a lullaby.

He has to piss but thinks he can hold out a little longer, at least until the next commercial break, before he stumbles off to find the bathroom.

The pressure from his bladder reminds him of the kid from the bar, Huck Finn sucking dick for twenty dollars, makes him remember the surprise on the boy's face when he punched him. Like they all think it's gonna be so goddamn easy, having your cake and eating it too, taking advantage of someone and then robbing them in the bargain. He wishes he'd hauled the kid in for soliciting. Let him scream about faggot cops all he wanted, no one would have ever believed him anyway. At least it's nice to tell himself that, and when he's this drunk he can almost believe it, can almost pretend no one whispers behind his back or snickers or suspects him of being anything but one of the boys.

Frank closes his eyes as the credits roll, thinks maybe he can put off pissing long enough for a nap. Outside the rain falls from a black sky, and the sound of it follows him down to a deep and mercifully dreamless sleep.

three

AN HOUR UNTIL MIDNIGHT, AND JARED AND LUCRECE SIT
together on the floor of the bedroom. Lucrece has carried away
the broken pictures and poured herself a glass of scotch. The
crow watches them from the bed. Sometimes it squawks
loudly, as if it's preparing to announce something urgent; each
time they turn and watch the bird, waiting for something more,
until it's clear it has nothing else to say for now.

Occasionally Jared begins crying again, deep, racking sobs
that seem as if they will tear him apart, and Lucrece holds him
until they pass and he is silent.

"I don't understand what I'm supposed to do," he says.
Lucrece looks at the big black bird, guarded reproach in her
eyes as if maybe she thinks it hasn't done its job and she'll have
to fill in the blanks it has left.

"What has the crow told you?" she asks Jared. He just stares
at the bird on the bed, watching its vigilant eyes. In a little
while he answers her, speaking slowly, as if he's uncertain of the
words or the way they fit together.

"Because there are scales and Benny's death left them
unbalanced." He stops, remembering a statue of Justice outside
the courthouse where he was sentenced to die, the ageless
bronze woman blindfolded and holding her sword and balanced scales. The memory of her and the sick irony there makes
him laugh.

Jared sneers at the bird. "No," he says. "It's more than that. If all that was required to bring back the dead was a little injustice, the fucking graveyards would be empty."

The crow caws in response.

"It's not the injustice," he says to Lucrece, to himself and the bird. "It *can't* simply be the injustice, *can* it?"

"Then what?" Lucrece whispers, afraid Jared knows the answer, more afraid he doesn't. She knows, has heard it in the bird's grating voice; she could tell Jared but knows that he should be the one to see it for himself.

"Fuck you both," he mutters, and she holds his face gently between her hands. His skin is cold. The coldness hurts her like a bad memory, or a memory so good it hurts to recall.

"It's your pain, Jared," she tells him, not letting him look away from her eyes. "It's your pain that is creating the imbalance, your pain that has to be satisfied before order is restored."

"That's bullshit, Lucrece . . . do you even know how ridiculous you sound?"

She ignores him. "Not just the pain, though. Your love for Benny. That's part of it too. That's the part you were supposed to carry with you to the other side. It's the pain and anger that you were supposed to leave behind. There's no room for them among the dead."

Jared pushes her away then, the sneer dissolving into hateful laughter, an ugly, predatory sound that Lucrece would hardly believe is human if she weren't seeing it come from his lips.

"There's no room for *anything* among the dead, Lucrece, except the hungry worms."

She cannot look him in the eye now, cannot face the ebony glimmer there. She knows that it's part of what he has become, part of what he will have to do if he is ever to find peace, but that knowledge makes it no easier for her to face.

"You can hear the crow, Jared. You know I'm telling you the truth."

He doesn't say anything. When she raises her eyes and looks back at him Jared is watching the bird perched on the footboard of the bed. His lips are pulled so far back that his teeth look like fangs, bared for fresh meat.

"An avenging angel," he snarls. "So the gods can rest easy and still keep their hands clean. Is that what you're saying?" The bird ruffles its feathers and shifts from foot to foot.

"That's all there is to it, *isn't* it? Find the bad guys and make them pay, so my niggling soul doesn't disturb the spooks roasting down in hell."

The crow tucks its wings close to its body and huddles as if it expects Jared to strike it.

"Yeah, well, you tell me what good that does Benny, you black-hearted son of a bitch. You tell me that it's going to *fix* what some depraved motherfucker did to Benny and *maybe* then I'll want to play along with your little game."

Lucrece can feel his fury in the close atmosphere of the bedroom, more immediate than the storm outside, can feel his anger crackling through the damp air around them.

"Nothing's going to help Benny, Jared. Unless you can find peace and return to him, nothing's ever going to help Benny." The last part catches in her throat like broken glass, but she knows it must be said.

"Right now Benny is *alone*, Jared, alone in the cold and the dark, waiting for you to come back to him."

And she braces herself, ready to feel his fist or ready to put herself between him and the bird again. But Jared sits very still and stares at the crow, the muscles in his face relaxing by almost imperceptible degrees.

"Ah, *God*," he says softly. She wants to hold him again, wishes there were words that she could say.

"But that's not all, Lucrece. If you can hear what he's saying, then you *know* that's not all."

"Yes," she says, because she can understand the bird voice, its shrill, uneasy mind, the way she understood the thoughts that Benny never spoke to her out loud, the way she knew when his dreams were troubled.

"You're supposed to know who killed him," Jared says to the crow, spitting out the words like a bad taste in his mouth. "That's the way it's supposed to work. You drag me back here and *show* me. But you *can't* show me the killer, can you? You can't show me shit!"

Lucrece risks one hand on Jared's right shoulder and he turns on her, the glare meant for the bird. She thinks maybe she can see hell locked up in those eyes, the pupils dropping straight down forever.

"I'm right, aren't I? It doesn't know, any more than the god-damn police knew."

"The crow is doing what it was made to do, Jared. Whatever else is going on here, it's just a crow and there are limits to its . . ." and she pauses, knowing how she must sound to Jared, pragmatic, irreligious Jared, that this is all just a bunch of crazy voodoo non-sense to him.

"There are limits to its powers. There's something else going on here, something that's getting in the way, that we have to figure out and get around."

Jared buries his face in his hands and she thinks that he's about to cry again. That would be better than the anger, some-thing she understands more intimately. She's spent all her life since her brother's death in the company of sorrow. She has become sorrow's most cherished concubine.

"I don't understand any of this," Jared says.

"And you mustn't waste your time trying," Lucrece replies, hoping that there's at least a little solace in her voice now. "You can get lost if you spend too much time trying to understand how this could be. You have to simply accept that it is."

"How do you know these things, Lucrece? Can you just tell me that? Can you tell me why *you* understand what this fuck-ing bird is saying?"

She pauses again, knowing the answer but afraid to turn it loose, faced suddenly with her own fears and self-doubts. Knowing that her response will bind her to this mystery with knots that no fingers, mortal or undead, can ever unravel.

"Yeah," she answers at last as she takes her hand from Jared's shoulder and begins unbuttoning the front of her dress. "I think that maybe I can." She pulls the dress down past her thin white shoulders, revealing the severe black silk corset underneath. Lucrece turns around so that Jared can see her bare shoulders.

"I had it done about a month after Benny's funeral," she

says. "I hoped that the pain and the healing would help *me* begin to heal some . . ." Her voice trails off as she feels his eyes on her back, tracing the intricate pattern of scars there. The picture the scalpel drew into her skin, the cutting that she meant to be a raven, after Jared's photograph. But the artist only had a picture of a crow to work from and didn't confess that he'd cheated on the design until later, after the gauze and surgical tape were hiding his fresh, weeping work.

"I think that's why I can hear your crow, Jared."

"Oh, Lucrece," he says, and his fingertips graze the crisscross of puckered white tissue.

"It helped a little," she says, and pulls her dress back up, hiding the cutting. "Maybe it's going to help a lot now. Maybe it's going to let me help you."

Jared rises and stands above the crow, and the bird cranes its neck to look up into his face.

"If you brought me back here for nothing, you bastard," he says, "I swear that you'll die very, very slowly."

"I think it's time to cut the macho bullshit, Jared," Lucrece says, her fingers working the last of the dress's pearlescent buttons. "And if you care, it's a she."

Jared glares down at her, uncomprehending, and the crow caws softly.

"The *crow*," Lucrece says. "It's a *she*."

Jared rolls his eyes. "Pardon me," he says.

The crow tells them that there's a little time then, and so Jared rests awhile in Lucrece's arms and listens to the rain, coming down harder now, playing the roof of the building like a perfect and soothing percussive instrument. He closes his dead man's eyes and tries to pretend that these are Benny's arms around him instead of Benny's twin's. She strokes his hair with her long fingers, fingers like Benny's grown softer and more hesitant, but close enough for the game in his head.

"I want to get this awful jacket off you," she says. "And this shirt." He is still in his funeral clothes, slit up the back for the morticians' convenience. "And then I'll find something else for you to wear."

• • •

Jared Poe met Benjamin DuBois at a gallery in the Warehouse District, a ramshackle barn of corrugated steel, punky masonry, and bare concrete floors set so close to the river that the air smelled like mud and rotting fish. It was a performance thing and he'd only gone because it was a friend's boyfriend's show and he'd run dry of excuses. With very few exceptions he'd always found performance art either a horrific bore or simply horrible, a last, pretentious refuge for talentless wanna-bes desperately trying to gouge a niche for themselves. Most of the time he'd end up feeling embarrassed for the performer, embarrassed for the audience trying to understand whatever foolishness was being acted out for them, and so uncomfortable that he'd sneak out halfway through the show.

And the scene that night was no exception, certainly not the worst thing he'd ever seen, but bad enough to make him wish he'd just made up a story about car trouble or leaky plumbing and stayed home. The artist stood on a small stage in the center of the warehouse, wearing nothing but an old alligator hide and a pair of expensive-looking loafers, reading aloud from the *Wall Street Journal*. Fortunately there was a bar and Jared stayed close to it, downing shots of tequila and trying to keep a straight face. But the mask became increasingly difficult to manage as the guy in the alligator skin droned on and on and the Cuervo worked its way through Jared's bloodstream to his brain.

In an effort to distract himself he began eavesdropping on a couple standing a few feet away from him, near the edge of the crowd. Jared had noticed right away how much they resembled one another, and the woman was so tall he thought maybe she was really a drag queen. They were speaking loudly to each other, almost shouting in order to be heard over the stock quotes being read through the microphone onstage, the nasal voice booming from speakers rigged high along the rusty walls. Both were dressed in impeccably tailored leather and latex Victorian costumes, their skin as white as chalk and their hair like black satin. To Jared they looked like some fetish freak's vision of Jonathan and Mina Harker, an unlikely juxtaposition of the prim and perverse, but they wore that vision well no matter how unlikely it might be.

"This is surely hell," the woman said. Her voice seemed to confirm Jared's suspicions about her gender.

"No, no," the boy said, leaning close to her ear and still having to shout. "This is a lot worse than *that*."

The boy wasn't exactly Jared's type. He'd always gone for the well-muscled submissives, the hard but yielding bodies that could take whatever loving tortures he might happen to devise. He'd always found the goth end of the SM and fetish scene a little tedious, too much window dressing for his particular tastes. But *this* boy was something different, something so unexpected with his high, sharp cheekbones and hooded eyes, and Jared was taken completely off guard by the stirring in his jeans. He asked the bartender for another shot of tequila and took a cautious step closer to the pair.

"Hell has better acoustics," the boy was shouting.

"And something worth hearing," the woman shouted back.

"Not impressed, I take it," Jared said, just loud enough to be heard, and they both turned and regarded him skeptically from kohl-smeared eyes.

"Oh, don't tell me," the boy said, one index finger held up for emphasis. "He's this poor, misguided fuck's lover and we've offended his feelings."

"Or maybe he's just a critic for some rag," his companion said. Jared realized, now that they were facing him, that the pair were identical twins.

"No," Jared said, smiling, playing the good sport to their jibes. "He's just the poor schmuck who didn't have any place better to be tonight, that's all."

"Oh," the boy said. "That's better. Then we don't have to make polite over this drivel." Jared shook his head, took a sip of his tequila before responding.

"Hardly. Can either of you make heads or tails of what's going on up there?"

The boy glanced back toward the gator-clad nude and

53

shrugged. "Well," he said after a moment, "we're of two minds on the subject. *I* think it's all an unfortunate misunderstanding. The real artist was held up in traffic or mugged or something, and *this* guy is just some unmedicated street person who conveniently wandered in. The similarity between his delusion and this crowd's expectation was so profound that no one's noticed yet. My *sister*, on the other hand, thinks it's a brilliant metaphor for the creeping gentrification of the—"

His sister interrupted him with a sock in the arm, not hard, but he made wounded sounds and rubbed at his shoulder. "Do you have a name?" she asked, holding out her gloved hand to Jared as if she expected him to bow and kiss it.

"Oh, yeah. Sorry." He shook the extended hand. Her leather glove was as supple as silk and her grip through it was firm but not mannish. "Jared. Jared Poe. I'm a photographer."

"Jared *Poe?* P-O-E Poe?" the boy said, still rubbing his shoulder and glaring sidelong at his sister. "That's a joke, right?"

"Nope," Jared replied, finishing his drink. "I'm afraid it's not. That's my real name."

The sister took a dramatic step back, spread her arms wide, and cleared her throat loudly before she began to speak, her voice broad and deeper than the unfortunate voice blaring through the speakers. She held her head high as she spoke, her eyes focused somewhere past the dust and rafters overhead, and delivered each syllable with stage-perfect diction.

"'But the Raven, sitting lonely on that placid bust, spoke only

That one word, as if his soul in that one word he did outpour.

Nothing farther then he uttered: not a feather then he fluttered—

Till I scarcely more than muttered: "Other friends have flown before—"'"

Then a hippie standing behind them turned and shushed her. The boy rolled his eyes and muttered, "Oh, *please*, like you might miss last week's pork futures." The hippie scowled and turned back toward the performer.

"That was actually very good," Jared said, and the boy

54

regarded his sister with eyes that were somehow jealous and proud at the same time.

"Lucrece is such a terrible show-off," he said.

"It's better than listening to that idiot," Jared said, using his empty shot glass to point in the direction of the Wall Street gator boy.

Lucrece sighed and offered Jared half a smile. "Well, that's a pretty sorry excuse for a compliment, mister, but thanks anyway." And then the hippie hissed, *"Shhhhhhhh,"* louder than before, and her brother stuck his tongue out in response.

"If you *people* aren't interested in the show, maybe you should go elsewhere," the hippie said.

"He has a point," Jared told the twins. "If I have to listen to any more of this crap I think I'll puke."

The hippie shook his head as he turned back toward the little stage. "I honestly pity people like you, who aren't open to new experiences."

"Oh, Jesus in a Ford pickup," Lucrece said, and she took her brother's hand and Jared's and towed them both through the haze of cigarette smoke and the whispering press of bodies toward the loading ramp that served as the gallery's only visible entrance and exit, leading them out into the night.

Outside, the sultry air felt almost cool after the crowded warehouse. They walked northwest along Market Street, away from the river and its fishy miasma. When Jared suggested that maybe this part of town wasn't the best spot for a stroll after dark, Lucrece laughed a soft, low laugh and asked him which part of New Orleans was. The brother, whose name he still had not learned, produced a small silver flask of brandy they shared as they turned off Market and wandered between other derelict buildings, crumbling red brick walls and tin roofs separated from one another by streets neglected so long they were more pothole than asphalt.

The heady combination of the booze and the company of the twins distracted and disoriented Jared. Soon he was uncertain precisely where they were. Nothing looked familiar, or rather everything looked *vaguely* familiar—some corner of the warehouse district that hadn't yet been made fit for yuppie habitation but had for the time being been left as a decaying signpost back to an era when the area had bustled with the noise and activity of forgotten industry.

"Where the hell are we going?" Jared asked finally, and he could hear the slur that had crept into his voice somewhere between the tequila and the brandy.

"What difference does it make?" the boy said, but Lucrece answered, "Our place. It isn't far now."

They came to the mouth of a narrow alley half barricaded with the husks of two burned-out cars and an abandoned refrigerator. As the twins slipped ahead of him, forsaking the weak cover of the streetlights, Jared paused, leaned against the hood of one of the old cars, and tried uselessly to clear his head. He'd never been far enough north to have walked on thin ice, but he thought it must feel something like this, uncertain steps taking him farther and farther from safe and solid ground. The boy turned and looked back at him from the shadows, the darker slice between high, dark walls. "Are you coming or not, Jared? It's not safe out here alone, you know?" He sounded impatient and amused, distantly petulant, and Jared realized that his dick was hard again. Hard for this pretty, taunting goth boy dressed up like some William Gibson version of 1890s London, and probably hard for his haughty bitch twin as well.

"Really, Jared. Benny's right. There are bad people out here." The voice came from somewhere close behind him. He spun around too fast, almost lost his balance, almost fell face first onto the broken pavement. Lucrece was standing by the old refrigerator, although he could have sworn she'd been the one in the lead, had already disappeared down the alley in front of her brother.

"How . . . how'd you do that?"

She just smiled at him.

"Like I said before," Benny sneered from the alleyway, "she likes to show off. She read a book once, that's all."

Lucrece stepped past Jared, still smiling her secret smile,

taking his hand again, and the three of them walked together into the gloom.

Jared's eyes are closed and he hasn't spoken for almost an hour. He is letting the memories settle down over him like silt on a muddy river bottom, like the rain falling out on Ursulines, falling on the roof and windows of the apartment. Lucrece has found a silver comb and is combing his long hair out across her lap.

"You have to tell me everything you know," he says at last, and the teeth of the comb hesitate, lingering in their gentle progress across his scalp.

"It's not much," she says after a moment. "I expect it's not much more than you know already, Jared."

He opens his eyes and watches Lucrece's face carefully as he speaks. "Harrod knew that I wasn't the killer, didn't he?"

She flinches when he says the DA's name, summoning the image of the gray-eyed prosecutor, John Henry Harrod, as shrewd as a butcher's cleaver or the grin of a hungry cartoon wolf.

"I honestly don't think Harrod really gave a fuck one way or the other. He needed a murderer and you were convenient. Nothing personal . . ."

"Bullshit," Jared says, closing his eyes again, knowing the acid tone of his voice hurts her and not wanting to see more pain on her face, knowing he's a coward to look away and looking away anyway. "Harrod was taking care of two birds with one stone. Get rid of the faggot artist and make all the faggot voters happy at the same time."

Lucrece begins combing his hair again, long smooth strokes as if she might still have a chance to calm him, to bring some stingy bit of comfort. Very softly she says, "The killings haven't stopped, Jared."

Now he does open his eyes again, stares speechlessly up at her, unbelieving, as she continues.

"The television and newspapers aren't making much of it.

They're trying to play it all down, I think, calling it a copycat killer. No one wants to think there could have been a mistake, especially since . . ." She pauses, turns her head toward the bed and the crow still perched on the footboard.

Jared finishes for her.

"*Especially* since the man they already put in prison recently got three inches of sharpened spoon shoved in his guts and is buried in Lafayette Cemetery."

"Yeah," she whispers, and the black bird caws.

The twins lived on the entire upper floor of one of the two buildings that flanked the alley. Jared looked back the way they'd come, the dirty, dim light at the far end of the alley, while Lucrece unlocked a steel fire door with an old-fashioned brass key from her purse. Beyond that there was a staircase hardly wide enough for Jared to climb without having to turn sideways. There was another steel door at the top, this one with a small peephole and three deadbolts. Lucrece selected more keys, slid back the bolts one after another, and the door made a dry gritty sound as it swung slowly open. She felt along the wall just inside and flipped a switch, turning on a string of naked incandescent bulbs strung up high among the rafters.

"Jesus," Jared muttered as he followed Benny across the threshold. "Wow. You guys don't do things halfway, do you?"

"What would be the point in that?" Benny asked, but Jared wasn't listening to him, entirely too amazed at what they'd made of the second story of the old warehouse—the refuse of a city turned into impossible elegance, garbage molded into the most unlikely opulence. There were pieces of junked cars and unidentifiable machinery welded into tables and cabinets, semitranslucent curtains of expertly pleated plastic hung for room dividers, broken glass mortared into the walls, glittering like jewels. The only piece of furniture in the place that seemed to be serving its originally intended purpose was a huge canopy bed near the center of the loft. Everything was lacquered in shades of black and red that glimmered wetly under the lights.

"Have a seat," Benny said, pointing Jared toward an armchair near the bed. "We'll get drinks." Jared obeyed, too drunk and stunned to do much else. The chair was upholstered in a deep crimson crushed velvet and its spindly frame had been fashioned from human-looking bones held together with epoxy and metal rods.

"Are these real?" he called after the twins, who were standing on the other side of one of the polyurethane curtains, indistinct, murky figures appearing to move beneath cold and oily waters.

There was the sound of ice cubes and Lucrece called out, "Yes, of course they're *real*." Jared stared down at the chair's armrests—long bones that ended in skeletal fists, one turned upward toward the ceiling, the other grasping for the bare floorboards.

"Real bones are a lot easier to come by in this city than artificial ones," Benny added.

"You know," said Jared, talking now because his voice was better company than his imagination, "there are people who would think this was some pretty sick shit."

Benny slipped through an invisible slit in the plastic, a drink in each hand. "And what about you, Jared *Poe*? Are *you* one of those people? Do *you* think this is some *pretty sick shit?*"

Jared accepted his drink, straight whisky over ice, sipped at it tentatively. Benny sighed loudly and shook his head. "Go ahead, silly. It's not laced, and we didn't bring you here to poison you."

The amber whisky burned pleasantly going down, a brand he didn't recognize, probably something more expensive than the stuff he was used to drinking.

"It is very, very impressive," he said, taking another swallow from his glass.

"Which?" asked Lucrece, who'd come up silently behind him. "Our apartment or your drink?"

"Whichever," Jared answered.

"We made most of it ourselves," Benny said, sitting down on the corner of the big bed closest to Jared. "Oh, but not this, of course," and he patted the bed. "We found this in an antique

59

store on Magazine Street. Saved up for months, but it's been worth it . . ." He let that last thought trail off ambiguously.

Lucrece sat down beside her brother and sipped from her own glass. Again Jared was struck by their resemblance, male and female reflections of the same exquisite face.

"So, Mr. Jared Poe, what is it you photograph?" Lucrece asked as she slipped an arm around her brother's waist.

"Well," he said, watching their every move. His erection was beginning to become uncomfortable, and he shifted in his chair of bones and velvet. "That depends on whether I'm trying to pay the bills or not. If the rent's due, it's mostly weddings and babies . . ."

Benny made a disgusted face and rolled his eyes.

"And the rest of the time?" Lucrece prompted.

"The rest of the time, well . . . I've been putting together a portfolio of nineteenth-century cemetery sculpture and architecture." Jared paused, then went on almost reluctantly, an ashamed or guilty admission: "And sometimes the people I find hanging out in cemeteries."

"*Ah,*" Benny said, his eyes suddenly brightening, eager. "See, Lucrece? I knew he wasn't just another loser art fag."

"Yeah, well, I wouldn't be quite so sure," Jared said, frowning. "You ever noticed how *many* people there are out there taking pictures of the local bone orchards?"

"The *question,*" Lucrece said, speaking not to Jared but to her brother, "is whether or not he's any good."

"Whether or not his *heart* is in it," Benny added. He finished his drink, set the glass on the floor at his feet. The ice cubes clinked faintly against each other.

"What do you mean?" Jared asked, and Lucrece shrugged.

"Anyone can point a camera and click, Jared," she said. "Fucking Yankee tourists on the sight-seeing buses do *that* every goddamn day of the week. The question is, whether or not you genuinely *understand*—"

"—the dead," Benny said, completing her thought. "After all, it's *their* houses that you're putting down on celluloid and paper, right?"

Jared watched Benny's eyes a second before answering, feeling suddenly lost and stupid, in too deep or maybe even completely out of his element. Benny's eyes were the same guarded, brilliant green as his sister's, the green of uncut emeralds.

"Right," he said at last, only half remembering the question. "Right."

"Because it isn't enough to *appreciate* the dead," Benny said. "To simply steal their likenesses and call it art. There has to be an—"

"—understanding," Lucrece said, and Jared realized their habit of finishing each other's sentences was beginning to give him the creeps.

"Any genuine aesthetic of the dead requires, no, *demands* that the artist treat them as something more than mere objects. They must be seen and portrayed as dynamic opposites of life, not empty vessels devoid of anything but the power to make us nervous, afraid of our own mortality."

"And he calls *me* the show-off," Lucrece said, distractedly stirring the ice cubes in her drink with one finger.

Jared was busy trying to process what Benny had said through the alcohol clouding his mind. He shook his head.

"No, I mean, that's really, um, articulate . . ."

"Yeah, ain't it amazing that someone can be this pretty *and* smart too?" Lucrece purred, smiling as she touched an index finger, wet with whisky and water, to her brother's lips.

"But surely we didn't bring him all this way just to talk shop, did we?" Benny asked her, and she shook her head and kissed him lightly on the cheek.

Jared's face felt suddenly hot, flushed, and he knew that he was blushing, and that the twins could probably see that he was blushing.

"That would be terribly, *terribly* rude," Lucrece said, and Benny turned his head, kissing her full on the lips now. The bulge in Jared's jeans responded as if an invisible line had been attached to the end of his penis and someone had just tugged at it sharply.

"I don't know," Benny said, pulling away. The stark light caught in a thin string of saliva linking their lips. "Maybe he's not up to it. Maybe we're wrong and he *is* just another poseur . . ."

Jared swallowed hard, his mouth and throat suddenly very dry. He wished his glass wasn't empty but wasn't about to break this moment by asking for a refill. He squirmed nervously in his strange chair.

"Or *maybe* he's not into boys," Lucrece said, her voice full of mocking regret, and her tongue flicked across Benny's lower lip. And then Benny whispered slyly, mischievously, "Or *maybe* he's not into girls."

"Bingo," Jared said. He'd set his glass in the upturned skeleton hand and covered his lap with his hands, embarrassed at his own embarrassment.

Lucrece sat back, scooting a couple of feet away from her brother, her face an almost comic mask of exaggerated rejection and disappointment. Benny let her go, but his eyes followed her retreat longingly. "Not even girls who used to be boys?" he said.

Jared caught the slicing, flinty edge of the question before Lucrece slapped her brother. It wasn't a playful slap, and the sound of her hand against his skin was very loud in the apartment.

"Bitch," she hissed, and Jared thought there was the faintest, calculated hint of a smile at the corners of her mouth.

"Touché," Benny said.

There are strings everywhere, Jared thought, *not just on the end of my dick.* This scene was something the pair had rehearsed over and over again, he realized, perfected in privacy and practice.

"Never mind," Lucrece said, getting up off the bed. "Fortunately I like to watch. You don't mind if I *watch*, do you, Mr. Poe?"

"Then you are identical twins?" he asked, wondering if perhaps that was pushing her too far, if maybe this spot really was too sensitive for Lucrece and he was blowing his chance at Benny. But she just shrugged, tossed her hair to one side, and said, "Once upon a time."

"Sometimes," Benny said, removing his leather overcoat, "I think my sister will never forgive me for not making the transition with her. For ruining the set, as it were."

"You never had the balls," Lucrece said, and now she *was* smiling, a careful, secret smile that said there was so much here that Jared could never even hope to understand half of it. "You never had the fucking balls."

As Benny began unbuttoning his vest Jared got up from the bone chair, moving slowly, as if he was being scored on every action and reaction, and joined the male twin on the bed. Lucrece left them alone briefly to pour herself another drink, then returned with the bottle and took Jared's place in the chair.

Jared rubs at his temples, wishing it were anything as simple as pain throbbing there. He stands above the crow and the bird looks back up at him with mindful, eager eyes. Lucrece is still sitting on the bedroom floor behind them, holding the silver comb.

"Where am I supposed to start?" he asks, the question posed to the bird or Lucrece, to himself or all three.

"I'm not sure," Lucrece says. When Jared turns around, she's holding strands of his dark hair between her fingers, staring at them. *The way someone might clutch a holy relic*, he thinks, and the thought makes him feel sick to his stomach. *What am I to her? What does she think I've become?*

"I think you're supposed to find Benny's killer and stop him. I think that's what you've been brought back for."

"And Harrod and the cops and that fucking judge, what about them? Aren't they part of this as well?"

Lucrece's eyes reluctantly release their hold on the precious strands of his hair, refocus on Jared standing at the foot of the bed. The bed he shared with her twin brother. The bed Jared first saw in that warehouse apartment so long ago. Lucrece's eyes look as hard and old as New Orleans itself, as wet as the night.

"I'm not sure, Jared. Maybe. But maybe not. The *crow's* supposed to know what happens next, and for some reason it doesn't."

"They set me up," he says. The bird looks away, pecks at the dark wood of the headboard.

"I think we have to be *sure*, Jared, before you do anything that can't be undone."

"Did the fucking cops bother to be *sure* before they arrested me? Before they told the goddamn papers *I* killed Benny? How sure were *they*, Lucrece?" He hears the sour, jagged tone wrapped around his words, the anger cranking itself up a notch.

"I don't think that you can punish everyone, Jared. A lot of people did a lot of stupid things. I think that you have to concentrate on what started it all."

"But you don't know that, do you?"

She sighs, a broken sound like a death rattle.

"No, Jared. I don't know that."

Jared turns away from her, away from the useless bird, and there's his reflection watching him from the mirror above Benny's dressing table—a dead man's pallid excuse for a doppelgänger, its skin like cold ashes. But there *is* fire there as well, bright vengeful coals in those dead and living eyes.

"Please, Jared. Just give me a chance to find out what I can. There are people I know who might be able to help."

Jared steps closer to the mirror and his reflection takes a step to keep up with him. There's a white Mardi Gras mask hanging limply from one corner of the glass, dangling by its elastic strap. Jared picks it up, stares into the vicious, clownish grin molded into the creased and wrinkled leather. The mask has a smile no human face could ever manage, its thin scarlet lips curled back upon themselves, a black smear across the empty eye sockets like the face of a rabid raccoon. Jared bought the mask for Benny from a street vendor, their last Mardi Gras together, and he remembers Benny's emerald eyes glaring at him through those slits.

"Yeah," Jared tells Lucrece as he slips the jester mask over his own, crueler face. "You talk to your witchy friends and see what they say. I'm not going to hold my breath, but you go ask."

Now his eyes fill the space meant for Benny's, his own eyes like last night's fire that only needs to be stirred, that only needs

64

a little tinder to become an inferno again. There's nothing else in his face any more alive than this mask, nothing else but his eyes worth showing, so he leaves it on.

"In the meantime, I have some questions of my own, Lucrece. And I know the people who have the answers."

four

THE GUTTERPUNKS CLUSTERED AROUND THE GATES OF JACK-son Square talk quietly among themselves, as secretive as any cabalistic order. The rain has slacked off a little, enough for them to slip out from under the eaves and doorways and huddle by the tall iron gates. They've come together in the lee of the cathedral, this evening no different than any other, waiting for the commencement of another night's petty dramas and business transactions. Some of them are homeless and some of them only pretend to be because they envy the independence and self-confidence, the freedom, of those who are.

"But, I mean, you know, you don't think he's some kind of pervert?" the tall boy in the long black dress, the boy who calls himself Michele, asks the others, glancing back over his shoulder at the man lingering outside the Presbytere.

"Jesus, will you please get some kind of fucking clue?" The girl who answered him lights a cigarette, exhales expertly through her pierced nostrils, and squints past the smoke at the man standing very still in front of the museum. "No offense, Mikey, but have you bothered to look in a mirror lately?"

"You ain't exactly David fuckin' Duke yourself," one of the boys says, and they all laugh. "You ain't, like, Jesse Helms's fuckin' dream girl yourself."

And Michele glances again over his lean shoulder at the

man in the expensive raincoat. "I bet you he's got money," he says. "I bet you he's got a lot of money."

"You gonna blow him or you gonna roll him?" someone says and they all laugh.

"Beggars can't be choosers, Mikey," the girl taunts, then she goes back to reading a ratty paperback novel she's been carrying around for days. There's only one enticing word, *Silk*, printed across the cover, and the face of a white-haired girl staring out through a dream catcher.

Michele knows they're all still waiting for him to prove himself, to show that he's really one of them, not the new kid anymore. This is his first week on the streets, but already he likes it better than his old life in Shreveport. At least this way he gets paid and has some say about the men he has sex with instead of waiting terrified for his stepfather to stumble into his room every night, drunk and so loud there's no way his mother *couldn't* hear. But never a word from her, never so much as a question, her denial as thick as the Max Factor she caked on her face every morning to try to look twenty-five instead of fifty, as thick as the gray shroud of suburban despair he escaped with a stolen credit card and a bus ticket south.

"Gotta learn to take it like a man," his stepfather liked to tell him if he dared to cry. "It ain't no different than the way the world's gonna treat you. It ain't no different than the goddamn world."

"Watch and learn, Robin," he tells the girl. They all laugh again as he steps away from the crowd, feeling immediately more vulnerable, separated from the pack, on his own. The man in the raincoat notices him and smiles tentatively, drops the cigarette he's been smoking to the cobblestones and crushes it out under the heel of one of his loafers.

It can't be more than ten yards from the gates to the spot where the man is waiting for him in front of the Presbytere, a short obstacle course of tourists and street performers, but the walk feels at least three or four times that far. Michele is sweating by the time he's standing beside the man.

"You're very pretty," the man says, and Michele smiles cautiously for him. "But I'll bet you hear that a lot, don't you?"

You think I'm stupid? the bold, streetwise voice in his head asks the man, the big, brave voice he's spent the past five days cultivating. *You think I don't know you tell that shit to every boy you want to sell you a little head?* But he bats his eyes, just once, shy like the brainless girls at his old school preening for the jocks. "No. No one ever tells me that."

"Well," the man says, "it sure as shit is a cruel old world, then, ain't it?" and in that instant the man sounds so much like Michele's stepfather that he almost backs out, puts his tail between his legs and runs back to the safety of the others, still watching him from the gates.

"Yeah," he says instead. "Yeah, mister, sometimes it sure is."

Robin watches from her seat on the stone steps outside the square as the man leads Michele into the narrow alley between the Presbytere and the cathedral. Part of her feels sorry for him, the same part that feels sorry for them all. *The weak part,* she reminds herself, and so she keeps her thoughts to herself and concentrates on the rap music thump-thumping from the boom box at her feet.

When they're done the man gives Michele a twenty and grunts as he wrestles his zipper closed again. Michele wants to spit, wants to get the flat, briny taste of the man out of his mouth. *Nice girls swallow,* he thinks. He doesn't remember where he heard that but thinks maybe he saw it on a T-shirt once. He's still on his knees, and the old cobblestones of Père Antoine Alley reek of rotting garbage and magnolia leaves and the piss of all the drunken tourists who've ducked into the alley to relieve themselves. The stones hurt his knees and he gets up slowly, checking to be sure he hasn't run his hose.

"I meant what I said," the man says. "I mean about you being pretty and all. You shouldn't even be out here on the streets. You should get yourself a decent job doing drag or something, you know? These streets will mess you up, kiddo. No one stays as pretty as you if they stay out here very long."

Then Michele is alone, watching as the man walks quickly

away from him toward the bright lights and noise and forgiving anonymity of Royal Street. Michele feels something cold against his face and he realizes that the rain's started again, just a light sprinkle so far, but there's thunder too and he knows it'll probably be pouring again in a few minutes. He looks down at the twenty in his hand, the crumpled wad of paper and green ink, and he thinks if he only had one of these for every time he went down on his fucking stepfather, shit, he'd have an apartment in the Pontalba.

He's heading back to the square, eager to show Robin and the others that he didn't wuss out, even more eager to be out of the stinking alley. Then the thunder rattles the sky above him again, rumbles like the growl of something vast and predatory, and Michele decides that he's at least earned a cup of coffee and ten minutes or so out of the weather. Just a short break before the next john, he tells himself. Maybe he'll buy Robin a cup too.

"Does the thunder scare you, Michele?" someone says, someone standing somewhere behind him. He spins around, stares into the shadows crowding the empty length of Père Antoine.

"No," he answers the darkness, and his voice sounds very small and vulnerable, not the big street-voice at all.

"Not even a little?" the voice asks, insistent and unconvinced. "All that power above your head, like the sound of the sky breaking. That doesn't frighten you?"

"It's only thunder," Michele says, straining to see the speaker, and then the thunder comes again: closer, more immediate, as if it's heard what he said, his casual denial of its authority, and is angry.

"Then you're a very brave little . . . girl," the voice replies, and the speaker steps out where Michele can see him. Another tall man, wearing a black windbreaker, his hair soaked, hanging across his face in stringy wet hanks. Michele cannot see the man's eyes.

"Do you *want* something, mister?" Michele asks. This time at least he almost *sounds* like he has his shit together, almost sounds the way he imagines Robin would. Never mind that this

70

guy is starting to seriously creep him out, that the urge to just turn and run back to the safety of the gates of Jackson Square and the company of the others is so strong it's almost impossible to stand his ground.

"I want . . ." the man begins, but his voice is lost in another clap of thunder.

"What?" Michele takes one step backward, wishing now that someone would come along, a bum or a haunted-streets tour or even a fucking cop, *anyone* to interrupt, to break the spell and get him moving.

"I want to talk to you, Michele," the man says. "There are things happening tonight that you and I must talk about."

"I don't have *time* for talk," Michele replies. "I have to make a living." When he turns around, the rain-dulled lights of the square seem so close. Just a few steps and he'll be among people again, back out in the open.

"You'll be paid," the man says behind him, "if that's what you're worried about. You'll get what you've got coming to you. For your time."

"No thanks, mister," Michele says. "I think you've got the wrong person." Now he actually *is* walking back toward the others, and he's amazed at how much brighter the lights are after only a single step away from the man's oily, vacant voice. He's already beginning to feel a little silly at letting himself get spooked so easily, knows how Robin would rag him if she found out. *You gotta get a thicker skin, girl,* he hears her say, *if you're gonna be turning tricks in the Quarter. There's a whole lotta weirdos out there . . .*

There is the deliberate sound of footsteps behind him then, and a sudden pricking pain at the base of his neck. *I've been stung,* he thinks, *Jesus, I've been fucking stung,* remembering once when he blundered into a nest of angry red wasps behind his grandmother's garage. And then the light is far away again, farther than he ever thought it could be. In another moment it is gone and he's alone in a cold and perfect darkness.

● ● ●

71

The man who wears the names of rivers knows that he is no longer like other men, that some part of his fearful work has changed him forever and he can never return to the simple, painless life he lived before. Sometimes the knowing of this hurts him so badly that he sits alone in a dark room for hours and cries for the loss of himself. It is a terrible thing, he knows, to have had so little say in the course of his own life, to have had so many things decided for him before he was even born. To be a soldier in an army of light and blood so secret that there can never be any acknowledgment of his achievements or failures, not even the most fleeting contact with his brothers and sisters in arms, for fear of discovery.

The invaders are everywhere, and Their agents are everywhere. A moment of weakness, one slip, could mean much, much more than the mere loss of his life. He has dreams where someone (never, never him) has been weak, one of the other nameless, faceless soldiers working secretly in the corrupting cities of the world. In the dreams They walk the streets without fear, spreading the androgyne contagion, and the sky burns with the roaring engines of Their warships.

He often wakes from these dreams screaming, curled in his sweat-soaked bed, the choking smells of diesel and burning flesh still hot in his nostrils. But he does not resist the dreams; he understands that they are an integral part of his vision, part of what keeps him strong and certain and pure. He writes down the smallest details of each dream, everything that he can recall, in special black notebooks he keeps in a windowless room in the center of his house.

For almost a week now there has been a new dream, and he knows that it means there is even less time than he'd thought. He has powerful black wings in this dream, the wings of a fierce avenging angel, and they carry him high above the blazing, dying city of New Orleans. The streets below are filled with fire and lakes of blood that burn like gasoline. The writhing bodies of the creatures in Their truest form, Their primary aspect, cling to every wall and rooftop, Their smooth and sexless bodies white as bone beneath the night sky, the wet red holes between Their legs like the beaked jaws of squid or octopi. In the dream Their voices have joined together into a single, hideous wail and Their black and swollen eyes watch jealously as he passes above Them. The end of the dream is always the same, the part where the man with river names looks over his shoulder at the shadow of the crow falling swiftly across the land.

Michele wakes up in a place that smells like disinfectant and mold and latex. He's lying on a bare metal table and there's insane light, white and blinding light that stabs at his eyes and makes his head hurt even worse. He's dizzy and sick and only wants to go back to sleep. Michele closes his eyes, shuts out the hateful light, and then the voice says, "It's time for us to talk, *Michael*."

He's trying to think of what to say, something nasty and appropriate—something Robin would say—when he hears a brittle, snapping noise. Suddenly his sinuses are filled with the scorching reek of ammonia. He coughs and gags as the last merciful shreds of oblivion are driven from his reach and there's nothing left but the light hanging above him and the cold against his bare skin. And the voice.

"There," it says. "You can understand me now?"

Michele tries to answer but his mouth and throat are too dry, not a drop of spit, and his tongue feels two times too big to be of any use.

"Just nod if you understand what I'm saying," the voice says, so Michele nods. He has realized that his hands and feet are tied firmly to the table with wide leather straps. Then there is a glass of lukewarm water being pressed to his lips and he swallows a mouthful.

"The sedative does that sometimes. It'll pass soon and you'll be able to speak."

The glass returns and this time Michele takes a deeper drink, notices that the water tastes faintly of chlorine, like swimming pool water. But it feels like heaven going down his aching throat. As soon as the glass is removed he tries to speak, but there's only an unintelligible rasping wheeze where the words should be.

"Like I said, it'll pass," the voice of the man tells him. He can dimly make out the man's form now, glimpsed through the glare of the light and his tearing eyes.

"Where am I?" Michele croaks. The form moves back a little, out of the glare just enough that its face begins to solidify, its features begin swimming slowly into focus. A thin and haggard face, a face of a very tired young man who looks years older than his age. Michele blinks again, then sees the man's eyes, flat blue-gray eyes like a stormy January afternoon sky, eyes at once cold and filled with the threat of violence.

"I ask the questions," the man says matter-of-factly.

"Is this . . ." Michele begins, but he has to swallow, his tongue working up a few precious drops of spit to wet his throat before he can continue. "Is it a hospital?"

"No," the man says. "But I did say that *I'll* be asking the questions, didn't I? You should save your strength. You're going to need it, Michael."

"Don't . . . don't call me that." Michele closes his eyes, remembering the face from Père Antoine, the rain-bedraggled hair and the sting in his neck, fear rushing up to overwhelm the confusion. It doesn't matter where he is, he knows. He's somewhere bad, somewhere *very* bad he shouldn't be.

"It *is* your name, isn't it? It is the name your parents gave to you." Now there is a small black flashlight in the man's hands. He uses it to examine Michele's eyes, just like a doctor, but Michele knows now the man isn't a doctor.

"It's not . . . my name anymore," Michele tells him, and closes his burning eyes when the probing fingers and black flashlight are taken away. "My name's Michele."

"But that's a girl's name, and you're not a girl, are you?" the man asks.

Michele ignores the question, as he has so many times in the past. "What are you going to do to me?" he asks. The man sighs loudly, and Michele feels the sudden gust of the man's breath blow cool across his bare chest.

"I am going to ask you questions."

74

"Is that all you're going to do? Ask me some questions?"

The man doesn't answer this time. Michele pulls cautiously at the straps at his wrists and ankles. The hard leather cuts into his skin like the blade of a dull knife.

"There's no point in trying to get loose. I'd just tie you down again. You must know that."

Michele stops wrestling with the restraints and moves his tongue across chapped lips that taste like sweat and lipstick. He swallows again, careful to be sure he has control of his voice before he speaks.

"If you weren't afraid of me," he says, "you wouldn't have tied me up in the first place." In response the man makes a sudden, dry sound that's part cough and part angry huff, then slaps Michele hard. Michele's head snaps sideways, smacks roughly against the cold metal tabletop. His mouth fills with the taste of his own blood.

"I have to take precautions, *boy*, but don't underestimate me, and don't overestimate yourself." The man pauses and Michele can tell that he's panting now, his breath coming out fast and hard, furious staccato gasps and wheezes like a winded animal or a frustrated old woman.

"If I thought you posed *any* immediate threat to me or to anyone else I'd have killed you in that fucking filthy alley. There could have been cyanide in that needle, if that's what I'd wanted, just as easy. *Easier.*"

The man pauses, gasps and wheezes his exasperation, and because Michele doesn't know anything else to say, because he's already pretty sure there's no way he's going to walk away from this, he says, "You're crazy, aren't you?"

Growling, the man lunges into the glare of the surgical light so that its glow crowns his head like a mad saint's nimbus. He seizes Michele's face in both his huge, clammy hands, one for either side, his thumbs poised above Michele's eyes like snakes readying to strike. The man's face is only inches from Michele's now, muscles straining against the rage inside. The man's breath smells bad, like rotten vegetables and wintergreen mints.

"You're going to have to do a lot better than that," he says, and his words seem to cling wetly to Michele's cheeks in spatters of spittle. "Jesus! Do you really think I haven't *heard* that before? You think that's all it's going to take to mess with my head?"

The man's hold tightens, his hands like a vise, steel jaws winding themselves closed. Michele thinks that maybe they could crush his skull like a punky old melon if that was all the man wanted, if he wanted this to end so soon, so easily. But Michele knows that the man doesn't want it to be over yet, that what the man wants could take a long, long time and be a lot worse than dying.

"It's just that I've known crazy men before," Michele says, having to strain against the grinding force of the man's hands to move his mouth. "They sounded a lot like you."

"*July second, 1947,* motherfucker!" the man screams into Michele's face, as if that's supposed to mean something to him, supposed to explain all this away. "July second, 1947, you deviant little son of a bitch! You *tell* me what the fuck fell out of the sky that night if you want to live! If you even want the *chance* to get out of here alive!"

Michele swallows and thinks of his stepfather and his shitty little life in Shreveport, thinks of the freedom he felt stepping off the bus into New Orleans, of Robin and the others. He closes his eyes.

"They have medication for people like you," he whispers. The hand on the right side of Michele's face releases its grip and there's a brief moment's relief from the pain before the fist smashes down across the bridge of his nose and the world mercifully swirls away again.

The man stares helplessly down at the broken, bleeding thing he's made of the pretty boy's face, the blood oozing bright from the nostrils, spilling to the shiny silver tabletop to make scarlet pools on either side of his head. The unconscious face still painted like a carnival mask, mocking him with its lie of femininity. Mocking his weakness, the sad fact that he could be so easy to manipulate. Even after all his work, all his careful tests and observations, that he could be made to doubt himself so easily. He looks down at the blood smeared across the knuckles of his right hand, his fingers still clenched, his nails digging themselves into his own flesh. The red stain of the boy's tainted blood says, *You are so weak. You are so very, very weak.*

The man steps away from the examination table and almost trips over a chair. It was such a risk, taking two in one night, first the transsexual, dead now and awaiting its burial, and now this molly boy, not even a larva yet, just a fucking child whore playing dress-up. And the man knows he's not *ever* supposed to bring anything back to the house except the ones who have gone across, all the way across. He's broken one of his own most sacred rules because of the dreams and the things he saw from his window, the bird-things in the clouds above the river, above the city. Because he needed answers and he was too afraid to wait.

You get scared and you get sloppy, he thinks. *You get sloppy and then you get dead.*

"July second," he says quietly, and laughs a cold laugh at his own stupidity. His hands rub nervously back and forth across his trousers. "This one doesn't even know who I am, much less does it know July second. It doesn't know *shit!*"

He paces around the table, circling the boy like a hungry but indecisive shark, wondering how he ever thought this child could be of even the slightest use to him, knowing that it was a choice made from necessity, from blind desperation. If only he could drive the awful dream images away long enough to think more clearly or if he could figure out why it feels like something has changed tonight. Why after so many years of careful, painstaking planning and plotting the rhythm of Their movements, rhythms as predictable as tides or seasons or the phases of the moon, why suddenly *everything* seems so utterly changed. He cannot even remember precisely when he was first cognizant of this new sense of urgency, sometime after he brought the transsexual into his house, sometime after the tests and questions began.

Something from the sky, perhaps. *The thunder?* he thinks, trying to remember what he'd asked the child on the table about the thunder and if it might have been important. The man glances at the clock on the wall and realizes that fully three quarters of an hour have passed since he knocked the boy unconscious. *How? How could it have been that fucking long?* He checks his watch to be sure.

The man stops circling and stands very still. He closes his eyes, concentrating on a calm, small place he keeps hidden deep in his soul, a spot so deep They could never find it. *Something for a rainy day,* he always thinks whenever he needs to remember that part of himself, and right now the rain is drumming hard and icy against the window of the room. There's peace in that space inside him, or as close as he will ever get to peace again. If he can have only a shred of that peace, he can get this shit under control again. And control is all that matters.

The man stretches the calm into something bigger and wraps that thing about him. He stands and listens to his heart and the clock on the wall, the rain coming down outside and the wet, uneasy breathing of the boy on the table. And slowly, but as steadily as the ticking cadence of the sounds filling his ears, he begins to see the simple solution written in the incontestable language of his resolve.

The man first saw Jared Poe two weeks after he'd killed the female-to-male transsexual who'd been interviewed on television. He'd always believed in providence, or something that might as well be providence, so he understood when he saw the flier thumbtacked to a bulletin board in the French Quarter coffeehouse. He was having a cup of black and bitter African coffee at his usual spot in Kaldi's when he noticed the piece of paper, black ink photocopied onto marigold yellow paper and stuck up alongside a dozen other fliers advertising rock bands and lost cats. He pulled the piece of paper off the wall and read it while his coffee cooled enough that he could drink it. PAINED EXPRESSION was printed large across the top in a severe Gothic script. Beneath that was a photograph, poorly reproduced, of a figure on its knees, head bowed. Someone else stood above with a bullwhip. The man was unable to identify the gender of either person.

He smoothed the flier out flat on the top of his table and read it carefully, repeatedly, so he would be sure not to miss anything important. Besides the heading and the photograph, there were a couple of paragraphs clipped from a review in *The Village Voice* announcing the discovery of "the worthy successor to Robert Mapplethorpe, Jared Poe of New Orleans." The article went on to describe the photographer's work as "sublimely twisted" and "derived but certainly not derivative . . . [Poe] understands the subtleties to be mastered in the complete deconstruction of gender and gender roles." There was a Warehouse District address printed below the photograph, a gallery called PaperCut, dates and times. The man, who was still calling himself Joseph Lethe then, folded the flier neatly and slipped it into the front pocket of his shirt.

The next Saturday he took a cab to the opening of Jared Poe's exhibition. PaperCut wasn't a *real* gallery, of course, just an empty old warehouse with a little (and *only* a little) of the grime scraped away, a sign hung discreetly out front. Inside were maybe fifty or sixty people and a maze of pegboards on which Jared Poe's sepia-toned photographs were displayed, each matted on brown paper and framed in rusty steel or shiny chrome.

Joseph Lethe stuffed a five into the Lucite donation box by the door and kept to the fringe of the scattered clots of people milling through the exhibition. His heart had started beating fast when the taxi driver had turned off Felicity onto Market Street, and now he was drunk on the adrenaline and his racing pulse. Here he was, walking among Them and Their acolytes, androgynous bodies in latex and leather and fishnet stockings. Faces painted white as skulls, eyes as dark as empty sockets. Bits of metal and bone protruding from lips and eyebrows, jewelry like the debris of an industrial accident. They took no notice of him, the assassin in Their midst, just carried on with Their preening and posing. He had never felt half so powerful as he did at that moment, surrounded by the enemy and so clearly invisible to Them.

Joseph Lethe had brought one of his yellow legal pads and a mechanical pencil. He stood before each of the abominations hung from the pegboards, astounded and entranced that They would allow Themselves to be displayed so openly, Their perverse likenesses put down on paper, flaunted. He made careful notes on the photographs, recording their titles and exhibition numbers, writing concise but careful descriptions of each and every one.

When he realized that someone was watching over his shoulder he turned around fast, one hand spread protectively over his notes. The intruder was a tall creature disguised as a woman, scarecrow-thin and pale as chalk, as if every inch of exposed skin had been airbrushed the same matte white. It was wearing a ratty black T-shirt with the sleeves and collar hacked away, skintight black stretch pants that revealed no evidence of its genitalia, if indeed it had any to conceal. There was a single red dot painted between its dark, thin eyebrows, like a Hindu woman's *bindi*.

It smiled, showing perfect, even teeth, and said in a velvety voice that was neither masculine nor feminine, "Do you write for a newspaper?"

"No, no," he replied, surprised at how calm his voice was, no trace of the panic welling up inside, the fear that he had been discovered after all. "I'm just a student."

"Oh," it said apologetically, and blinked once.

Its eyes seemed wrong in no way that he could put his finger on. He looked quickly back at the photograph he'd been busy examining when the creature had interrupted him.

"He really is very good, isn't he?" the creature asked. "I mean, he's not just another bullshit wanna-be taking fetish snapshots for the lookieloo norms."

"Yes," Joseph Lethe agreed coolly, careful not to sound *too* enthusiastic. "He is good. He is, well . . ."

The creature finished for him. "Genuine," it said conclusively. "He is genuine."

Joseph Lethe stared intently at the photograph, praying the thing behind him would go away, that its curiosity was sufficiently satisfied. This print was titled *Skylla and Kharybdis*. Like most of the others he'd looked at so far, it showed two murky figures, one on either side of the picture. The figure on the left had both its long arms flung wide, its head back and its small breasts bared. The figure on the right had its back turned to the first and was curled into a hard knot of muscle and shadow. Something small and hard and indistinct hung between them, suspended on a taut piece of wire.

"'God or man,'" the creature behind him whispered, "'No one could look on her in joy.'"

"What?" he asked. "What did you say?" He turned to face it again, but already it was moving away from him, inserting itself seamlessly into a small cluster of bodies farther along the aisle of pegboards.

He wiped at his forehead and realized for the first time how hot it was in the warehouse, that there was no air-conditioning, only huge and ancient-looking fans rotating slowly high overhead. He was drenched in sweat. Joseph Lethe clutched his yellow legal pad and moved along to the next print.

This one was titled *The Pleasures of Teirêsias* and was the first that he'd encountered with only a single figure, or what he at first *mistook* for a single figure. He leaned close and could see that it was in fact a double exposure, with two bodies occupying the same space. He thought perhaps there was a male body superimposed over a female, but it was hard to be sure. Both forms were draped with strips of raw meat and the viscera of slaughtered animals, and the figures stood in a dark slick of blood that had run down their naked bodies and pooled about their bare feet. Only their faces were clear, unblurred by the photographer's trick, their two heads, male and female, turned in profile to the left and right, respectively.

And he realized something else then. All the photographs so far had shown the same couple, a boy and a girl whose features were so perfectly matched that they had to be brother and sister, maybe twins. He felt a small chill across the back of his neck like a sudden gust of cold air. Joseph Lethe wiped at his sweaty forehead again, wiped his hand on his pants, and wrote down the title of the photograph.

Past a final divider of pegboard, toward the back of the gallery, there was a folding table set up where wine was being served in Dixie cups along with dry-looking slices of a white cheese on wheat crackers. Joseph Lethe knew better than to eat or drink anything here, so he ignored his parched throat. But he did approach the table and the people gathered there, all talking excitedly at the same time. He hung back at the edge, waiting for a good look at the artist himself, who was seated at the table. It had taken Joseph Lethe a little over an hour to complete his catalog of every photograph on display, forty-three prints altogether, and he held his legal pad tucked safely under one arm.

Shortly after he'd realized that the same two models had posed for all the photos, he'd begun paying attention to the titles. There was clearly a pattern, and patterns were always the key to understanding, to putting a new part of the intrigue into context. Most of the titles had been taken directly from Homer, *The Iliad* and *The Odyssey*, the rest named for other random bits of Greek mythology. Only one broke the pattern, so he knew it must be the means of access to this cipher of light and shadows. The crucial photograph had been given the incongruous title *The Raven*, a reference to the poem, he assumed, and a pun as well—Jared Poe's *The Raven*. But Joseph Lethe also suspected that indicated that the poem would prove to be the Rosetta stone for the entire exhibition.

The Raven showed the male model only, his face made up like a woman's. His hands had been bound with electrical tape and insubstantial wings somehow had been made to sprout from his skinny shoulder blades. It was the only photograph in which either of the models had been permitted to look into the camera. One corner of the boy's rouged lips was turned up in a snarl or sneer, an animal expression of threat or defiance, and his eyes sparkled with a wicked, secret glee—like the eyes of the creature that had spoken to Joseph Lethe minutes ago, simply *wrong* in a way he couldn't yet explain. He'd made a note to concentrate more on Their eyes in future examinations.

A breach opened in the crowd and he could see that Jared Poe was busy talking to a plain-looking woman taking notes. He was nothing like the monster that Joseph Lethe had prepared himself for, none of the expected cross-dressing or physical modification. The photographer appeared to be in his mid-thirties, maybe a little older, dressed simply in a black T-shirt and blue jeans. The only notable thing about his face was a two- or three-day growth of beard. However, there was only a fleeting second or two for Joseph Lethe to wonder that a man who appeared so normal could be behind the profanities he'd just witnessed, a moment of surprise before he noticed the figures seated just behind and to either side of Jared Poe.

They were the strange brother and sister from the photographs. There could be no mistake about that, and he felt as if he'd seen something he wasn't supposed to, as if he should look away or hide his eyes. He prayed that the shock of seeing the pair in the flesh had not shown on his face.

The woman was seated on the left and the boy on the right, holding the photographer's hand tightly. The models were wearing matching black dresses, simple clinging things that showed off the lines of their bodies, the scant differences of muscle and fat that distinguished one from the other. They *were* twins. He was certain of that now, and he was almost as certain that they were identical twins as well, although he knew that natural opposite-sex identical twins were a biological impossibility. Then the woman raised her head and looked straight at him and there were those eyes again. That indefinable wrongness in her outwardly friendly glance. The sudden heat he'd felt earlier in the evening returned, washing his skin in goose bumps. He flinched, barely managing not to look away. He felt as though she were peeling him with those eyes, removing the onion layers of clothing and skin and deception to see what lay underneath. Joseph Lethe felt sick and dizzy.

"You don't look so good," a voice said. He knew it was the creature that had spoken to him before, knew that there were *two* pairs of those terrible eyes on him now, probing his body and mind and soul, and that knowledge made him want to run.

The sensation of those eyes made him want to take steel wool and borax to his skin to be rid of their touch.

Instead he stood very still and kept his eyes on the female model. She smiled at him, a gentle smile that he knew was meant to put him at ease, to lull him into a false and treacherous sense of security, but he knew also that she'd seen the truth. She understood precisely who and what he was, and in a moment she would stand and point, or whisper into the photographer's ear . . .

"You don't look well," the creature said more loudly, somewhere very close. "Would you like something to drink?"

"I'm *fine*," he replied, turning away, pulling himself free of the female twin's gaze. He imagined fishhooks imbedded just below his skin yanking free as he moved away from her, tiny bits of himself clinging to rusty metal. She would reel them in, would have them as proof of his existence. As he walked quickly back through the aisles of pegboard the photographs seemed to peer out at him now like accusing gargoyles, hungry sentinels that might spring to life at any moment to tear him to ribbons.

But he made it past them, through the door and out into the warm and sticky night. Joseph Lethe kept moving until he'd put a full block's length between himself and PaperCut, the things gathered inside, and those hideous photographs. Then he stopped, breathless, leaning against a telephone pole, his sides aching and the panic beginning to fade by degrees. He looked up into the summer sky, past the halo of streetlights and into the dim splash of stars, pinpricks so far away and all that hellish nothing in between. He shuddered, remembering the twin's eyes, her expression of smug triumph. It would come back to him again and again as surely as the constellations spread out above the delta and the winding Mississippi. It would be with him forever.

He'd fucked up, had allowed curiosity to make him careless, had walked straight into a trap set for him and him alone. It was so plain now, so fucking *obvious*, an elaborate banquet of misinformation and red herrings that They'd known all along would be irresistible to him. They'd drawn Their one nemesis out into the open, and now They'd seen his face, knew the smell of his fear.

From now on his work would be different. It would no longer be the simple game of him picking Them off at his leisure. He had become, in a single reckless evening, the hunted as well as the hunter. That They had allowed him to escape was an indication of nothing more or less than Their deserved confidence that They could take him whenever They were ready.

Joseph Lethe closed his eyes and became Stanley Hudson, hoping that the switch might buy a little of the time he needed. He kept his eyes shut until his breathing and pulse had slowed almost to normal again. Then he removed the folded sheet of yellow paper from his pocket and stared down at the photocopied excerpt from the *Voice* article. It only took him a moment to find what he was looking for, the brief mention of the photographer's studio apartment on Ursulines Street.

Stanley Hudson refolded the flier and returned it to his shirt pocket. He glanced once last time in the direction of the gallery and disappeared into the night.

Stanley Hudson spent almost a whole week locked away in his tall, dark house by the river, eating nothing that he had not purchased in a can and carefully microwaved first. He spent a week studying his explicit notes on Jared Poe's photographs, a week trying to find some way to turn the tables back to his advantage, to unravel the net that had been cast so expertly over him.

Maybe, he decided, the photographs weren't entirely useless after all. The exhibition itself was an act of misdirection, of that much he was now certain, but the individual photographs might still prove useful—*if* he could read between the lines, if he could even discover which lines to read between. He suspected that the answer lay in the placement and composition of the last print he'd seen, *The Raven*. It was meant to throw him off the track, but maybe in that act of bravado They had shown something far truer of Their nature than all of his experiments could ever hope to reveal. If he only had the actual print in his possession, or even a Xerox, if only he didn't have to work from memory and his ultimately inadequate notes, he might begin to understand its significance.

When he felt that he could wait no longer, that every day he spent huddled over his notes was another nail driven into the lid of his coffin, Stanley Hudson packed the simple, deadly things he needed into an old leather satchel he'd bought years ago in a junk shop, all the sharp and shining things that would be required, all his needles and wire and surgical thread. But because this move against Them was not meant merely to demonstrate his superiority, not meant merely to eliminate the immediate threat to his life and mission, he also packed an assortment of specimen jars and preserving fluids. Because in Their desperation to entrap him, They had carelessly revealed one of Their most terrible perversions of the natural order, and his work required that he must never forget his role as a scientist as well as a soldier.

The very last thing that went into the old satchel would serve no greater purpose than to show Them that he was not the fool they'd mistaken him for, that They had given him the clue that in time would be Their downfall. He laid the two pages he'd sliced from his thick paperbound edition of *The Unabridged Edgar Allan Poe* on top of the rest. Then Stanley Hudson snapped his black bag shut.

He waited until he was sure that the photographer was gone, that he wasn't just *pretending* to have left the apartment, before he stepped out of the recessed doorway where he'd spent most of the morning and crossed Ursulines. It took him only a couple of minutes to pick the lock on the wrought-iron security door, would have taken him half that long if he hadn't had to keep checking to be sure no one watched. The tumblers clicked and rolled beneath his skillful ministrations, and he eased the door open slowly so it wouldn't clang against the wall of the small entryway before the stairwell, shut it even more carefully behind him.

The stairs were wooden, so he slipped his shoes off and climbed them in his sock-clad feet. There was only one door at the top, and he breathed a hushed sigh of relief that there was no chance he'd be breaking into the wrong apartment. He pressed his ear against the door and listened, past discordant strains of rock music playing loudly inside and the thumping of his own heart, for some sign that he'd guessed correctly, to be *sure* he hadn't gone to all this trouble for nothing. After a moment there was the unmistakable sound of footsteps, someone walking across the creaky pine floors on the other side of the door, and Stanley Hudson went to work on the deadbolt.

"I don't . . . know . . . what you're talking about," Michele slurs, his voice thick and syrupy from the numbing drugs the man has given him to keep the pain to a dull and distant roar. Michele has begun to think of the pain as The Pain, as a starving, fire-eyed thing with too many heads and too many mouths, chained to a wall, and the chain slowly coming free of the masonry. It seems now as if The Pain has been with him all his life. He knows now that there is only one way it will ever finally tear itself loose and gobble him up, like the Big Bad Wolf and he's just Little Red Riding Hood with an Adam's apple and a dick and there will never be peace anywhere again except in the acid darkness of its belly, the dissipating pit of its gut.

"I don't know . . ."

The man stops cutting then, abruptly, as if he's finally accepted that Michele is telling him the truth. The scalpel clangs loudly into the metal tray with all the other instruments and the man's red latex hands pass between Michele's eyes and the parts that have been cut loose and hang on hooks above the table where he can see them, has to see because the man took his eyelids right at the start.

"Of course you don't, child," the man says gently. Then he is filling a syringe with a clear liquid. He plunges the needle into the exposed muscles of Michele's abdomen, and The Pain lunges forward one last time. The sounds of its claws and the

87

crumbling stone are very loud, drowning the raw world of meat and steel.

"But even unknowing pawns have their uses, Michael," says the man. Then he whispers indistinctly, something that sounds like "Forgive me," before The Pain opens its jaws wide and Michele slips easily, gratefully, down its gullet.

Stanley Hudson had thought he would find both the twins waiting in the apartment above Ursulines and was disappointed that there had been only the boy. It was the girl who had recognized him, who had violated him with her smirking, triumphant stare. But he would catch up to her later, he told himself, when he was finished with the boy named Benjamin.

He paused in the room where every surface was stained in complementary shades of red and black, paused and corrected himself. He would catch up to *it* later. Benjamin had told him everything he wanted to know, had confessed how his identical twin brother had gone to Trinidad, Colorado, six years earlier for the surgery, the final step in the conversion, surrendering its humanity for whatever dark rewards They promised Their disciples. *It is approximately 260 miles due south from Trinidad, Colorado, to Roswell, New Mexico,* he absently reminded himself, glancing once again past the slaughter on the canopy bed to the print of Jared Poe's *The Raven*. The dead boy still stared out at Stanley Hudson from the photograph, but any menace that face might have harbored had been negated by the cleansing rites of the knife.

He leaned down, reaching into the leather satchel at his feet, and removed the pages he'd cut from *The Unabridged Edgar Allan Poe*. He silently counted the lines as he scanned the opening stanzas of the poem. When he reached the twenty-sixth line, he marked it with a yellow highlighter pen he'd found earlier in Jared Poe's office. And then he read the line aloud.

"'Doubting, dreaming dreams no mortal ever dared to dream before . . .'"

DILLONS THE BOOKSTORE
14-16 Bold Street
LIVERPOOL
L1 4DS
Tel: 0151 7086861

153 CASH-1   9920 0022 001

LAZARUS HEART, THE   QTY 1   5.99
                TOTAL   5.99

                TOTAL   5.99

CARD NUMBER   675940421731139754
ISSUE NUMBER   1
EXPIRY DATE   0999
AUTHORISATION CODE   00002607
SWITCH   SALE   5.99

THANK YOU FOR SHOPPING AT DILLONS

                      25.04.99 11:25

Twenty-six times two, he thought, *is fifty-two,* and he counted down to line fifty-two and subtracted six lines, one for each year since the living twin's conversion, and read line forty-six out loud as he traced over it in neon yellow.

"'But, with mien of lord or lady, perched above my chamber door—'"

Stanley Hudson sighed wearily and stared again at the photograph watching him from the other side of the room.

"'With mien of *lord or lady,*'" he repeated slowly, satisfied that his message would be understood, that They would know he'd caught on, had made all the appropriate connections. He stood and walked around the end of the bed, stepping carefully over the boy's bowels and kidneys, the upper portion of his liver, and used a piece of Scotch tape (also borrowed from Jared Poe's office) to stick the highlighted pages to the blood-speckled glass protecting the photograph. Then he left the yellow pen in the mess heaped in the center of the bed, removed his surgical gloves, and went to the apartment's bathroom to wash his face.

That night when Jared Poe was arrested for the murder of his lover, Stanley Hudson had just allowed himself to become Joseph Lethe again. He watched the news reports on the old black-and-white television in his kitchen while he ate his dinner of canned beef stew, listened to the anchorman's account of the boy's grisly death and a short interview with a New Orleans homicide detective.

At first he felt jealous and angry, jealous that the credit for *his* work was going to the deviant photographer, though that was what he had intended. But then the reporter asked the detective if there was any connection between the death of Benjamin DuBois and the Bourbon Street Ripper killings, and although the detective refused to comment, Joseph Lethe had seen the hopeful, guarded glint in the cop's eyes. As the anchor segued into a story about an alligator attack in Bayou Segnette, he chewed a mouthful of mealy beef and potatoes and reminded himself that there were more important things than his pride.

By killing the twin he had scored a double victory against Them, had taken not one acolyte but two. Because now the photographer, who had been chosen to spread Their monstrous images, to subliminally disseminate Their lies through his perverse "art," would be locked away in prison, useless. And if the police believed that Jared Poe was also responsible for the other killings, then it bought Joseph Lethe a lot more time. He washed the stew down with a sip from a can of warm Canada Dry ginger ale and allowed himself a cautious smile.

Joseph Lethe wraps the boy whore's body in garbage bags and binds them together with a whole roll of duct tape, until the mess is contained in a neat package. Because this one cannot be buried conveniently in the yard, because the yard is only for the ones that have gone completely across, he carries the body down all the flights of stairs that lead from his examination room to his garage and dumps it into the trunk of his car.

The thunder growls, reminding him of the storm and his visions. He opens the garage door and stares out into the storm-haunted darkness. There's still an hour left until dawn, plenty of time for him to finish the job. The fear and confusion, the dangerous uncertainty that plagued him earlier in the evening and threatened to erode his will, are gone now, washed away by the meticulous, familiar ritual of the boy's vivisection.

High above New Orleans a brilliant fork of lightning stabs down at the world. Joseph Lethe sees the outline of a gigantic ebony bird spreading its wings wide above the rain-lashed city. *A sign*, he thinks, and a warning too. That something is coming, something new and terrible sent to stop him. Something that he must lure into the open so that he can confront it, destroy it, as he destroyed Their plans against him a year before. He closes the trunk, checks to be sure it's locked, and gets into his car.

five

"NO," LUCRECE SAYS, BUT JARED IS ALREADY THROUGH THE bedroom window, following the crow. He doesn't pause to consider the unseen force that threw the windows open as the bird fluttered cawing above the bed. And he does not pause to question gravity or the distance down to the street; he moves now on instinct alone, an instinct that either he's carried back with him from the grave or flows into him from the crow. He hears the French windows bang closed behind him, shutting out the storm again, shutting out Lucrece. There is a faint sense of vertigo, not of falling but of the risk of falling, and the commingled flapping from the long tails of the latex frock coat and the bird's broad wings.

Then there is a flat and solid rooftop beneath his feet. Jared turns, looking back toward the apartment. He can see dim, unsteady candlelight behind the curtains. He imagines movement on the other side, Lucrece coming to see if he's lying broken on the street, but the crow caws again, a harsh, demanding sound. Jared looks away, stares instead down at the bird perched on the edge of a sagging, leaf-clogged gutter.

"What now?" he asks.

The crow shakes herself, throws a crystal spray of raindrops from her feathers. She peers up at him, her eyes eager, impatient but indecisive.

"That's what I thought," Jared says, tasting the rain on his lips, the faint oily taint of petrochemicals in the drops. "You're turning out to be pretty goddamn useless, you know?" The crow blinks, squawks again, as if to say, *I already dragged your sorry dead ass all the way back from hell, didn't I?* She shakes herself a second time and looks south toward the lights of Bourbon Street.

"You can't find the guy who killed Benny, and you don't know why. Well, while you're figuring it out, I have some other scores to settle. Any chance you can help with *that?*"

The bird looks away.

"I think you have to," Jared says. "Maybe you're not *supposed* to, but I can make you. Because you know where they are, and you know they damn well deserve it."

The crow huddles into herself and emits a small, mournful croak. He sees that she is shivering, but he is no longer capable of anything like pity, least of all for this black bird that dragged him out of oblivion.

The rain is cold, though, and he does wonder a moment that he can still feel cold. Then another wave of loss and anger washes over him, a thousand times more chilling than the storm, more bitter than the polluted rain. Hurt so big and heavy it can only cripple him or drive him on.

"Is that *all* there is to keep me moving?" he whispers, suspecting that the bird doesn't have the answer but needing to ask anyway. *The loss and the anger*, he thinks, fingering the words like bullets, and says, "I'm wasting time, aren't I?"

The crow replies by spreading her wings and hopping from the rain gutter into the air above Ursulines Street, heading away from Bourbon. Jared lingers only a moment, glances one more time toward the apartment before he follows, moving like something only a little more substantial than shadow across the roofs and the empty spaces in between.

At first Jim Unger thinks he has screamed himself awake, but Julie's still asleep beside him, so maybe the scream never made it out of the nightmare, out of his throat. He's shivering, drenched in slick, cold sweat. He fumbles in the dark for his cigarettes on the bedside table, lights a Camel, and inhales deeply, checking the LED readout on the clock radio. It says 3:37 A.M. in squarish phantom-green numbers. Unger takes another drag off his cigarette. His head is still too full of the dream, the red cascade of images and sounds, and his heart is racing as though he's just run a marathon.

In the dream he was back in the apartment on Ursulines, the one where his part in the arrest and conviction of Jared Poe began. Except *this* time he was the first one through the door, the first one to see the blood and viscera dripping down from the walls and ceiling. In the dream he was the one to find the pages taped to the photograph and he was standing there, reading them out loud, just the highlighted lines—he can't remember them now, but in the dream they were so fucking clear—and someone was snapping pictures. The flash went off like white bolts of lightning, one after another, and he asked whoever was doing it to please fucking stop so he could fucking concentrate.

And then there was the sound of something at the window and he turned to see. Behind him the idiot with the camera was still snapping away, *flash, flash, flash,* and he heard Fletcher saying, "Jesus, Jimbo, don't open it. Don't let it *in* here," and Vince Norris said, "Well, ain't this some pretty faggot shit we got here? Fuckin' *sick* sons of bitches, if you ask me."

"Shut up," he hissed, reaching over the bits of human body scattered across the bed, reaching for the windows to open them, to let it in so it would stop making those *sounds,* like the night coming apart at the seams, like a thousand sharp beaks or claws working at the glass.

"Jesus, Jimbo," Fletcher said. "You *wanna* let it in here with us? Is that what you want?" But his hand was already grasping the blood-smeared handle, already pulling one of the windows open wide. From the other side came an irresistible grinding force, and a sudden wet flood of entrails and feathers flowed in over the headboard of the bed. He caught a fleeting glimpse of something else out there, something vast and restless on scaly stilt legs before he woke up, the scream dying on his lips, mercifully taking any impressions of the thing outside the window away with it.

Unger gets out of bed, careful not to wake his wife, not to interrupt her dreams. He crosses the room to the coat hook on the back of the closet door, the hook where he always keeps his shoulder holster and service revolver. He takes it out and checks the chambers, all six loaded, then slips it back into its leather cradle.

Just the simple action helps a little, makes him feel more real, more grounded. He takes another drag off the Camel and looks over his shoulder, across the room toward the single window hidden behind the ugly purple drapes that Julie brought with her when she moved in. He can hear the rain pounding at the glass, enough like the sound in his dream that he makes the connection. A few seconds later there's a flash of lightning.

It's been almost a week since he got the news about Poe, how some big Cuban had cut him open and he'd died before anyone in the prison infirmary was able to stop the bleeding. *Good fucking riddance*, he said. *Saves the taxpayers the cost of juicing the pervert bastard.*

"You're a coldhearted SOB, James Unger. Anyone ever bothered to tell you that?" Pam Tierney had said that, and he looked at her and smiled, thinking, *Yeah, bitch, and everyone in this department knows you're a fucking bulldyke*, but all he said was, "Honey, I don't get paid to be a sweetheart."

"Well, you'd sure be one sad, penniless motherfucker if you did," she said.

Detective Jim Unger sits down on the floor beside the closet door to finish his cigarette, within easy reach of his gun. He counts the seconds between each flash of lightning and the thunderclaps that come after, and he keeps his eyes on the window.

He'd been on the force almost ten years, had spent the last four of those on homicide, and in that time Jim Unger had seen

94

some pretty awful shit. Gunfights, knifings, strangulations, an ax murder, bodies hacked up and dumped into the bayous to be chewed on by gators and crawfish—he'd once seen the corpse of a woman that a perp had tried to dissolve in a bathtub full of muriatic acid. But nothing, absolutely *nothing*, had prepared him for what was waiting in the bedroom at the top of a squeaky stairwell near the corner of Ursulines and Dauphine that muggy August afternoon. And nothing ever *could* have.

Vincent Norris was still his partner then, lanky white-haired Vince who'd moved from the wastes of north Texas to New Orleans to be a cop, who talked like a bad actor in an old cowboy picture. Vince had never learned to laugh at all the sick shit they had to deal with day in and day out, had never managed to set up that necessary buffer between himself and the job.

They reached the scene way ahead of the coroner, just minutes after a hysterical old woman had flagged down a patrol car. That was almost three months before Vince had his nervous collapse, or whatever the hell the doctors finally decided to call it, and left the force.

Vince phoned him once from the hospital in the middle of the night, his voice groggy from all the tranquilizers they had him on. He spoke quietly and very slowly, hesitantly, as if he was afraid someone might overhear.

"How you doin' out there in the real world, Jimbo?" he asked.

"Doing fine, Vince," Jim replied. "Doing just fine. Are they treating you all right in there?"

There was silence from the other end of the line, so long that finally Jim said, "Hey, Vince. You still with me, pal?" And Vince came back, but now he was whispering.

"They're giving me these little *pills*," he said, "Three times a day, Jimbo, these little red *pills*," and he paused again. Jim could hear the muffled tattoo of footsteps in the background before Vince continued.

"They don't help," Vince said, and now Jim was straining to hear him. Vince didn't just sound like he was whispering; he sounded like he was speaking into the telephone from the bottom of a very deep well, as if someone had dangled the receiver over the side of a pit and Vince's words were crossing all that darkness.

"I can still see it, Jimbo," he said. "I can still see what was up there."

Jim swallowed, his throat gone almost too dry to speak. There were goose bumps on his arms, like an allergic reaction to what he was hearing.

"You gotta trust those doctors, Vince. They know what they're doing," he said, trying for Vince's sake to sound as though he believed what he was saying.

"It takes a little time, but you'll—"

Click. The line went dead. Unger sat there for a while, sipping Scotch whisky and staring at the silent phone.

When Jim Unger was a rookie a desk sergeant told him, "You let all this bullshit get to you and you'll be picking petunias off the wallpaper." He had taken the advice to heart. He'd spent the years letting the things he saw, the atrocities that human beings were capable of doing to each other and to themselves, numb him, build up a thick callus around his soul. And maybe that's why he would only have nightmares about what they found in Jared Poe's apartment.

There were two squad cars outside when he and Vince arrived, their lights washing the darkening street red and blue. Vince went up the stairs first. A cop named Fletcher met them at the door to the apartment.

"You guys better brace yourselves good," he said, "'cause you ain't even gonna believe this one." Fletcher looked green, and he must have seen the unspoken skepticism in Jim's eyes, because he said, "My partner's in there puking. I *ain't* kidding you. This one is un-fucking-believable."

That was when Jim first noticed the smell, the cloying stink of blood and shit and raw flesh, the way he imagined a slaughterhouse might smell. Vince covered his mouth with one hand and mumbled, *"Je-sus."*

"I almost think someone used one of them wood chippers on the body," Fletcher said, shaking his head as he led them through the stinking apartment to the bedroom.

"Oh, goddamn," Vince Norris muttered, and he managed to get out of the doorway to the bedroom and halfway to the bathroom before he vomited, so at least he didn't contaminate the scene.

"I *said* I wasn't fucking kidding," Fletcher said defensively, and stepped aside so that Jim could get a better view.

Jim almost asked where the hell the body was, but he stopped himself as his first impression began to fade. A better question, he realized, would be where the hell the body *wasn't*. The walls, the furniture, the floor, the goddamn ceiling, *everything* was painted with a sticky, wet veneer of human gore. It was like looking into the belly of some bizarre and gargantuan creature whose insides just happened to resemble a bedroom. The only things he could recognize as actual human parts were on the big canopy bed: the victim's feet and hands, tied to the bedposts with nylon cord that might have been white once, but was now the same crimson as everything else.

He turned away, fighting his rolling stomach, determined not to be sick. "That's not even fucking possible," he said to Fletcher.

"If you'd asked me half an hour ago, I'd have agreed with you one hundred percent."

"I need a cigarette." Jim moved back toward the front door, trying to put some distance between himself and the smell. Vince was on his knees now, dry-heaving, and that sure as hell didn't help any. Jim leaned against a chair and lit one of the menthols he kept for the really bad cases, inhaled the smoke and stared at the floor and the scuffed toes of his shoes. The taste of the cigarette did little to mask the blood-and-vomit reek filling his nostrils.

"Where the hell's everyone else?" he asked Fletcher, exhaling. "There were two cruisers out there."

"They're downstairs with the old lady," the beat cop replied. "The one who found it. She lives downstairs. I think maybe she owns this place."

97

"She found that?" Jim asked.

"Yeah. There was blood dripping out of her fucking ceiling, if you can believe *that* shit. She came up to see what was going on, found the door unlocked. They're trying to keep her calm until an ambulance gets here."

"But she didn't see anyone else up here? Just . . . that?"

"Not that she's told us about so far."

Jim sighed, breathed out smoke that tasted like cough drops, and looked over at Vince.

"You gonna be okay over there?"

Vince wiped his mouth with the back of his hand, started to answer, nodded instead.

"I know the coroner's office is just gonna *love* the mess you've made on the floor," Jim said.

"Fuck 'em," Vince muttered. Then he was gagging again.

"Find him a wet towel or something, will you?" Jim said to Fletcher. They heard the ambulance, and Jim took another drag off his cigarette.

"You may as well take your time, boys," he said.

There was the sound of a toilet flushing from behind a closed door that Jim assumed led to the bathroom. A moment later the door creaked open and a younger officer he didn't recognize stepped out. The kid's face was the color of old feta cheese.

"Think you're gonna live through this?"

"Maybe," the kid replied, smiling weakly. "Maybe not." Vince slipped quickly past him and shut the bathroom door again.

When the paramedics started up the stairs Fletcher played interception and routed them back to the old lady's place. They gave her oxygen and a mild sedative, but nothing so strong that she wouldn't be able to talk when the time for questions came. The coroner's wagon arrived shortly after the ambulance. Jim Unger had stepped outside, hoping the night air would drive some of the fetor of the apartment from his nostrils, where it seemed to have taken root like a creeping red fungus. There'd been very few times when he'd thought of the air in the French Quarter as fresh, but this was one of them. After the abattoir upstairs, the ever-present background scents of sewage and river water, ripening garbage and mildew seemed familiar and soothing.

The coroner was a heavyset third-generation Irishwoman named Pam Tierney. Jim Unger knew she considered cops a necessary evil at best, thugs who were only there to keep her crime scene from getting trampled before the *real* detective work could be done. He'd actually seen her slap a policeman's hand for touching a coffee cup that lay near a body. "Just keep your hands in your pockets," she'd said. "I don't think that should be too hard for a bright young man like you."

She stood in front of him now, peering expectantly at the windows of the second-story apartment.

"Word on the radio is you got something special waiting for me up there."

"Oh, I think they ordered this one just for you, Tierney," he said, making no effort to hide his feelings for the woman. Jesus, half the ward knew she was a fucking dyke, that she was currently shacked up with some artist chick from New York City.

"So what are we waiting for?" she asked impatiently, and he shrugged his shoulders, flicked the butt of his third menthol into the gutter.

"Ladies first," he said, and followed her up the stairs, praying silently that this would be the day that old blood-'n'-guts Tierney finally took a ride on the porcelain bus. When they reached the door to the bedroom, Jim didn't look in again, stared back instead at Vince and Fletcher loitering about the living room. Vince still looked way too sick to care, but Fletcher rolled his eyes, shook his head.

Pam Tierney didn't say a word for a good three or four minutes, just stood very still, staring into the blood-soaked room. When she did turn back to Jim, the only sign that the sight had affected her was a loud, exasperated sigh.

"Wow," she said softly, and laughed, actually fucking *laughed*, a short, dry, unhappy sound that made Jim Unger want to hit her.

"Any particular thoughts as to the cause of death, Detective?" she said, stepping around him, heading for the kitchen.

"How about a goddamn hand grenade?" Fletcher said as she passed him and Vince and his partner. The partner was sitting on a black leather sofa, looking through a photo album.

"Yeah, Fletcher. That's a real good one. You must've been working on that one all afternoon." Then to the partner, "Hey, what the hell are you doing?"

The kid flinched and looked quickly up at her, startled, his eyes wide as those of a little boy caught with his arm up to the elbow in a jar of Oreos.

"Unless you're some sort of freak of nature and were born without fingerprints, I'd really like you to put that down and get up off the couch. Can you do that for me?"

"Better listen to her, Joey," Fletcher said. "Her bite's a lot worse than her bark."

But the young cop had already set the photo album back on the coffee table where he'd found it and stood up so fast he looked like some sort of mechanical wind-up toy.

"Thank you," Pam Tierney said, and disappeared into the kitchen.

"What's her problem?" the kid asked.

"Her girlfriend's probably on the rag this week," Fletcher said.

At that moment Tierney's two assistants reached the top of the stairs, both of them loaded down with cameras and cases of forensic equipment. They stood in the doorway, looking lost and wrinkling their noses at the smell.

"Where's the body?" one of them asked, and everyone, even Vince Norris, started giggling.

"If you girls will try not to touch anything for about five minutes," Jim said, "I'm gonna have a few words with the Dragon Lady in there."

He found Pam Tierney at the stove, emptying a package of Community Coffee into an iron skillet. The gas flame licked at the bottom of the pan and the air was already redolent with the rich, scorched smell of burning chicory and coffee grounds.

"What the hell are you *doing?*" he asked her, staring dubiously at the skillet.

"The guy who trained me up in Baton Rouge used to do this whenever we got a real stinker, especially the ones that had been underwater a while. Personally, I think it smells a whole lot worse than what's in there," and she motioned toward the front with her head. "But I can't have everyone puking all over the place while I'm trying to work." She adjusted the flame beneath the skillet and fanned the dark smoke toward the ceiling.

Jim coughed, squinted at her through the haze.

"Are you gonna try to tell me that shit in there didn't bother you?"

Pam Tierney turned to face him. He noticed that her eyes were watering, but he assumed it was from the sizzling coffee grounds.

"What do you *want* me to do, Unger? Barf all over the floor like the Three Stooges in there? Fuck yes, it *bothers* me, but I'm the one who has to go back in there and pick through whatever's left of that guy."

Jim glanced back toward the bedroom. "I think it was a woman," he said. "There's black nail polish on the fingernails and toes," but Tierney shook her head. She left the stove on and squeezed through the narrow entrance to the kitchen, edging past Jim Unger. She barked some instructions to her assistants and they began setting up, unpacking. Then she turned back to Jim, still standing in the door to the kitchen.

"Come here a second, Sherlock. I want to show you something."

Jim groaned, but he walked across the room to where she was standing at the edge of the bedroom, pointing down at something lying near her feet on the gore-smeared floor.

"You ever seen one of those on a girl?" she asked him. Jim bent closer for a better look before he realized that the sausage-sized lump of meat on the floor was a penis with a small bit of the scrotal sac still attached. The head had a large stainless steel ring through it. Jim Unger felt the hot rush of acid and half-digested lunch forcing its way back up from his stomach and dashed for the toilet.

"That's what I *thought*," Pam Tierney called out after him, just before the smoke alarm in the kitchen went off.

As Jim Unger lights his second Camel a flash of lightning illuminates the room like noonday sun. Two seconds later the thunder catches up and the concussion rattles the windows of the house. On the bed Julie stirs. "What was that?" she asks.

"That was just thunder, honey."

"Oh," she says doubtfully, then, "Why aren't you asleep?"

"I had a bad dream." Though it is the simple truth, it sounds wrong coming out of his mouth. *You thought you heard something. That's what you meant to say, wasn't it? That's what you* wanted *to say.*

"Oh," Julie says again, sounding more convinced this time as she rolls over in bed, turning her back on him.

"Just take it easy, Mrs. Poche. We're not in a hurry here," Vince said for the fifth or sixth time. The old black woman stared out at him through the fish-eye lenses of her spectacles. Jim Unger was losing interest, was staring through Mrs. Poche's lace curtains at one of Tierney's ghouls snapping photographs of the sidewalk.

"Shouldn't I call my lawyer?" she said again. Vince shook his head.

"You're not a suspect, Mrs. Poche," Vince said.

Why not? Jim asked himself. *Why the hell not?* It would make as much sense as anything else here.

"We just want to know if you saw or heard anything unusual this afternoon."

The old lady stared at Vince as if he'd sprouted a second head from the middle of his chest, then rolled her dentures back and forth in her mouth.

"There was *blood* drippin' outta my *ceilin'*," she told him. "I thought that was pretty damn *unusual*."

"She's got you there, Vincent," said Jim, closing the curtains. The downstairs apartment smelled like dust and medicine, the miasma of age, and it was starting to depress him.

"If you'll just tell us anything else you saw, ma'am, it'd be real helpful," he said to Mrs. Poche. She looked away from Vince, locked her bewildered gaze on Jim instead.

"It was awful," she said again. "I'm just glad none of my grandbabies were here. Can you imagine if they'd had to see somethin' like that?"

"Ma'am," Jim interrupted, trying to sound polite but losing his patience, "did you see anyone come in or out of the apartment *before* you went upstairs?"

The old lady frowned and rolled her dentures.

Jim looked back up at the maroon stain on her living room ceiling. It was about as big as a large pizza, and he guessed it was situated somewhere just below the foot of Poe's bed. There was a much smaller, matching stain on the floor; sooner or later, the guy on the sidewalk would be in to photograph both.

"All I saw was Mr. Poe, and it's his apartment, so I don't see nothin' unusual about that. He comes and goes all the time."

"And what *time* did you see Mr. Poe leave?" Vince asked her, pretending to write down everything she said on the memo pad open across his knee.

"Oh, wait a minute now. If you're thinkin' Mr. Poe had anything to do with this, you're wrong, young man. Mr. Poe, well, he's a prissy boy, but he wouldn't *kill* nobody. 'Specially not Benny. Benny was his fella, you know?"

"What time did you see Mr. Poe leave the apartment, ma'am?" Jim asked, still staring at the stain on the ceiling. The room upstairs had been unbearable, but the dark stain seemed to have the opposite effect; his eyes kept coming back to it.

"Ain't nothin' at all wrong with bein' a prissy boy," Mrs. Poche said, crossing her wrinkled hands on her lap. "That's what Oprah said."

"Yes, ma'am," Vince sighed. "She's entitled to her opinion. But didn't you *see* or *hear*—"

"What I *saw* was all that *blood* drippin' outta my *ceilin',"* she said, pronouncing each word slowly, as if she'd decided the two detectives were hard of hearing. Then her front door opened and Fletcher said, "Come on, guys. I think we got him."

The first time Jim Unger saw Jared Poe, the photographer was sitting handcuffed in the backseat of a patrol car, staring straight ahead as if his eyes were focused on something far away that no one else could see. If those eyes had been empty, blank, it might not have bothered the detective, but they weren't. They almost seemed to glimmer in the shadows, and it was difficult to look at his face for very long.

"Another car picked him up all the way over on Conti," Fletcher said, "just wandering around talking to himself. He won't talk now, but his driver's license says he's Jared A. Poe and gives this place as his home address."

The man in the back of the patrol car didn't respond to the sound of his name. The front of his white T-shirt was stiff and crusted with blood, as were his jeans. His hands and arms were the color of dried rose petals.

"He's gotta be our perp, Jim," Vince Norris said. "The old lady said the boyfriend's name was Poe."

"Has he been Mirandized?" Jim asked Fletcher, and the beat cop shrugged.

"Probably, but what's the point of asking this fag anything? He's a total veggie, Jimbo."

"He's *gotta* be the fucking guy," Vince insisted. "Just look at all that fucking blood on him. You think he got that from a nosebleed or something?"

Jim stooped down next to the open door of the patrol car, close enough to smell the drying blood that soaked Jared Poe's clothing. "You've been placed under arrest," he said, "on suspicion of murder. Do you understand these charges, Mr. Poe?"

Jared Poe blinked then, just once, and turned his head slightly toward the three officers. "I understand," he said. His voice came out brittle, like thin glass. "I understand," he repeated. "You think I killed Benny."

"Holy fuck, Batman, the fruit can talk," Fletcher said, and laughed.

"Vince, will you please get him the fuck out of here before he blows this," Jim said, trying not to look away from Jared Poe's glimmering eyes.

"I'm right, aren't I?" the man in the back of the car asked them. "All of you think I did that to Benny."

"Listen, buddy." Jim leaned closer, trying to sound calm, trying to sound reasonable. "What do you *expect* us to think? We know he was your boyfriend and you got blood all over you. We got a witness that saw you leave the crime scene. I'm guessing we're gonna run some tests and we're gonna find out that blood came out of the guy upstairs. Now, if you *didn't* kill him, you better tell us where all this red stuff came from."

"I didn't kill him," Jared Poe said. He closed his eyes, turned away from the detective.

"Oh, yeah? Then I'm the goddamn Sugar Bum Fairy," Vince Norris sneered.

"Detectives," someone called, and Jim Unger looked over his shoulder. The guy who'd been taking pictures of the sidewalk earlier was standing in the door to the stairwell. "Pam says she's got something up here you guys ought to see right now. What do you want me to tell her?"

"Tell her to hold her fucking water," he shouted, and the guy disappeared back up the stairs. Jim looked at Jared Poe, who still had his eyes closed. There was blood on his face, too. Long steaks of it, like Indian war paint, and a dark smudge across his lips.

"You could make this easier on both of us," he said, but Poe didn't answer him. When Jim slammed the door of the patrol car a second later Poe didn't even flinch.

"Get him out of here," Jim said to Fletcher, and then to Vincent Norris, "Come on. Let's see what kind of nasty shit the Dragon Lady's got waiting for us this time."

●　●　●

"Fuckin' wacko," Vince said for the third time as Jim handed the plastic evidence bag back to Pam Tierney. Inside the bag there were two pages torn from a book, "The Raven" by Edgar Allan Poe. A couple of lines had been marked with a bright yellow highlighting pen.

"'With mien of lord or lady . . .'?" Jim Unger read out loud. "Is this even supposed to make *sense*? Like he was leaving us a message or something?"

"Maybe," the coroner said, frowning down at the pages. "Or he was trying to tell *himself* something, or the dead guy. Shit, who knows. I'm not a psychologist."

Jim glanced at the framed photograph again. Tierney or one of her boys had removed it from the bedroom. Now it sat on the floor, leaning against the coffee table. There were crusty streaks of gore on the glass, partly obscuring the image inside, the winged androgyne snarling for the camera. They'd found the poem Scotch-taped to the front of the picture, and Jim didn't really give a shit *what* the killer was trying to communicate with the highlighted passages. There was an excellent partial thumbprint right in the middle of the sticky strip of tape.

"If the print matches, I'd say it's a pretty safe bet you got the right guy," Tierney said.

"Yeah," Jim replied. "Well, let's all just keep our fingers crossed." He glanced over his shoulder at the bedroom. Someone had turned on a floor lamp in there, and he could see the shadows of the men still working through the mess, shifting patches of darkness straining to pass for human, shadows stretched from floor to ceiling, as fluid and insubstantial as ghosts.

The next morning Jim Unger and Vince Norris questioned Jared Poe in a stuffy interrogation room that smelled like floor cleaner and stale cigarettes. What was left of the victim still awaited them in Tierney's office in the basement of the Criminal Courts Building. The autopsy was scheduled for one o'clock. With any luck they'd have a confession by then.

"Okay, Mr. Poe, let's just try to make this as painless as possible," Vince said, lighting a Pall Mall and blowing smoke at the tiled walls. "I can't say I slept real fuckin' well last night and you *sure* as hell don't look like you did either, so I think we'll all be better off if we skip the bullshit."

Jared squinted at the detectives. There were dark circles under his bloodshot eyes, like bruises, and the fluorescent lights in the room lent his skin a sickly greenish cast. He was unshaven and dressed in prison denim, a shirt that looked too large with a big stain on the front.

"That blood we took off your hands and clothes matched up with the victim's, Jared," Jim Unger said, placing a manila folder on the table between them. "And we have a shitload of fingerprints *and* a witness who puts you at the scene of the murder. We *know* you killed Benjamin DuBois, Jared. Are you absolutely sure you don't want a lawyer present before we—"

"I said I don't need a lawyer," Jared replied, blinking at them.

"Yeah, I know what you said. But I have to be sure—"

"I didn't kill him." Jared closed his eyes, shielded them from the light with one hand. "I don't need a lawyer."

"We've seen the scratches on your back, Mr. Poe," Vince said. "What do you think we're gonna find under Mr. DuBois's nails?"

Jared Poe answered slowly, as if he was having trouble remembering how to talk, or what words were for.

"We had sex yesterday morning, before I left," he said without opening his eyes. "I didn't kill Benny."

"Then how did you get his blood all over you, Jared?" Jim asked, pushing his chair back from the table a little, trying to see Jared's face better.

"I *found* him," Jared said, and swallowed hard, like someone who was trying not to cry, or throw up. "I found him and I was trying . . . I was . . . Jesus . . ."

"So you admit you were there?" Vince asked. He was standing closer to Jared now, leaning on the table, the cigarette's filter clenched between his teeth. Jim thought he looked like a cartoon vulture.

"I was at the CAC. The Contemporary Arts Center on Camp Street. I'm . . . I was going to have a show there. I was there all day taking measurements."

"But you just said that you and Mr. DuBois had sex that morning," Vince interrupted.

"Yes, before I left."

"But no one *saw* you there? There's no one to corroborate what you're telling us?"

Jared moved his hand so that the bright light washed freely across his face again. "No," he said after a moment. "No, I don't think so. But *why* . . . why do you think I would ever hurt Benny?"

"You tell us, Jared," Jim said, and Vince clicked his tongue loudly against the roof of his mouth.

"I don't have time for this crap, Mr. Poe," he said. "And Detective Unger here, he doesn't have time for this crap. You think a jury's gonna buy any of this? We've seen those pictures you take. That's some pretty twisted shit, Mr. Poe. It looks to me like you have a real hard-on for hurting people."

Jared Poe closed his eyes again.

"So how's it gonna look to a jury, hmmm? Normal guys who don't like to fuck other men up the ass, who don't get their jollies taking obscene pictures of boys dressed up like women? You know, I worked vice two years and I've never seen anything one *tenth* as disgusting as that stuff."

Jim Unger held up one hand to silence Vince, to signal that it was his turn now. Vince grunted and turned to stare at the one-way mirror on the other side of the room.

"You can't tell us you'd never hurt Benny, can you, Jared? Because you hurt him on a regular basis. Isn't that right? Every time you fucked him you hurt him. Benny *wanted* you to hurt him . . ."

"What's the point in my telling you anything at all, Detective?" Jared Poe asked. His weary bloodshot eyes made Jim Unger want to look away. "You've already made up your minds. The only thing you want to hear from me is a confession. All that's going to satisfy you is to hear me say that I did . . . that I did *that* to Benny."

"Seems pretty fuckin' reasonable," Vince said without turning around. "Under the circumstances."

"But it's never going to *happen*, Detective."

"Then you better have another good long think about that lawyer, Jared," Jim said, standing up, sliding his chair back under the edge of the table. "Because regardless of what you *say* or how many times you say it, you look guilty as sin to us. And I'm betting you're gonna look just as guilty to the DA's office and a jury."

Vince dropped the butt of his Pall Mall to the floor and crushed it out with the toe of one shoe. "And we ain't talking about life in prison, Mr. Poe. We're talking about death by electrocution. You do understand that?"

"Come on," Jim said, reaching for the doorknob. "Let's give him some time alone. I'm sure he's gonna figure this all out sooner or later. A man can't be up to his ears in his own shit and not smell something sooner or later."

Jim Unger finishes another cigarette and stubs it out in a ceramic ashtray the color of dead sunflowers, something Julie's niece made in school, a bright present filled with butts and tobacco ash and burned-out matches. There's another flash of lightning and he thinks about turning on the television. Maybe the weather reports would take his mind off the dream, off these things he shouldn't be remembering anyway, gnawing over like a dog with an old meatless bone. The storm is real, solid, *immediate*, the sort of threat he can at least comprehend, not like these haunted patches of memory trapped inside his head or the lie that there was something more he could have done for Vince Norris.

The news of Vince's suicide reached Jim the day after he heard Jared Poe was dead. It had been months since Vince's release from the hospital, but his mind was still broken, barely held together from day to day by pills and biweekly visits to a therapist. He was living with his mother in Slidell, and Jim had kept promising himself he'd do more than check up on him, that he'd make the drive across the lake and spend an afternoon with Vince. But he'd put it off and put it off and finally the call came from a friend in the St. Tammany Parish Sheriff's Department. By the time Jim got to Slidell they'd already taken Vince's body away. There was only the blood he'd left behind in his bedroom and his mother, sitting alone and staring vacantly out a kitchen window at a backyard gone wild with dandelions and polk salad. There were still a few cops on the scene too, and one of them, a detective named Kennedy, took Jim aside.

"There's something in there I need your opinion on," he said, pointing down a long gloomy hallway toward Vince Norris's room. Jim had already looked in the room and he didn't really relish the thought of going in there again.

"What? Look, I don't really—"

"I know he was a friend of yours," Kennedy said. "That's why I was hoping you could help make some sense of this."

"Make sense of *what?*" but the detective was already on his way back down the hall, back to the room where Vince Norris had cut his own throat with a jagged shard of broken mirror. And Jim followed, wanting to be back in his car and putting as many miles between himself and this house as he could, as fast as he could.

The detective led him through the bedroom door and Jim was trying to tell him again that he'd already been in there, had already seen everything there was to see and didn't care to see any of it again, thank you, when Kennedy pointed at the low ceiling and then crossed his arms.

"That," he said, and Jim looked up.

The grade-school crude outline of a bird, a huge bird with wide outstretched wings and a beak like a dagger, had been traced onto the ceiling directly above the bed. The blood was already dry. Jim Unger stood speechless and staring, dizzy. Suddenly the room seemed cold.

"No note or nothing. Just this," Kennedy said. "We think he did it with his fingers, before he cut his throat. All the fingertips on his right hand were scraped raw."

"Can you keep this out of the report?" Jim asked, unable to

look away from the unsteady maroon smears across the white plasterboard, remembering Vince's tranquilized voice over the telephone: *I can still see it, Jimbo. I can still see what was up there.*

"If you know something about this, I'd like—"

Jim interrupted before he could finish. "I'm asking you if you can *please* keep this out of the fucking report." The hot surge of anger broke the spell. He turned away, better to see Vince's blood soaking into the shit-brown shag carpet and the bed.

"But—"

"Just say yes or no, Detective. But it doesn't mean anything, okay? Vince wasn't well. He had bad dreams."

There was a long silence between them while the other detective watched Jim, then glanced back at the grisly outline on the ceiling.

"Yeah," Kennedy finally replied. "Yeah. What the fuck. You got it." Jim said thanks, or he meant to say thanks, before he stepped back out into the hall. And there was Vince's mother, waiting for him, blocking his escape. She wore a dead woman's face, too much sorrow in her eyes for anything like life.

"You *tell* me," she said, and she sounded old, old as the festering swamps and the skies above them, old as the first mother who ever lost a son. "Vincent was so afraid and he wouldn't ever tell me or his doctors what he was scared of. But you know, don't you? I want you to *tell* me."

He could have told her, could have sat her down and told her about his own bad dreams, about the dripping red nightmare they'd walked into on Ursulines, details he suspected Vince had never shared with anyone. And it might have made a difference.

"I'm sorry, Mrs. Norris," he said instead. "I swear to God I wish I did know, but I don't. I'm very, very sorry." Then he stepped past her and didn't stop moving until he was out of the house and across the weathered concrete driveway to his car. He looked back then, just for a second, and she was watching him from between the living room drapes, her accusing face grown as old as her voice had sounded.

• • •

He doesn't turn on the television, but leaves Julie sleeping on their bed and goes downstairs to the living room. He removes his revolver from its holster and takes it with him. He doesn't like to be too far away from it anymore.

Outside the house the storm is battering the city. Jim thinks he'll just sit in the kitchen and have a beer and watch it for a while through the bay windows, hopes that the alcohol will be enough to make him sleepy again. He has a prescription bottle of Valium in the medicine cabinet, little blue bits of calm, but he doesn't like to use them, doesn't like their unreal, detached brand of comfort.

The rain is making a sound like giant fingers drumming against the roof as he pops open the can of Miller and sits down. The gun lies on the table in front of him and he stares past it into the wet, storm-lashed night. The beer feels reassuring going down and he drains half the can in one long swallow.

"You gotta get it together, Jimbo," he whispers, wiping his mouth. The night outside is lit by another brilliant flash of lightning. A split second of daylight pours over the world and he freezes, the can halfway to the tabletop, the back of his other hand still damp with beer and saliva.

What the fuck was that, before he can prevent the thought, before he can tell himself it was only a trick of the sudden light shining through the driving rain, just a mistake made by his tired eyes. The thunder rumbles overhead. Jim Unger puts the can down, picks up the .38, and steps around the table to the window.

What the fuck do you think *you saw out there?*

"Nothing," he says out loud, "absolutely nothing at all," but then the lightning comes again, crackles above the Metairie subdivision and makes a liar of him. Because what he *thought* he saw is still standing a few feet from the kitchen window, staring in at him through bottomless cat-slit eyes. Eyes punched into a grinning harlequin face, wrinkled flesh the color of something that's been in the tub too long.

112

"Holy *Jesus* . . ." he whispers. He brings up the gun, but the thing outside is faster, much faster. The glass shatters, explodes around him in a roar of wind and a drenching diamond spray of slicing glass and rain. Jim feels the gun slip from his grip, hears it clatter across the linoleum as he tries to protect his face from shards of flying glass. Above the noise of the storm and breaking window panes there is another sound, a frantic fluttering, the terribly familiar sound of angry, black wings. *I'm still dreaming*, he thinks as he stumbles backward into the table.

"Detective Unger," a voice says from somewhere very nearby, a voice that seems to weave its substance from the cacophony of unseen birds.

"Who the fuck *are* you?" Jim screams into the night sweeping through the broken windows. His arms and the backs of his hands are cut and bleeding, and he can taste blood in his mouth. But none of it hurts, not yet. There's no room in him for anything but the fear, a hundred times more demanding than the pain from any mere physical wound could ever be.

"I know it's been a while," the voice says. He realizes that it too is familiar. "But it hurts to think you could have forgotten me *already*."

"You stay the fuck away from me," Jim growls, trying to sound cool, trying to sound like he's not about to shit himself. He glances at the floor for some sign of the dropped .38, but the lights above the sink have started to flicker and the floor is covered with glass and water that catch the unsteady light and wink it back at him, making it impossible to find the gun.

"You don't seem very glad to see me," the voice says, coming now from somewhere behind him. Jim turns his back on the gaping hole where the window used to be, and the thing with the smirking harlequin face is silhouetted for a moment in the flickering light before it bleeds away into the shadows.

No way, no fucking way any of this is happening, Jim tells himself. It is a hollow reassurance at best.

"I've got a gun, you weirdo son of a bitch," he says, and takes a step toward the door that leads from the kitchen into the carport. There are things out there he can defend himself with, sharp things.

"No, Detective. This time *I* have the gun." Suddenly there is cold metal pressing hard against his temple.

"Don't waste precious time asking yourself *how*," the voice says, speaking directly into his ear now, and he knows there's no point anymore pretending that it isn't the voice of Jared Poe. No point pretending the dead man isn't standing in his kitchen with his own fucking gun pressed to his head.

"'Cause *how* doesn't matter right now. All that matters is whether or not I think you're telling me the truth."

He's shoved into one of the chairs, one hand on his shoulder as cold as the barrel of the .38, one hand as hard and indisputable as tempered steel forcing him to sit when every muscle in his body is telling him to run.

"I think you remember how this works, so let's try to make it as painless as possible," the voice says. Then strong fingers are tangling themselves in his hair, pulling his head back so he's staring straight up into the pale grinning face. Now he can see it's just a cheap Mardi Gras mask, not a real face at all.

"You're not Poe," he says. "If you're Poe, take off the mask, you fucking coward."

"Wrong," the white face says without moving its lips, and the butt of the pistol comes down fast across the bridge of his nose, cracking bone, tearing cartilage. Warm blood spurts down his chin. Jim Unger screams as the searing pain fills his head, but a thunderclap devours the sound.

"Now, see what you made me do?" The barrel of the gun is already jammed against his temple again. Jim gasps and more blood spills out of his nostrils and into his mouth, gagging him.

"You *knew*, didn't you?" the man behind the mask asks. "You knew I wasn't the one who killed Benny."

"Bullshit," Jim Unger coughs, spitting out a mouthful of blood and snot, blowing a finer drizzle of gore from his broken nose. His eyes are watering and it's hard to see the mask, just an alabaster smear now against the flickering dark.

"Don't lie to me, you fucking pig." Now the gun is pressed against the tip of Jim's chin, pointing upward. "I have no reason in the whole fucking world not to pull this trigger and blow your brains out, so don't you fucking *lie* to me."

Jim hears the weakness in the voice then, the strain of anger. A chink that might let him past the mask, might even give him a chance if he doesn't screw it up.

"What difference does it make?" he asks. "Even if we didn't get the killer, we got another sicko off the street, right?"

"You really think this is all some sort of fucking *game*, don't you?" The hand holding the gun is trembling with rage that wants out, anger like a starving dog on a very short leash.

So much anger can make a person careless. Jim swallows, hating the bitter, salty taste of his own blood.

"Either way, I was just doing my *job*, right?" he says.

"Wrong," Jared Poe snarls back at him, a voice that could be Jared Poe's if such a thing were possible. The gun is suddenly past Jim's lips, chipping teeth as the stubby barrel is forced across his tongue. Thunder rushes from the sky to cover the deafening boom of the gunshot.

Four blocks west of Jim Unger's house Jared finally stops running, collapses into a row of oleander, and lies staring up into the rain, the belly of low, roiling clouds stained orange by the Metairie streetlights. Benny's mask is still clutched in his right hand. The rain has already washed most of the cop's blood off him, washes his own blood from the hundred scrapes and gashes left by his dive through the window.

Is there anything he could have said that would have stopped you from killing him? he thinks, but it sounds like Lucrece asking the question, Lucrece speaking from behind his eyes.

"What difference does it make?" he asks her, knowing that there won't be an answer. The crow lights on the ground beside the oleander bushes and Jared turns his head so he can see her. The water rolls off her black feathers; a single raindrop catches on the end of her beak and hangs there like a jewel until the bird shakes it off.

"And where were *you*, bitch? I thought you were supposed to be here to help me."

The bird caws and spreads her wings, blinks her golden eyes

in a way that is somehow indifferent and accusatory at the same time. Not that Jared has to rely on anything as subtle as body language. Her voice would be impossible for him not to hear, not to understand.

"Yeah? Well, fuck you too," Jared says, and rolls over again to stare into the storm.

AFTER JARED AND THE BIRD HAVE LEFT HER ALONE IN THE apartment, Lucrece sits at the window and watches the rain filling the gutters on Ursulines. She knows that she should be moving, should be asking the questions that Jared's impatience and rage have kept him from considering, not sitting on her ass while what little is left of her world careens toward fresh disaster. But she feels too stunned, entirely too overwhelmed.

There's a limit, she thinks. *Even for me, there must be a limit.*

Since Benny's death her life has become a downward spiral toward a despair so complete and crushing that it could be the lightless bottom of the ocean, that absolute pressure on every inch of her body and mind and soul. She wasn't even given a chance to grieve for the loss of her twin, her bright shadow, before she had to begin fighting to save Jared's life and was thrown into the merciless arena of lawyers and police and courtrooms. And the press too, because it was just too good a story not to smear across every paper and tabloid and television news broadcast: the transsexual sister pleading for the life of the accused homosexual murderer of her cross-dressing twin.

When the police were finally finished with Jared and Benny's apartment, she was the one who scrubbed her brother's blood from the floorboards and windows, the one who dragged the gore-crusted mattress away and painted the walls that could never be cleansed of their stains. She felt like a traitor, covering over those last lingering traces of him. She was the one who handled Benny's funeral when the coroner's office finally allowed what was left of him to be entombed in the plot Jared had bought the year before in Lafayette No. 1.

And Lucrece did almost all of it by herself, because while Jared had attracted plenty of art-crowd hangers-on and wanna-bes, the three of them had very few actual friends, people willing to stand by her through the shitstorm of publicity and pain that her life became in the days after Benny's murder. Those days that had turned to long months of the same droning, unrelenting hurt.

When the trial was over and Jared was sitting on death row at Angola, Lucrece was left to stand guard over the apartment. She gave up the old place in the Warehouse District. The only hope remaining in the world was that some overlooked bit of evidence would free her brother's lover before his execution left her finally, irrevocably, as alone as someone could become.

Against that day she had nothing but Jared's pearl-handled straight razor and the knowledge of her limits, the certainty that she would not be left lacking an out, a way to stop the pain when it was clear that there was nothing left for her to do. When there were no more stingy strands of idiot hope to dangle from, no more far-fetched fantasies of justice to keep her reeling from day to day.

Then Jared was killed in some sort of brawl, a fight with another inmate, or maybe he was simply attacked; she still isn't clear on the details. They didn't matter, anyway. All that mattered was that the end came a whole lot sooner than she expected and Lucrece was caught off guard. Jared was supposed to die after all the slow and impersonal rituals of legal execution, after the obligatory appeals and protests. Instead he bled to death in a prison exercise yard. Or so she was told. The news reached her in a midnight phone call from one of Jared's attorneys. For a long time afterward she sat staring at the telephone as if maybe it had been a mistake, maybe in a moment someone would call back and tell her no, it had been a *different*

Jared Poe, sorry for the confusion. Or even a practical joke. Lawyers could be pretty sick fuckers, after all, and she'd have gladly forgiven them and laughed, she would have actually fucking *laughed* at that point.

Eventually she went to the bathroom medicine cabinet, where she kept the razor, and she sat on the toilet seat and stared at it the way she'd stared at the phone. She wasn't afraid of dying. If she ever had been, that fear had been stripped from her. Lucrece folded the blade open and it glinted dully in the dim bathroom light. She even made a couple of tentative cuts along her arms, preparing herself for the pain of the deep longitudinal slashes that would be necessary to ensure permanent oblivion.

But then someone had whispered into her ear, so close that she could feel cold breath against her cheek. A single question from a gentle voice so much like Benny's that she let the razor slip from her fingers and clatter to the tile floor.

Who's gonna bury Jared if you go?

It might have been in her head, the product of a traitorous or cowardly imagination, a hallucination manufactured in a last-ditch effort to save her own hopeless life. But she waited, very still, patiently listening for anything else the voice might have to say.

"Haven't I done all that I can do?" Lucrece whispered back to the empty apartment. "*Haven't* I?"

There wasn't an answer, although she sat there on the toilet seat for almost an hour longer, listening to the murmuring background noises of the creaky old building, the street sounds of the Quarter going on about its business around her. Without her, if need be. Eventually she picked up the razor and folded it closed, returned it to its shelf in the medicine cabinet. She was damned to a few more days of life, a little more sorrow, by the image of Jared's lonely funeral, the casket being carried into the mausoleum and no one in attendance who wasn't paid to be there.

Outside the storm howls like a hungry giant. Lucrece puts one hand out flat against the windowpane. It feels like she imagines herself, polished flat and smooth, transparent and cold as the rain beating against it from the other side.

Why did I have to keep going after *the funeral? That's a fair question, isn't it?*

But there are no more answers now than there were that night when she sat with the open razor glinting at her feet. Only the mindless storm and the indifferent night, the sound of her heart, a restless reminder of her own irrelevant mortality.

If Lucrece had been any less warped by the world and her time in it, if she had not already been forced to accept so much loss and horror, then Jared's return might have been one step over the limit of what she was capable of enduring, the part of the story where the author loses her to disbelief and she closes the book for the last time. As it is, it only feels like the next impossible episode in a story that has grown ever more ridiculous since the day she was born into a body that wasn't even suited to her most basic needs.

That's the only truth she can read from the rhythm of the rain against the window, the only divination to be gleaned from the interlacing paths of water down the glass. Just the cruel, simple fact of her continuing survival and the comfortless understanding that there is still something left for her to do before she can finally let go and follow her twin.

"Please, Jared," she says, pulling her hand back from the window, letting the curtain fall back in place to hide the storm. "Give me the time I need to figure this out. Don't make me have to be here for nothing . . ."

And the thunder makes a sound like an old man laughing.

The Eye of Horus is a couple of blocks west of the apartment, a tiny curiosity squeezed in between a gallery and an antique store specializing in art deco lamps. By the time she reaches it Lucrece is soaked despite her black raincoat and umbrella. She stands dripping beneath a candy-striped awning, peering into the shop's single dusty window. The glass is decorated with two carefully rendered Egyptian hieroglyphs, stylized hawks bracketing Gothic letters that spell out the shop's name. Lucrece used to come here often, with Benny or alone, when she was still designing clothing, used to buy what she needed in the way of feathers and bird bones from Aaron Marsh, the proprietor.

Sunrise is still a couple of hours away and the French Quarter is idling, drowsy, most of the soggy night's revelry over but the new day as yet undelivered. Lucrece raps her cold knuckles against the door again. A bell on the other side jingles faintly, but there's no sound or movement from within the darkened shop. She's starting to shiver. She stomps her feet against the sidewalk, realizes that the rainwater has gotten into her boots as well. She knocks harder, rattling the little stained-glass panes set into the door.

"Come on, Aaron," she says, "I *know* you're in there some-where." She bangs at the door again.

This time a dim, yellowy light flickers on somewhere toward the back of the Eye of Horus and there are stumbling noises. Someone curses. A moment more and she hears the click of a deadbolt being turned before the door opens a crack, still held by a safety chain. Aaron Marsh peeps out at her cautiously, like a rat, his scraggly white beard and blue eyes bright even in the shadows.

"What the hell do you want?" he growls past the chain. "Do you have any idea what *time* it is? Go away or I'll call the police."

"I'm sorry, Aaron," Lucrece says. He recognizes her then, repeats her name a couple of times and makes a disgusted, inconvenienced snorting sort of sound.

"Lucrece," he says. "Lucrece DuBois? What do you want?"

"I need to talk to you, Aaron. About crows."

Aaron Marsh snorts again, the noise a surfacing hippopotamus makes.

"I thought you were *dead*," he says gruffly, suspiciously, and Lucrece shakes her head.

"No," she says. "That was my brother. But that's why I'm here, because of Benny."

"But you just said that you wanted to talk about crows," he says, squinting to get a better look at Lucrece. His arched eyebrows are the same bristling snow white as his long beard.

"*Please*, Aaron. I'm freezing to death out here." She stomps her feet again, not entirely for effect.

He mumbles something to himself that Lucrece doesn't understand, but unfastens the chain and opens the door the rest of the way, stepping aside to let her pass. He's wearing a paisley housecoat and slippers, and his eyes are sleepy and alert at the same time. Lucrece steps gratefully into the musty, warm shop. Aaron shuts the door behind her, locks it again. The air smells like old feathers and dust bunnies, cedar and pipe tobacco—gentle, nostalgic odors from a time when her life made sense.

"You're dripping all over my floor," Aaron says, and of course she is, the water streaming off her raincoat and her hair onto the red and gold Turkish carpet. The dim lamplight from the back of the shop makes Aaron look only a little older than he actually is, somewhere on the brittle edge of sixty. He makes Lucrece think of a slightly deranged Walt Whitman. He takes her coat and holds it gingerly between two fingers, drapes it across a brass coat hook nailed up near the door, points to another hook from which Lucrece hangs her umbrella.

She glances about the Eye of Horus, which doesn't seem to have changed much since her last visit at least a year and a half ago. Rows of tall oak and walnut display cases and bookshelves line the walls, cases filled with painstakingly mounted skeletons of eagles and herons and a hundred different species of song-birds; taxidermied wonders, stuffed owls and ducks and a flock of extinct passenger pigeons, and his most prized possession in a case in the center of the shop, not for sale at any price but he can't resist showing it off: a stuffed dodo. There are jars filled to overflowing with peacock and pheasant and ostrich feathers, drawers occupied by every conceivable sort of egg, each care-fully drained of its embryonic contents and protected in beds of cotton and excelsior.

Before he moved to New Orleans sometime in the nineteen fifties, Aaron Marsh was professor of ornithology at a small-town university somewhere in eastern Massachusetts. And then there had been a sex scandal, a flunking student who got revenge by confessing to the dean or headmaster or whomever that he was Aaron's homosexual lover, and Dr. Marsh was out on his ass. So he'd come south, to a warmer, more forgiving place less prone to witch hunts, and he'd opened the Eye of Horus.

"Well, would you like some tea?" he asks grudgingly, but most of the crankiness seems to be gone now. "A hot pot of green tea will warm you up."

"Yes," she says. "I'd like that very much, thank you." Aaron shuffles past her toward the curtain of amber beads that separates the shop from a narrow flight of stairs leading up to his apartment overhead. Lucrece follows slowly behind him, admiring Aaron's treasures even through her mental fog of cold and fear. She passes the big dodo standing its silent, perpetual guard like a character from a Lewis Carroll story. Its glass eyes seem to watch her skeptically, ready to pounce if she makes a wrong move.

When Lucrece reaches the bead curtain Aaron is already at the top of the stairs speaking softly to someone. It hadn't occurred to her that he might not be alone, and she wonders if they'll have the privacy she needs to ask her questions. The stairs creak loudly beneath her wet shoes.

"I think you'll live," Aaron mutters. "Now go back to sleep and stop being such a bitch."

By the time Lucrece mounts the last arthritic stair to the short second-floor hallway Aaron has disappeared into the kitchen at the other end of the hall. To her right the bedroom door is standing open and there's a lamp burning on a small table by a huge, sagging canopy bed. An annoyed-looking young man is sitting up, blinking at her.

"It couldn't wait until morning?" he asks.

"No," she replies. "I'm sorry, but it really couldn't."

The man makes a dismissive gesture with one hand and lies down again, covers his head with a pillow.

"I'm sorry," Lucrece says again, feeling awkward. Then Aaron is calling her from the kitchen and she can hear water running, filling a kettle. "Just ignore him," Aaron shouts, but she pulls the bedroom door closed and it creaks louder than the stairs.

• • •

The strong green tea does warm Lucrece. She sips her second cup while Aaron rambles on about the shop, holds the little china teacup in both hands and rolls it back and forth between her palms. The taste and smell of the tea is nostalgic too. She wonders if there's a thing left in the world that hasn't become tainted by her sadness.

"But you wanted to talk about crows," the old man says at last, peering at her from under his eyebrows as he blows on his own steaming cup of tea.

"Yes," she says, setting her cup on the table. "What do you know about crows and the dead, about crows and ghosts?"

Aaron frowns and tugs at his beard.

"You got me out of bed at four A.M. because you wanted to hear fairy tales?"

"It's very important," she says, stealing a glance at the grease-stained clock above the stove. It reads 4:20. She wonders how long Jared's been gone, where he might be now. *Or maybe I imagined the whole goddamned thing,* she thinks. *Maybe I'm just a crazy woman wandering around in the rain talking about birds.*

"Mythology and folklore are not my areas of expertise," Aaron replies, and slurps his tea.

"But you must have picked up a lot in your studies. You must have heard a lot of strange things."

"*Strange* things," he says, and laughs, closing his eyes a moment as if savoring the flavor of the tea or losing himself in some bit of memory. "Everyone sees and hears strange things, Lucrece. If they live a little while and keep their eyes open. Especially when one is a young boy in New England. Or an old man in New Orleans."

"Did you ever meet Jared Poe?" she asks, afraid she's losing her nerve. "Benny's lover, the photographer?"

Aaron narrows his eyes, blows on his tea again.

"You said crows."

"I know," Lucrece replies.

"I met him once," Aaron says, setting down his cup. "And I know he was killed in prison. I heard that on the radio a week or so back. The Bourbon Street Ripper killed in a prison brawl."

"Yeah." Lucrece begins to wish she'd gone to someone else. Someone more inclined to believe ghost stories than this outcast scientist, this snowy-haired man who might have invented doubt for his own particular pleasures.

"What's he got to do with crows, Lucrece?"

"Jared came back home tonight," she says, just like that, the whole thing out at once before she can change her mind. "He came back, with a crow."

Aaron Marsh doesn't say anything, just stares down at his cooling tea, the antique china cup decorated with cobalt blue sparrows painted beneath the cracked glaze.

"Why would I make something like that up, Aaron?" Lucrece whispers.

"That's not for me to say." Aaron sighs loudly and folds his hands in front of him. "In India the crow is the bird of death. Many cultures make that connection. It's natural enough, since crows are carrion-feeders. Crows are seen to feed on the dead, so we get legends and traditions of the crow as a sort of guide for souls, escorts between the land of the living and the land of the dead . . ."

"But does anyone ever mention it working the other way round?" Lucrece asks him, and he looks up at her. His eyes are almost the same shade of blue as the birds on the little teacups.

"I suspect that you have acquaintances better suited to answer a question like that," he says. "There's no shortage of occultists and spiritualists in this neighborhood."

"But I trust *you*, Aaron, because I know you won't just tell me what I want to hear, or listen to me and only hear what *you* want to hear. You're a scientist."

"I *was* a scientist," he corrected. "Now I'm an old homo who sells pigeon feathers and powdered chicken bones to would-be voodoo priestesses."

"And apparently spends a lot of time feeling sorry for himself," Lucrece adds, not bothering to hide her growing impatience and doubt.

"Yes, well," Aaron says.

"I'm sorry to have bothered you." She gets up to leave, not

125

wanting to waste any more of his time or hers, but Aaron immediately motions for her to sit down again.

"I *can't* tell you a great deal," he says. "But there's a German. Weicker, I think . . ." He worries at his beard. "Hell. Hold on a minute. I'll be right back."

Lucrece sits back down as Aaron stands and leaves her alone in the kitchen. She sips her tea and listens to his footsteps moving along the hall and then down the creaky steps to his shop. The man behind the bedroom door calls out, "What the fuck does she *want*, Aaron?"

"I said to go to sleep, Nathan," Aaron Marsh calls back, his voice muffled by distance and the storm, the rain drumming endlessly on the roof, a car passing out on Dumaine Street. He sounds a lot farther away than just downstairs. In a few minutes her cup is empty, only a few black specks of ground tea leaves left in the bottom. Soon she hears him on the stairs again, and when he steps back into the kitchen he's carrying a dusty old book bound in black cloth with faded gold printing on the cover and spine.

"I was right," he says. "Weicker. *Der Seelenvogel in der alten Literatur und Kunst.*" Aaron holds the book up so she can see the title printed on the cover, even if the German doesn't make any sense to her. "He writes a good bit in here about birds as death spirits and images of death, images of the soul, psychopomps and what have you . . ." He trails off, flipping through the brittle old pages.

"And crows?" Lucrece asks.

"Almost all the Corvidae. Crows, ravens, rooks . . . many of them are often portrayed as death birds. Ah, yes, here." He begins to read aloud, tracing a line of text with one finger. "'*In habentibus symbolum facilis est transitus.*'"

"I don't speak Latin either," she says. Aaron frowns at her, a very professorial frown, as though she hasn't done her homework or has been caught passing notes. But he apologizes and then repeats the line in English.

"'For those who have the symbol, the passage is easy.'" He pauses, then adds like a footnote, "The passage from the land of the living to the land of the dead."

"And what's the symbol?" Lucrece asks him, but he only shrugs.

"That depends. It could be many things." He goes back to the book. "Weicker records something here, a bit of a fairy tale that he thinks may originally be Hungarian or Wallachian." Aaron reads slowly now, translating for her as he goes. "'These people once believed that when a person died, a crow carried their soul to the land of the dead. But sometimes something so bad happens that a tremendous sadness is carried with it and the soul cannot rest. Then sometimes the crow can bring that soul back to the land of the living to exact vengeance against those responsible for its disquiet.

"'So long as the spirit pursues only those responsible, the crow protects it from all harm and it is invulnerable to harm by man or beast or any other evil spirits. But should the spirit turn aside from this narrow path, the crow may be forced to abandon it and the spirit will be left to wander the living world alone, forever, as a ghost or revenant.'"

Aaron pushes one finger at the bridge of his nose, force of habit, adjusting glasses he isn't wearing as he closes the book and lays it on the table between them.

"So," he says, "in this instance I suppose the symbol is the soul's pain and that pain's connection to the living."

"Jesus," Lucrece whispers, and stares down at Aaron Marsh's black book.

"It's only a *fairy tale*, Lucrece. These same people thought that the souls of suicides came back as vampires."

For just a second she wants to tell him more, tell him every detail of Jared's appearance in the apartment and the thoughts she read in the crow's nervous bird mind. Wants someone else, *anyone* else, to know the things she's seen and felt. The second passes. There might not be much time if she's going to help Jared.

"Thank you, Dr. Marsh," she says, sliding her chair away from the table. "It was very kind of you to try to help and I'm very sorry for waking you and Nathan . . ."

"A fairy tale, Lucrece. That's *all*," he says. She smiles for him, though it feels like a sickly grimace.

127

"I should be going now," she says. For a moment he looks uncertain, as if he might be thinking of calling a doctor or the police. But she steps past him toward the hall and he follows, mumbling about the storm, what he's heard about it on the radio. Together they descend the creaky stairs and walk back past the moth-eaten dodo in its glass and maple prison. Aaron opens the door for her while she's putting on her wet coat and retrieving her umbrella.

"Be careful," he says as she steps across the threshold, into the rain blowing in under the awning.

"It's only a fairy tale," she tells him. He nods, a small, optimistic nod that says he at least wants to believe she means what she's telling him. "I'll be fine."

And then he says good-bye and the door to The Eye of Horus jingles shut again and Lucrece is alone on the wet, dawn-hungry street.

It's hardly an hour after dawn, and if Frank Gray has had worse hangovers, his head hurts too badly to let him remember them. His partner is driving. As the police cruiser turns right off Canal onto St. Charles, rain hits the windshield so hard he's amazed it doesn't crack. His head feels that brittle, as if simple drops of water could break it into a thousand pieces. His stomach rises and falls like the gusting wind.

"*Christ*, Wally," he says, his voice ringing inside his head, bouncing off the walls of his crystal skull. "See if you can *miss* one or two of those potholes, okay?"

Wallace Thibodeaux has been his partner for over a year, a burly gray-haired black man ten years his senior. And Wallace Thibodeaux hates drunkard cops almost as much as he hates dirty cops. He has told Frank so on more than one occasion.

"So what was it last night, Frank?" Wallace says, squinting to see through the rain, using one hand to wipe away some of the condensation clouding the inside of the windshield. "Gasoline and turpentine? Aqua Velva with a Drano chaser?"

Frank stares out at the white-columned houses lining the

street, half obscured by the driving rain, and grunts for an answer.

"Well, sir," Wallace says, "if you got anything in you left to puke up, you better get it done before we get to the park, 'cause I got a feeling this one's gonna be bad."

"I'm fine," Frank says, and rubs at the throbbing place between his eyes.

"Yeah, you *look* fine. Fine is just exactly how you look." A streetcar rumbles past, a blur of red and green and spinning wheels, and Frank moans.

"You drive like an old woman," he says. "We're getting passed by fucking streetcars."

"I can't see shit, Frank. In case you haven't noticed, we're having a goddamn hurricane."

Frank remembers passing out in front of the television, remembers the Weather Channel and the pretty white swirl of clouds on the blue satellite photos of the Gulf of Mexico. "Oh, yeah," he groans.

Frank half dozes for a few minutes. When he comes to, they're passing Tulane, its not–quite–Ivy League facade of respectability like a shield against the corruption and slow, inevitable rot pressing in from all sides. Wallace pulls in behind a tomato-colored Honda and parks, stares across the street, past the streetcar tracks, at the entrance to Audubon Park. There are already four patrol cars parked on the river side of St. Charles, probably more inside the park. The rain dulls their strobing red and blue lights to something Frank can stand to look at.

"You sure you're gonna be okay, Frank?" Wallace asks, buttoning his raincoat. "I don't wanna have to be explaining why you're puking all over the place."

For an answer Frank opens his door and steps out into what seems at first like a solid wall of falling water, rain that would make Noah proud. He is soaked to the bone in seconds. But the cold and the wet make him feel a little more alive, and he thinks that maybe he can deal with this after all.

Wallace has an umbrella but the rain's blowing right up under it. They cross the neutral ground, splashing through the ankle-deep puddles and swollen gutters, and they stop at one of the patrol cars. The cop in the driver's seat cracks his window an inch or two.

"Did we beat the coroner?" Wallace asks the man inside the car. Frank looks up into the rain, opens his mouth, and sticks out his tongue like when he was a little boy. But the rain doesn't taste the way he remembers, tastes faintly of oil or chemicals, and he spits on the asphalt.

"Yeah, I think so," the cop tells Wallace. "But I better warn you guys, if you ain't heard already, this is a messy one. I mean a real gut-churner. I'm just glad it's fuckin' rainin' and the sun's not out, know what I mean?"

"Yeah," Wallace says. "I know what you mean." Frank spits again, but the chemical taste of the rain clings to the inside of his mouth like fried-chicken grease.

The cop rolls his window up again and Frank follows Wallace into the park, between the masonry pillars framing the park entrance. The rain begins to taper off to a simple, steady downpour.

The fountain is only thirty yards or so into the park, marble and concrete and a verdigris nude for a centerpiece, a bronze woman balanced on a bronze ball, her arms spread wide as if she has summoned this storm for her own secret purposes. There are two bronze children at the edges of the fountain, small naked boys astride turtles, one on either side of the woman. The fountain has already been cordoned off with bright yellow crime-scene tape strung along an irregular ring of wooden barricades. The tape flutters in the wind, ready to tear free at any moment and go sailing away into the voracious storm.

Frank and Wallace flash their badges. One of the beat cops nods and steps aside just as a particularly strong gust seizes Wallace's umbrella and turns it inside out.

"Fuck," he says, and Frank manages a small laugh that makes his head throb.

"You were getting wet anyway, Wally."

But Wallace just frowns humorlessly down at the ruined umbrella and tosses it to the ground, where it shudders and rolls about in the wind. The black umbrella makes Frank think of some sort of bizarre alien bat. He looks away, steps over the crime tape, and gets his first look at what's waiting for them in the fountain.

"Jesus H . . ." Wallace turns away, coughs into his hands. But Frank cannot look away. He stands staring at the pink-red water and the raw, floating things in it.

"Pretty amazing, huh?"

Frank only nods, doesn't turn to see who's spoken.

"Who got here first?" he asks, swallowing hard, struggles against the nauseous acid rising into his throat. It's only a matter of time until he loses, but at least he can say he fought the good fight, and maybe Wallace will cut him a little slack for the effort.

"Me and my partner. We didn't touch nothin'," the cop says. "Of course, with all this goddamn rain, I'm not sure that's gonna matter a whole hell of a lot."

"Who made the call?" Frank asks, biting down hard on his lower lip, a little pain against his rolling stomach.

"Right there," the cop replies, pointing beyond the fountain to an old man in an expensive-looking raincoat and green galoshes. He's sitting on a metal park bench holding a shivering Chihuahua on a leash. The dog is also wearing a raincoat, banana-yellow plastic. The pair are completely surrounded by cops with umbrellas, huddled protectively above the old man and his little dog.

"He called 911 about half an hour ago."

Frank holds up one hand to silence the officer and takes a step closer to the fountain.

"They ain't paying me enough for this bullshit," Wallace says somewhere behind him, but Frank can't look away from the water stained the color of cherry Kool-Aid. It's almost like one of those 3-D puzzles, a senseless collage of reds and blacks and whites, and if he could just look at it the right way it might resolve itself into something human, something that might have once been human. A blue-gray loop of bowel, a mat of black hair like a patch of some strange algae, teasing bits that almost make sense of the whole.

"There's some Hefty bags over there," the cop says, and

nods toward the gnarled oak on the other side of the fountain. "They've still got some blood and stuff on them, so I'm thinkin' the killer must have used them to haul all this mess here and dump it in the fountain."

Someone tugs at Frank's sleeve. He jumps a little, but it's just Wallace, one hand still covering his mouth and nose, only glancing at the fountain.

"Let's step back a minute, okay, Frank? Give yourself a break. You're starting to look kinda green . . ."

He pushes Wallace's hand away. Only one more step to the edge of the fountain and he's looking directly down into the stew of rainwater and meat, bone and gristle, organs and muscle hacked apart like butcher's scraps. The wind gusts hard enough that for a second Frank thinks it will lift him like a stray newspaper and toss him high to snag in the branches of the craggy trees or carry him far above the city, far away from the atrocity spread out before him. But when the wind dies down again he's still there.

"Jesus, Frank. *Please* . . ." Wallace moans. Frank blinks, wipes the polluted rainwater from his eyes. That's when he sees the writing scrawled along the top edge of the fountain, the clumsy leaning letters in something black and greasy, something the storm can't wash away. Words a foot wide, so that he has to walk around the fountain to read it all. Wallace trails close behind him, cursing Frank and the goddamn weather and the sick son of a bitch who would chop someone up and leave them floating in a city park.

"Poe," Frank says. At last he can look away, as if he's passed some sort of test. He stares up through the swaying limbs into the storm clouds rushing overhead.

"What the fuck are you talking about?" Wallace gags on the last word and has to turn away.

"'On the morrow *he* will leave me,'" Frank begins, repeating what he's read in the oil-black graffiti, reciting now from grade school memories. "It's from Poe. You know, 'The Raven'? By Edgar Allan Poe? 'On the morrow *he* will leave me as my Hopes have flown before.'"

"Whatever . . ." Wallace starts and stops, swallows before he

132

can finish. "Whatever you say, Franklin." Then he steps away from the fountain, steps back across the barrier of tape, and vomits into the grass. Frank doesn't move, doesn't take his eyes off the clouds. In a moment he realizes that his head has stopped hurting.

In the kitchen of his big house by the river the man who is Jordan today finishes his breakfast of canned corned beef hash and canned creamed corn as he listens to the radio. The old portable Sony on the counter is the only radio in his house, and he's carefully wrapped all of it except the bent rabbit ears in three layers of aluminum foil, has drawn the appropriate symbols on the foil in red and black Magic Marker so he's absolutely certain there's no danger of errant signals or amplified cosmic rays or subliminal telepathic waves getting through to him from the Outside. He always keeps it tuned to WWOZ 90.7 because jazz is the only music he likes, the only music he's relatively certain is free of Their influence.

But now he's listening to the news, mostly reports on the tropical storm that's about to be upgraded to a hurricane. Hurricane Michael. He thinks how appropriate that will be, vengeful heaven sweeping across the Gulf of Mexico toward the seething Babylon of New Orleans. If he really believed in God or gods, he might think of the storm as a divine reinforcement sent to counter the black bird-thing from his dreams and visions. But he is not a religious man, so the metaphor and its abstract comfort will have to suffice.

Jordan scoops up another forkful of the sweet yellow corn and listens as the soothing male voice reports the discovery of a body in Audubon Park just after dawn. No details. No whisper of the time and skill he expended on the boy, but Jordan has come to expect that sort of carelessness. They're afraid to tell the truth, afraid to scare the masses living always between the rock of Their occupation and the hard place of his resistance.

"Sources indicate that the body was badly mutilated, but New Orleans police have declined to confirm or deny this information at the present. They have also refused to comment on whether or not there may be a connection between this crime and the Bourbon Street Ripper slayings."

That gets a cautious, guarded smile from Jordan, a self-satisfied smile that makes him feel a bit ashamed. *Someone's noticed*, he thinks. *They can try to cover it up, but someone* always *notices.*

"In possibly related news," the report says, "the body of Detective James Unger of the Sixth Ward's homicide division was found this morning in his home in Metairie, dead from a single gunshot wound to the head. Sources close to the police department report that Detective Unger may have taken his own life in the wake of his partner's suicide five days ago, though the possibility of foul play has not been ruled out. Both detectives were responsible for the arrest of Jared Poe, who was convicted of the brutal murders that became known as the Bourbon Street Ripper slayings.

"In sports today, the Saints lose their first preseason game—"

Jordan gets up and switches off the radio. He stands by the kitchen counter listening to his heart thudding in his chest, and his head feels light and heavy at the same time. What wrinkle in the game is this? Both the detectives dead, the detectives who had so expertly and unwittingly diverted any suspicion from Jordan, who fell for the clues he left behind in the Ursulines Street apartment. They were dutiful foot soldiers in his war. They got Jared Poe off the street.

They got the fucking pervert killed, Jordan thinks. *That's what they did.*

He knows he should have seen this coming. Dirty little reprisals for his recent actions, and surely something to do with the visions of the black, wicked thing above the city. The thing that is so close now he can feel it watching his every move. Payback for Jared Poe's death, Their prized evangelist lost to Them, and *someone* has to suffer.

"Fuck," Jordan whispers, his voice unsteady, and he looks down at his hands. They've gone the color of cottage cheese and developed a tremor, but he isn't sure whether he's afraid or just excited that his campaign has drawn such powerful forces out into the open. Perhaps it is even pride that They could fear him so much. That he has hurt Them so badly and They have not attempted to take Their pound of flesh from him, have struck out instead against innocent and ignorant pawns. Men unknowingly in his service, soldiers taking the heat, buying him a little more time.

In the end it will all come down to timing. He knows that. Jordan turns away from the radio and begins clearing the table.

By eleven o'clock Tropical Storm Michael has graduated to Hurricane Michael and the television and radio stations have begun talking about evacuation procedures, breaking into soap operas and talk shows to track the storm's steady westward swath across the Gulf. Satellite pictures of a great white spiral with an ocean-blue cyclops eye, a vast organism of cloud and wind and lashing rain, rushing past Mississippi toward the Louisiana delta, the swamps and the wide, dirty river, all the bayou towns with flooded streets and downed telephone lines. Even the dark ancient powers nestled between rotting cypress stumps and moldering Vieux Carré rooftops take notice of this force and steel themselves against its arrival.

seven

THE WORLD'S COMING UNDONE, FRANK GRAY THINKS. THE
thought frightens him so badly that he tries to pretend it's just
something he heard someone say once, nothing *he's* responsible
for. But that's not the way it feels to him, standing beside his
partner in Detective James Unger's kitchen with the storm
whipping back and forth beyond the all-too-insubstantial walls
of the Metairie house.

In the last twenty-four hours the world has somehow begun
to unravel away around Frank like an old sweater, a few loose
threads neglected too long and now the whole thing's coming
apart at the fucking seams. Something that started with the kid
in the bar maybe, the bathroom blow job gone crazy, the first
step on a crooked trail that has somehow led him here.

"We should get going," Wallace says. Frank turns to look at
him. Wallace looks sick, scared, fed up with this long day of
blood and wind that's only half over. "Our asses got no business
even bein' way out here."

That was true enough. But when the news about Unger
came in from dispatch Frank had to see for himself, to hell with
jurisdiction. He knew how important Jim Unger's testimony
had been in convicting the man the NOPD sent up for the
Bourbon Street killings. And now here's Unger, lying on the
floor of his own kitchen with his brains splattered like tapioca
all over the linoleum.

"What the hell's going on here, Wally?" Frank asks, but Wallace just sighs and stares out the shattered bay windows. The kitchen is drenched from the blowing rain.

"Jesus, Frank, it's not our case. It's not our goddamn problem what it means."

"Maybe not," Frank says.

"Ain't no fuckin' maybe about it, Frank. This is *not* our turf and Unger is *not* our case."

Frank stares back down at the body sprawled on the floor, still half seated in a chair tipped over backward so that its bare knees are aimed at the ceiling, the butt of the revolver protruding from what's left of its mouth.

"We got enough trouble of our own to worry about with that bullshit back at the fountain."

"Just think about it a second, Wally—"

But Wallace has him firmly by the arm and he's already leading Frank out of the house, past the annoyed-looking Jefferson Parish cops and the ambulance in the driveway, back to their car, parked by the curb.

"You didn't even *like* that son of a bitch, Frank," Wallace says as he opens his door. Frank's still standing in the rain, staring back at the house, trying to put the pieces together in his head. Trying to find a resolution for the basic contradictions and apparent coincidences bouncing around in his skull. Finally Wallace tells him to just get in the goddamn car, so he opens the passenger door and slides in as the Ford coughs noisily to life.

"So you gonna tell me what that was all about?" Wallace asks, pulling away from the dead man's house. The wipers come on, swiping like skeletal wings from one side of the windshield to the other, but they're practically useless in the downpour.

"I'm not sure," Frank says.

"Come on, Frank. Don't make me beg. My ass is cold and wet and I'm not in the mood for it today."

The entire world, unraveling like an old sweater, Frank thinks again. Never mind the care, the paranoid calculation, that he's put into keeping it all together for so long.

138

"Do you think Jared Poe was the Ripper?" he asks as Wallace stops for a red light.

"Do I . . ." Wallace begins. Then the light changes, a vivid blur of emerald green through the rain. They cross the intersection carefully, heading back toward I-10 and the city.

"Oh, I see," Wallace says, wiping condensation from the windshield with one hand. "You think Jim Unger poppin' hisself has something to do with this morning."

Frank wants a cigarette but he knows that Wallace is trying to quit and so he doesn't reach for the half-empty pack of Luckies in his shirt pocket.

"First," he says, "Poe goes to prison and the killings don't stop. I mean, yeah, okay, they stop for what? A few weeks or a month?"

"You ever heard of a copycat killer, Frank?"

"That's what I thought too. But that shit about the poetry they found with Benjamin DuBois's body, that never showed up in the press, Wally."

"You've lost me, Franklin," Wallace says as the Ford glides up the entrance ramp onto the interstate. "Man, I cannot see *shit* out here."

"There was a copy of 'The Raven' by Edgar Allan Poe found with DuBois's body. Some lines were marked . . ."

"You're sayin' that shit written on the fountain was from the same poem."

"Yeah," Frank replies. "It was."

"And you want to know how the copycat knows about the poem from the DuBois case."

Frank fishes the Luckies from his pocket and punches the car's cigarette lighter. "I'm sorry, man," he says, but Wallace shakes his head.

"It's been what, a week since Poe was killed up at Angola, right?" Frank says, taking a cigarette from the pack and putting the rest back in his pocket.

"Yeah," Wallace answers, cracking his window. The air rushing in makes a loud, unpleasant sound, and they both flinch at the icy drops of rain sucked into the car. "That's about right."

"And the next fucking day Vince Norris cuts his throat. Vince Norris was Jim Unger's partner."

"Vincent Norris was also as crazy as a loon, Frank." Wallace makes circles around one ear with an index finger.

"Then we get the body in the park this morning . . ."

"If you wanna call that a body," Wallace says, and swipes at the windshield with his hand again.

". . . along with a line from 'The Raven,' and barely an hour later we hear that Jim Unger's dead."

"So now you're thinkin' maybe it wasn't Colonel Mustard in the library with the wrench after all."

The cigarette lighter pops and Frank lights the Lucky Strike from its glowing red-orange coil.

"You're the most sarcastic fuck I've ever met, Wally," he says, trying to sound as though he isn't afraid, as though none of this shit's getting through his defenses. Frank exhales and looks out at the storm, the clouds, and the wind-tossed trees. The wind buffets the Ford and he can tell Wallace is having trouble keeping the car on the road.

"It's one of my finer qualities," Wallace says with a grin. "Keeps me from havin' to go suckin' on my own rod, like the recently deceased Detective Unger back there."

Frank takes another deep drag off his cigarette and watches the clouds, remembering what the storm looked like on the Weather Channel satellite photos.

When Jared opens his eyes the crow is still huddled on his shoulder, crouched close to his face as if maybe she can steal body heat he doesn't have to give.

"Where are we?" he asks her. The crow makes a soft bird sound deep in her throat.

It's still raining. Jared is starting to think that maybe it's been raining forever and his memories of sunlight are as unreal as his memories of life. He hasn't been asleep, but he feels as though he has dreamed. He doesn't remember leaving the row of oleander bushes in Metairie, but the street signs tell him that he's back in the French Quarter. The cobblestone street shimmers under an inch of water, a straight and narrow river fed by the sky and gutters and the crystal cascades falling from the roofs. He wants to lie down in the street, imagines the water carrying him away in small bits and pieces, taking apart his body and mind, all the pain, until there's nothing left but a greasy, iridescent stain. Before long that would be gone as well.

"Hey, mister!" someone yells. Jared sees a black face gazing out from an upstairs window. The face floats and bobs inside a rectangle of shadow framed in pink stucco, and then the man shouts at him again.

"Ain't you got the sense to come in outta the rain? Ain't you heard there's a hurricane comin'?"

I ain't even got the sense to stay dead, Jared thinks. *What do you expect from a zombie that ain't even got enough sense to stay dead?*

"And why you dressed like that? This ain't Mardi Gras, you know! Hey! Your bird's gettin' wet!"

Jared waves at the man, turns away from the window. Rain rolls off Benny's black latex frock coat and is lost in the downpour, drips from the jester mask that Jared doesn't remember putting back on. He wades to the sidewalk and stands in the minimal shelter of an awning outside a shop that sells herbs and voodoo potions. There are no lights on inside the shop. Jared stands there a moment, staring at his reflection in the shop's display window.

Deep into that darkness peering, long I stood there, wondering, fearing . . .

Jared touches the sharp chin of the leather face hiding his own. His reflection follows his example.

"You gonna get washed away, mister!" the man shouts behind him, and then laughs, a hoarse braying laugh. "Michael gonna wash you *both* all the way to the sea!"

A long black car rolls by, parting the river that flows down Toulouse Street, spraying the sidewalk and Jared as it passes. He turns, catching a brief glimpse of the driver through the Oldsmobile's window. The face is narrow, pinched, with hollow, hungry cheeks; that face tugs at his lazy memory and now Jared knows why he's come back to the French Quarter. Knows a name to put with the face: John Henry Harrod, the district

141

attorney who personally handled his prosecution, the man who sat on the other side of the courtroom and nailed together his doom from scraps of coincidence and lies while Benny's murderer walked the streets somewhere, unpunished, exonerated by default, and free to kill again.

The Oldsmobile turns into a private driveway and Jared and the crow are alone again. For the moment, at least, the man in the window seems to have lost interest in them.

"I bet that son of a bitch isn't on the agenda either, is he?" Jared asks the crow. He already knows the answer before she replies.

"Then we'll just take another little detour while you're figuring out exactly who the hell *is*," Jared says. The bird responds with an earsplitting *caw-caw* that makes Jared's head ache.

"Fine with me. Thanks for finding the asshole—I can take care of the rest myself." He reaches up and brushes the bird off his shoulder. She flutters under the awning for a second before flying away through the rain toward the rooftops.

"Hey, man! There go your bird!" the face in the window shouts. Jared ignores him, walks to the spot where the car turned in, a black iron gate set into a high brick wall. Jared grips the bars and presses his face to them, stares through a thick grove of windblown banana plants and rhododendrons. He can see the Olds, parked and empty now, in front of a cottage almost completely hidden by the garden. The storm makes wet flapping sounds in the big leaves of the tropical plants, sounds like the desperate flippers of deep-sea things beached and drowning in air.

Just like prison, he thinks. The thought makes him take a step back from the bars. No, sir. *Not* just like prison. Nothing is ever going to be just like prison again.

And scaling the wall is more of an idea than an effort, a problem he solves without knowing or caring precisely how. But he lands slightly off balance, slips, and realizes too late that someone has taken the precautionary measure of studding the top of the wall with jagged shards of broken glass, translucent teeth secure in cement gums, glass that slices his hands as he falls. Jared lands in one of the rhododendrons and clutches his injured hands to his chest. There's a deep gash across his right palm and a puncture straight through his left. The blood flows out as if from stigmata and is immediately thinned by the rain, diluted before it drips to the broad green leaves and the dark and muddy earth.

A ghost that bleeds, he thinks. *What fucking good is that supposed to be?* He squeezes his palms shut, squeezes hard against the pain. The big leaves overhead bestow a little shelter from the storm and Jared lies there until he finds the will to get up, the will to keep going. It helps to recall the thin face from the black Oldsmobile, the face from the courtroom, so he stares up into the angry sky and thinks about John Harrod.

Eventually, inevitably, they put Lucrece on the stand.

Early on, when his own attorneys had suggested her as a character witness, Jared had flatly refused. When they'd asked again, he had threatened to change his plea to guilty unless they shut up about her. No way he was going to put her through that. "And besides," he'd added bitterly, "she's just another freak for this fucking sideshow. What good is one freak's word in defense of another freak? We're all in this together, you know?"

So it was the prosecution who finally put Lucrece in the center ring, District Attorney John H. Harrod, who'd backed former Ku Klux Klansman David Duke in his 1991 bid for the governorship of Louisiana. Who'd more recently made political allies of Ralph Reed and his Christian Coalition and who'd gone as far as pledging to "clean up" the Quarter. Of course, he hadn't actually done much in the way of fulfilling that pledge: just a couple of porno busts staged for the media, the arrest of one shopkeeper who sold glass pipes, more hookers and hustlers spending the night in lockup. Harmless token gestures amplified by the press and nothing much more, until one of the highest-profile homicide cases in the city's murder-haunted history had fallen into his lap. A string of brutal killings apparently committed by a man one local radio pundit had already labeled "a pornographer of the sickest sort, masquerading as an *artiste.*"

The fact that all the killer's victims were drag queens, cross-dressers, or transsexuals made the matter a little delicate. After all, Harrod couldn't very well be seen as defending the sort of perverts he'd promised to rid the city of. But it had taken only a little semantic footwork to fix that. The very fact that New Orleans harbored the sort of deviant individuals who attracted sexual predators like Jared Poe was surely proof in and of itself that the city needed to be cleaned up.

And Lucrece had been only a little more grist for his political mill, one more life he could ruin in the name of wholesome family values. So he put her on the stand, the prosecution's last witness before they rested their case against Jared Poe. His lawyers objected, claiming Lucrece was irrelevant and prejudicial and still too grief-stricken by her brother's death to possibly be of any help to anyone. The judge overruled the defense's objection. Lucrece did as she was told, swore on the Bible she didn't believe in, sat up straight, and tried to make a brave face for John Harrod.

Harrod lingered over his papers a moment, pretending to ponder some detail or another, giving the jury time to get a good look at Lucrece. She'd dressed as conservatively as her wardrobe permitted: a plain black dress with a long skirt, her hair pulled back into a neat chignon. She had removed the omnipresent black from her nails and lips and wore none of her usual jewelry except a simple garnet ring that Benny had given her years ago.

It made Jared sick and furious to see her put on display like that, straining to pass as normal for a lot of norm motherfuckers who had already made up their narrow minds about her. To see her going through hell to try to save his ass when this trial was just a nicety anyway. He stood up, wrestling free of one of his lawyers.

"Please don't do this, Lucrece," he said, but the judge was already banging his gavel, calling for order. There were hands on Jared, pulling him back down into his seat.

"It doesn't matter *what* you say, Lucrece," Jared pleaded. "They'll make it mean whatever they want! Whatever they need it to mean! You can't save me!"

"Oh, Jared," she whispered, close to tears, and then the judge threatened to have Jared removed from the courtroom if he couldn't control himself. That was enough to shut him up, the thought of Lucrece being left alone with Harrod, alone with his manipulating questions and innuendo and no one there who gave a shit what he said or did to her.

Harrod glanced at Jared and smiled, and Jared bit a ragged hole in his bottom lip to keep himself from telling the DA to go fuck himself.

"So," Harrod said, straightening his tie, "*Ms.* DuBois. You're the *sister* of the deceased, correct?"

Lucrece swallowed once and said, "Yes," very quietly.

"Excuse me, Ms. DuBois, but I didn't quite hear you and I'm afraid the rest of the court may not have heard you. Could you please repeat your answer?"

"I said yes," Lucrece said, and Harrod nodded.

"Thank you, Ms. DuBois. But the truth is that you weren't always Benjamin DuBois's sister, isn't that correct? You weren't *born* his sister."

Lucrece didn't answer this time, looked nervously down at her hands and then out at the crowded courtroom.

"Ms. DuBois? Do you need me to repeat the question?"

"No," she said. "I heard you."

"But you didn't answer me, Ms. DuBois." Harrod took a step closer to the bench. "Were you *born* Benjamin DuBois's sister?"

"I guess that's a matter of opinion," Lucrece replied.

"Isn't it true that the name your mother gave you at birth, your *Christian* name, is Lucas Wesley DuBois?"

"I changed my name. Legally," Lucrece said.

"When you stopped being Benjamin DuBois's brother and decided to be his sister," Harrod said, looking toward the jurors' box as he spoke.

"Mr. Harrod, I *am* a transsexual. I underwent sex reassignment surgery years ago. Is that what Jared's on trial for? My sex change?"

There was tense laughter from the crowd and Harrod smiled again, nodded, and turned to face Lucrece.

145

"No, Ms. DuBois. I just wanted to be sure that these men and women understood your relationship to the deceased, that's all."

"I was always Benny's sister," she said.

Speaking straight to the jury, Harrod responded, "I guess that's a matter of opinion." He was rewarded with a second round of laughter.

"Now, Ms. DuBois, how would you characterize your relationship with the accused?"

Lucrece hesitated a moment, aware that every question was a snare, every answer a weapon to be used against Jared.

"Jared is my brother-in-law and friend," she said.

"He's your brother-in-*law*?"

"He was . . ." and Lucrece stopped, took a breath, and continued. "He *is* my brother's husband."

"But not *legally*, Ms. DuBois," Harrod said. "Because marriage between two men, two *homosexual* men, is not legal in the state of Louisiana. So Jared Poe cannot possibly be your brother-in-*law*, now can he?"

Harvey Etienne, one of Jared's two attorneys, stood up and objected. He tapped the eraser end of a pencil against the table as he spoke.

"Your Honor," he said, "this line of questioning is immaterial. Unless I'm mistaken, homosexual marriage is not on trial this afternoon."

The judge frowned gravely, peered down at Harvey Etienne through his thick bifocals.

"I see no particular harm in allowing counsel for the prosecution to pursue this line of inquiry as long as Mr. Harrod does eventually get to the point."

"As I will shortly, Your Honor," John Harrod assured the judge.

"Then proceed, Mr. Harrod," the judge said, and Harvey Etienne sat down again.

"So . . . your brother and Mr. Poe were *not* married—"

"Benny and Jared *were* married," Lucrece growled, interrupting Harrod. "I don't give a shit what the fucking state of Louisiana says, they were married."

"Ms. DuBois," the judge said, leaning his black-robed bulk

toward Lucrece, "I would strongly caution you to watch your language in my courtroom."

"I'm sorry," she said, not sounding it one bit.

Harrod coughed dryly into one fist and continued.

"Then, Ms. DuBois, would you say that you respected your brother's relationship with Mr. Poe the same as you would any *legal* marriage?"

"Of course I did. I *do*."

"Because in your opinion the homosexual union between your late brother Benjamin and Mr. Poe was as sacred as any legal, state-sanctioned marriage, am I correct?"

"Yes," Lucrece hissed. Harvey Etienne put one big restraining hand on Jared's shoulder.

"Tell me, Ms. DuBois, do you believe that adultery would be a violation of that union?"

This caught Lucrece off guard. *"What?"*

"Just answer the question, Ms. DuBois," Harrod said, standing very near her now. "Do you believe that a marriage, even an illegal homosexual marriage like your brother's, would be violated by the sin of adultery?"

"What are you trying to get me to say, Mr. Harrod?"

"All in the world I want from you, Ms. DuBois, is a straight answer to my question."

She watched him for a moment in silence. Jared could see how hard Lucrece was breathing, could see the fire sparking in her pale green eyes. Harvey tightened his grip on Jared's shoulder.

"Because if you *do* hold that union sacred, Ms. DuBois, I'd be very curious to know how you justified your own relationship with Mr. Poe."

John Harrod was resting one hand on the oaken rail of the witness stand, his eyebrows arched in expectation of her answer and a smug, victorious smirk on his lips. He bent close to Lucrece and spoke as low as he could and still be heard by the entire courtroom.

"I'm waiting, Ms. DuBois. I'm sure everyone in this room is waiting to hear your answer."

"*Objection*, Your Honor," Harvey Etienne said, standing

147

again but still pressing down hard on Jared's shoulder. "This is immaterial and prejudicial, *and* the state has offered no evidence whatsoever to substantiate such a charge."

"Come on, Ms. DuBois," Harrod urged through a big Cheshire-cat grin. "Just tell the truth. That's all I'm asking you do. Just tell us the truth."

"Your Honor!" Harvey Etienne shouted, and the fat judge struck his gavel three times in quick succession. It made a sound like gunfire. He wiped one sweaty hand across his exasperated face and turned toward Harrod.

"I presume this *is* leading somewhere, Mr. Harrod," he said.

"It goes directly to motive, Your Honor." Then, looking over his shoulder at Jared and his lawyers, he added, "*And* I have witnesses. Witnesses who will attest to knowledge of a sexual relationship not only between Lucrece DuBois and Jared Poe, but between Ms. DuBois and her own brother."

"You're a sick, hateful son of a bitch," Lucrece said. Leaning slightly forward in the witness box, she spat in his face. There was a brief shocked silence in the courtroom.

"That means a lot, Ms. DuBois," Harrod said at last, taking a handkerchief from his pocket. "Coming as it does from a confirmed sodomite such as yourself."

Jared lunged across the table, dragging Harvey Etienne after him, and the court exploded in a turmoil of shouting and camera flashes.

"You leave her the fuck alone, you bastard," Jared screamed over the pandemonium. "You leave her alone *now* or I'll fucking kill you."

Then Etienne was hauling him backward across the table, scattering briefs and legal pads. An expensive briefcase clattered loudly to the marble floor and vomited more papers. There were other hands on him, pulling him back toward the chair where he was expected to sit still and listen while John Henry Harrod lied and twisted the truth to fit his needs, while he hurt Lucrece. Jared lunged again and was rewarded with the sound of his collar tearing.

But Harrod had turned his attention away from Lucrece, took one cautious step toward Jared.

"It *is* true, isn't it, Mr. Poe? It's true that you killed Benjamin DuBois because you'd decided that you *really* wanted his sister and neither of them could keep their hands off each other. You were *jealous*, weren't you, Mr. Poe?"

"Shut up!" Lucrece screamed from the stand. "Please make him shut up!"

Jared tore free, tumbled headfirst off the other side of the table, and was on his feet in an instant. He caught a fleeting glimpse of one of the court bailiffs, and there was a sudden crushing pain across the back of his skull. As he fell there was only the sound of Lucrece crying and, much farther away, the wood-on-wood crack of the judge's gavel.

Angola Prison lies at the end of State Highway 66 by a sharp bend in the Mississippi River, surrounded on three sides by deep and drowning waters, hemmed in on the fourth by the rugged, rattlesnake-infested Yunica Hills. Eighteen thousand acres of Louisiana wilderness set aside for the punishment and rehabilitation of evil men and crazy men and men who are simply too stupid not to get caught.

As in so much of Louisiana, so much of the South, time has *almost* stood still here. Angola is not so different than the day it opened its gates in 1868, barely three years after the Confederacy surrendered at Appomattox. A vast cotton and soybean plantation on the banks of the river, hidden away from the rest of the world by all-but-impenetrable stands of oak and slash pine, a world with its own secrets, rules, and deadly rituals.

Jared Poe arrived at Angola on a muggy October day, an afternoon still plagued by summer's heat, but the sky was a bright autumn blue. As the bus carried him through the front gates Jared craned his neck to look back the way they'd come, straining for one last pointless glimpse of lost freedom through a wake of exhaust and red clay dust.

The jury had needed only two hours to find him guilty of Benny's murder, two hours to decide how and where the rest of

Jared's life would be spent. The judge had taken even less time to decide how it would end.

Death row wasn't far from the front gates, just past watchtowers four and five, four concrete walls the same sickly green as pistachio ice cream or Irish Spring soap. Jared wondered if they'd always been that color or if the merciless delta sun had faded them as it did men.

There was nothing notable about his arrival, a dull ceremony of chains and keys and paperwork that concluded with Jared being led to his cell through a gauntlet of six barred doors; above one of them someone had painted DEATH ROW in tawdry crimson, on the off chance, he supposed, that a man might think he was somewhere else. Abandon all hope, ye who enter here, and all that good shit. The air in the cell block smelled faintly of vomit, disinfectant, and tobacco smoke. Finally they locked him into the six-by-eight-foot cell that would be his last home. "Get used to it," the guard said as he slammed the door closed and electronic locks clicked solidly into place.

Jared sat in silence for the first five minutes, staring down at his prison-issue shoes, waiting for some small part of the nightmare to begin to feel real to him. When a voice whispered his name from the cell next door, he got up from his bunk and walked to the bars.

"Did someone say something to me?"

"Yeah, I said something to you, faggot," the voice replied in a heavy Hispanic accent. "You that Poe motherfucker, ain't you? You that fag sonabitch we been seein' all over television, ain't you?"

"Yeah," Jared answered. "Yeah, I guess I am."

"Yeah, well, you just listen to me, Anglo. There ain't no television celebrities in here. So you might have been some bad-ass spooky voodoo sonabitch down in New Orleans, but in here you just another piece of white meat waitin' your turn to ride Gertie. *Comprende?*"

And then someone down the row of cells was yelling, "Why don't you shut your wetback mouth, Gonzalez? I got a fuckin' migraine and all I can hear is your big fuckin' mouth jabberin' away down there."

"Hey, man! *Fuck* you!"

"No, Gonzalez, fuck *you*! Fuck you *and* your burrito-eatin' whore-bitch of a mama!"

Jared went back to his bunk and sat down, listened until Gonzalez and the other man got tired of yelling at each other, then listened to the other sounds, all the captive sounds inside the cement box. Eventually he began to make a mental list of the ways someone could kill himself in here if he *really* wanted to, if there was finally no other sane choice left. He stopped at fifteen.

The long weeks became months, days creeping by at a caterpillar's pace, but then so many of them were gone and Jared was at a loss to explain how the monotonous routine of television and pasty, tasteless meals could have devoured so much time.

He was allowed to leave his cell only for brief showers and calls from his lawyers, who made uncertain promises about his appeal. Lucrece called only once and he made her promise never to do it again. Never mind how much hope he might have gleaned from the sound of her, he would not have it.

"Christ, Jared," she'd said, "I can't just let you sit there and fucking rot."

"Neither of us has much of a choice in the matter. I love you, Lucrece, but *please* don't do it again." Then he'd hung up on her. There was no room for hope in this shithole. That's what those sloppy red letters over the door on the way in were meant to remind you, just some illiterate fuck's hateful idea of a joke, the allusion to Dante surely accidental, but Jared had learned a long time ago that intention and message do not always go hand in hand.

Jared also got three short trips a week outside the pistachio building, a handful of minutes at a time in the exercise yard so he could stare through the fence at the forested hills on the other side or the empty sky overhead before the guard herded him back inside again.

One day he'd been half asleep in his bunk, had been rereading a tattered Clive Barker paperback and dozed off, and then Gonzalez was calling him, a loud whisper through the concrete. Jared got up and found the small polished piece of metal that he could hold between the bars for a mirror so he could actually see Ruben Gonzalez while they talked.

"Hey, man. They took Hector." Jared watched the blurry reflection of his neighbor's face in the scratched and dented surface of the mirror.

"When?" Jared asked, because he was expected to ask, not because he actually gave a shit. Hector Montoni had been convicted of raping twelve children in Baton Rouge and Biloxi, of murdering the last three. He'd made videotapes of every one of the assaults.

"Jus' about fifteen minutes ago, man," Ruben said. "He's *over* there by now. He's in the death house by now." Gonzalez stepped away from the bars, out of the range of Jared's mirror. For a while he mumbled prayers in Spanish.

Jared went back to his cot and picked up the copy of *The Great and Secret Show*, read one paragraph before Ruben started calling him again. This time Jared didn't bother with the mirror. He lit a cigarette and sat down on the floor beside the bars.

"Two thousand volts," Ruben Gonzalez said. "That's a lot, huh? That's a whole lotta juice to shoot through someone, ain't it?"

"Yeah, it is," Jared said.

"They say it tears *holes* in your body, man. They say it jumps right outta your eyeballs like lightning and blows off the ends of your fingers. Jesus fuck, why don't they just fuckin' shoot us or somethin', you know? Somethin' a little more humanitarian."

"Humane," Jared corrected. "Something a little more *humane*."

"Hey, screw *you*, you faggot sonabitch. You just sittin' over there so goddamn cool, man, like a fuckin' ice cube 'cause you got them fat-cat lawyers workin' for you, right? 'Cause you ain't used up all your appeals."

"Maybe," Jared said, and took another drag off his cigarette, blew smoke through the bars.

"*Maybe?* What kind of macho bullshit is that, man?"

"*Maybe* I just don't give a shit, that's all."

Ruben laughed a humorless laugh on the other side of the wall. "Yeah, right. You gonna give a shit when they come to drag your murderin' faggot ass out to that van and drive you off to the death house. You ain't gonna be sayin' maybe then, asshole."

"Maybe not," Jared said, and crushed out his cigarette against the floor.

"Fuck you, man." Ruben Gonzalez fell quiet for a while then, five or ten minutes, and eventually Jared heard him praying again and went back to his book.

A few months later Jared Poe was led out to the exercise yard for the last time. It was a sweltering late-August afternoon filled with mosquitoes and the threat of rain, thunderheads piling up off toward Weyanoke and the state line farther north. He stood near the fence watching the clouds, not smoking, just breathing cleaner air into his lungs, washing a little of the prison out of him with air that smelled like pine sap and sunlight.

And then the guard disappeared, the first time that had ever happened, and Jared was left alone. For the first time since the judge had read his sentence Jared felt an icy twinge of fear in his gut, a sudden rush of goose bumps along his exposed arms. He stood with his back to the fence and watched the dark doorway leading back into death row. It yawned back at him like an open mouth, the toothless mouth of something ancient that could swallow a man whole and leave no trace but his absence.

When the Cuban stepped through that black hole Jared knew this was a setup. He didn't have a fucking clue who the big man was or what business there might possibly be between them, but he *knew* it had to be a setup.

The man stood by the doorway a moment, staring across the gravel yard toward Jared. His dark eyes were filled with something that transcended hate, something that had lain a long time in the shadow of that gaze, getting fat on bad memories.

Even before he saw the stainless-steel glint of the sharpened spoon in the man's hand, he knew the Cuban was there to kill him.

"Why?" Jared asked. The man raised his head a little, flared his nostrils wide as if he were sniffing the air to get Jared's scent, to be sure he had located a proper object for his hatred and the damage it could do.

"You're Poe. You're the queer bastard that killed all those people in New Orleans," he said.

Jared had long ago become too used to the presumption of his guilt, far too numbed to the denial of his innocence, to bother contradicting the Cuban.

"I'm Jared Poe," he said.

"You killed my brother," the man said, and took a step closer to Jared. "You killed my little brother and left him floating in the river like garbage for the fish to eat."

Jared caught a glimpse of the guard watching from just inside the doorway, a pale figure in the gloom, his eyes much too fascinated by what was about to happen to look away.

"I didn't kill your brother," Jared said, surprised at how calm he sounded, how steady his voice could be with his death standing only a few feet away. "I know you're not going to believe me, but I didn't kill anyone."

"*Liar,*" the man said, spitting the word out like a bitter taste, and then he mumbled something else in Spanish that Jared didn't understand. He moved quickly, and even if Jared had been inclined to run, even if what he'd told Ruben Gonzalez all those months ago had been a lie, there would have been nowhere to go. So Jared took one small step backward and braced himself.

The Cuban's makeshift dagger went in just above his navel, made a little popping sound as it punched through skin and muscle to the vital organs underneath. The Cuban pulled the blade out and drove it back in a second time. Jared's knees buckled. He could feel the warm blood pumping out through his T-shirt, soaking into his jeans, spilling like piss down his leg. He saw it red and sticky on the man's hand and dripping in dark spatters to the white limestone gravel.

"I didn't," Jared whispered, sinking to the ground. "I didn't kill anyone."

"No, man," the Cuban sneered. "That ain't why they put motherfuckers in here, for doin' nothing to people."

The Cuban turned and walked away, left Jared kneeling in the dirt and blood, his life pouring out of the hole in his belly. He looked up once. The Cuban was gone and the guard was still standing in the shadows, watching, smiling. Jared fell over on his side, starting to feel the pain in his guts through the shock, and in a little while someone called for a doctor.

He supposes some people in his present situation—if in fact anyone has ever *been* in this crazy situation before—would have gone back to Angola and killed the Cuban. Jared cannot see the point. The Cuban was as much a force of nature as this storm, a happenstance that killed him before the state of Louisiana could. Mostly, though, he can't imagine killing the Cuban because he doesn't blame the guy for killing him. The Cuban had genuinely believed he was killing the man who'd tortured his brother to death. In his place, Jared would have done—*would* do—the same.

Jared stands on the roof of the little cottage behind the glass-studded wall. The roof is only slightly pitched, and there is a skylight that must have been added fairly recently. The rain falls on him, a thousand tiny hammers every second, and rushes around his feet on its way to the overflowing gutters. The lightning and thunder dance above the city, all flash and bluster.

Jared kneels beside the skylight and looks inside.

In a room painted the color of dead violets John Harrod is fucking a black girl up the ass. She grips the shimmering silk sheets in both hands and bucks in time to Harrod's thrusts. Her mouth is open, but Jared can't hear her over the storm. Harrod's lips are curled back to show his perfect white teeth, the tip of his tongue protruding between them like a bit of some invertebrate trying to escape its shell.

155

Jared puts one hand against the glass. *You bastard*, he thinks. *You goddamned hypocritical bastard*. There are suddenly too many things in his head at once, images of Benny and the trial, the thing that the killer left of Benny, the Cuban and Lucrece and a smiling portrait of John Henry Harrod with his wife and two children. Jared pushes slightly against the skylight. He can feel that it would break very easily.

The crow lands on the skylight and caws loudly at Jared, loud even over the roar of the storm. The wind rips at them both, threatens to pluck them from this rooftop and fling them into the taller buildings, press them flat like stray leaves or newspapers against the old brick walls.

"What the fuck do you want?" Jared sneers at her from behind the mask, a sneer to match Harrod's down below. The crow tucks her wings close to her body, huddles against the glass, making a smaller target for the wind.

"I *have* to do this," he tells her. "That motherfucker isn't going to get away with what he did."

And then he hears Lucrece, her voice as clear as if he was back in the apartment with her, as if she were standing in front of him with no wind to rip away the sound.

"This isn't going to bring Benny back to you," she says, and the big black bird cocks her head to one side.

"So now you're a fucking ventriloquist?"

The crow loses her footing and is blown a few inches across the slick glass.

"It doesn't *matter*." Jared isn't sure whether he's speaking to the crow or Lucrece or both, and he doesn't really care. "Because of Harrod, the monster that killed Benny is still out there somewhere . . ."

"You can't do this," Lucrece says as the crow struggles to keep her grip on the skylight, her tiny claws skating on the glass. "Killing Harrod will only make a monster of you too, Jared."

He laughs at her, that she could possibly be so fucking naive after all she's seen, after her life and her brother's death. The laugh feels good, like he's coughing up something poisoned, something burning deep in his belly.

"Get a clue, babe. Haven't you looked in a mirror lately? We're *all* monsters."

"You can*not* do this, Jared," she says again.

"Watch me," he replies. With one arm he sweeps the crow aside, gives the wind a helping hand. The bird flutters away into the murky sky.

Jared smashes the skylight, one punch and it shatters just as easily as he imagined it would. The glass and the rain pour down on Harrod and his whore. Jared follows right behind.

He lands on his feet beside the bed. The woman is already screaming. There are jagged shards of glass protruding from her back and buttocks, and she's frantically scrambling away from Harrod, clawing her way toward the bed's wicker headboard. Harrod turns to face Jared, his trousers in a pile around his ankles and his wet, uncircumcised penis dangling loose inside its condom, already going limp, shriveling up like a salted slug.

"At least you wore a goddamn rubber, you filthy pig," Jared says. He's still laughing, practically giggling now; whatever's broken loose inside him is still getting out, a fury he's carried to the grave and back, and the laughter seems to make as much sense as anything else. "Wouldn't want to risk AIDS. That's a fag death."

"Who . . . who . . . who . . ." Harrod says, the word coughed out through the perfect, astonished O of his mouth.

"Wrong bird." Jared snickers and shoves Harrod, presses one hand against the man's bare chest and sends him stumbling backward to crash against a vanity. Bottles of perfume and tubes of lipstick clatter to the floor. One of the bottles breaks and the room is instantly filled with the sickly, funereal smell of flowers.

"Who . . ." Harrod says again. Now he has one arm up to protect his face.

"You're a slow learner, aren't you, Mr. Harrod?"

"Get out of here!" the girl on the bed screams. "Get out of here, motherfucker! I'm calling the fucking police!"

Jared ignores her and steps past the foot of the bed. Harrod is cowering in front of the vanity, nowhere left for him to run. His breath is labored, uneven.

"*Look* at me, John Harrod," Jared says. He is trying hard to stop laughing. He bites down on his tongue, but that's funny too. Harrod peeks up at him, terrified eyes peering past the shelter of his hairy forearms, and that's absolutely fucking hilarious.

"I know a rhyme, John Harrod. Just a little nursery rhyme my mother taught me. You're not afraid of a little nursery rhyme, are you?"

"Get out of my house!" the woman screams behind him. Harrod doesn't say a word.

"'There were three crows sat on a tree,

They were as black as black can be.

One of them said to his mate:

What shall we do for grub to eat?'"

"I *said* to get the fuck out of my house, you fucking weirdo! *Now!*" Jared hears the box springs creak behind him. He leans over and punches Harrod, feels the bridge of the man's nose break. Blood gushes down Harrod's chin, falls in bright spatters to the polished floorboards. Harrod gasps and cups his hands together to shield his wounded face.

"Sorry. But you really weren't paying attention, were you? I don't have all day. There's a hurricane coming . . ."

"Who the hell *are* you?" Harrod whispers. He sounds as afraid as Jared has ever heard anyone sound, a complicated, suffocating sort of fear that Jared is gratified to hear.

"Well, that's the question, now isn't it? But where was I?" Jared scratches his head like the Tin Man in *The Wizard of* Oz.

"What do you want?" Harrod begs. "Just please tell me what the fuck you *want!*"

Jared finishes the rhyme:

"'There's an old dead horse in yonder lane,

Whose body has been lately slain.

We'll fly upon his old breastbone,

And pluck his eyes out, *one by one*.'"

Harrod begins to cry. Jared kneels next to him in mock concern. "Jesus, that's an awful thing to teach a little kid, don't you think?"

Harrod makes a choking noise and looks at the blood in his hands.

"Now maybe if she'd read to me from the Bible like your mother must've done for you, maybe then I'd have turned out to be a *good* man just like you, Mr. Harrod."

"All right, you asshole, I've had *enough* of this shit!" Jared turns toward the naked woman on the bed just as she pumps the huge shotgun in her hands. There are shells scattered like candy across the rumpled sheets.

Jared drops to the floor and rolls away from the bed, away from Harrod. The boom of the gun is deafening in the small bedroom, thunder trapped and wanting out. Jared knows he's been hit before he even stops moving. He staggers to his feet as she's reloading, ejecting the spent shells and slipping two new ones into the chamber. There's a hole in his side as big an orange and he gets a whiff of his own ruptured bowels.

"Jesus Christ, Harrod. Where'd you *find* this bitch?" Jared dives for the bed. The woman raises the shotgun, takes aim down the long double barrel, but a fraction of a second later he's wrestling the gun from her hands. She screams again and slides to the floor.

"This hasn't got anything to do with you, lady, so stay the fuck out of it and you're not going to get hurt."

Seeing his chance, Harrod kicks the tangle of his pants away and makes a dash for the door. He is gone before Jared can do anything but curse his pale, skinny, fleeing ass.

John Harrod slams the door behind him as he exits the cottage, the pièd-a-terre where he's installed a succession of women for three years now, mostly blacks and Latinas. The storm seizes him immediately, broadsides him. He slips down the front steps and lands in a muddy heap between the Oldsmobile and the house. His ears are ringing from the shotgun blast and his mouth is full of blood from his broken nose.

He almost panics when he reaches for the keys and his fucking pants aren't even there, but then he remembers the extra set tucked above the sun visor. He slides in behind the wheel and pulls the door shut, locking out the storm and the crazy son of a bitch in the white Mardi Gras mask.

John Harrod folds down the visor and the keys tumble out into his naked lap, cold metal against his bare thigh. He tries to start the car with the trunk key on his first attempt and it takes him a moment to find the right one. His heart is ticking off the seconds like a countdown. Then there's a sharp scratching sound and he squints through the rain beating down on the windshield. There is a big black bird standing on the hood of the car, staring in at him.

There were three crows sat on a tree,
They were as black as black can be . . .

"Oh, God," he mutters. He turns the key in the ignition and stomps the gas pedal. The car roars to life momentarily; then the motor coughs, sputters, and dies. The crow spreads its wings and caws loudly, hops toward him, and pecks at the windshield.

Harrod turns the key again, mashes the accelerator to the floor. This time the engine only chugs weakly a couple of times before it's quiet again. The Oldsmobile begins to fill with the smell of gasoline and he knows that he's flooded the engine. When he glances out the windshield the bird is gone. Harrod breathes a nervous sigh of relief and tells himself to calm down. *No way that fucker could have gotten the gun away from Tonya without getting his face blown off,* he thinks. *All you gotta do now, buddy, is calm the fuck down.*

And then something dark drops out of the sky and crashes down onto the hood of the Olds. The car rocks violently from the impact. Where the bird was seconds before, the man in the grinning white mask stands now, pointing the Remington shotgun straight at Harrod's head.

And pluck his eyes out, one by one.

Harrod screams, opens his mouth wide and screams like a woman, as the man turns the gun around and slams the butt against the windshield. It cracks, spiderwebs, and on the second blow caves in, spraying Harrod with diamond bits of safety glass. The rain and wind spill through the hole. Harrod reaches for the .38 he keeps hidden beneath the seat.

"Benjamin DuBois!" the man howls above the wind. He's stooping now, peering in at Harrod through the hole he's made in the windshield. "What does that name *mean* to you, you fucking coward?"

"It means you're a dead son of a bitch," Harrod says. He shoves the revolver through the hole and pulls the trigger and the gun goes off in the man's face.

"Fuck," Harrod grunts, wiping blood from his eyes, blinking through a blurry, red haze. The man in the mask is on his knees now, one hand covering his face; blood drips between his fingers, runs across the hood of the car.

"Now," you goddamn freak," Harrod growls. "Now maybe you'll tell me what the fuck you want."

The man lowers his hand slowly and there's a neat hole in the mask, right between his eyes. Blood flows from the eyeholes of the mask like tears.

"For you to be waiting for me, Harrod," the man says, raising the shotgun again. "For you to *be* there waiting for me when I get back to hell."

The last thing John Henry Harrod sees is the barrel of the Remington 870P sliding in through the hole in the windshield, raindrops glistening on steel. He closes his eyes before the thunder.

Jared lies curled on the hood of the black car, his finger still wrapped tightly around the trigger of the shotgun. He never thought there could be pain like the pain behind his eyes, the hurt filling up his skull. The hit he took inside the cottage was nothing by comparison, an irrelevant, dull ache next to the pain in his head. He moves and the world spins. He is still again.

But the son of a bitch is dead. This is a small comfort, an aspirin for an amputation. Jared cranes to see the stump of Harrod's neck, a jagged few inches of spine jutting out between dead shoulders and then *nothing*, nothing but the gore dripping from the ceiling of the car. Everything inside the Oldsmobile seems to be covered in a fine crimson mist, a fog of blood and brains and vaporized bone. The only thing he can recognize as human is one ear stuck to the mangled headrest of the driver's seat.

Jared hears the crow before he sees her, the hoarse caw cutting through the whistling wind before she lights in front of him. She stares at him a moment, then stabs the hood of the car once with her ebony dagger beak.

"You have to get out of there," Lucrece says, and the crow pecks the metal again.

"He's dead, Lucrece. I killed him," he whispers to the crow. "He's dead."

"That doesn't matter now, Jared," Lucrece replies, her voice urgent, firm, frightened. "There will be cops coming soon. They can't find you there. Get up. Get moving . . ."

He closes his eyes. The afterimage left by the pistol is still there, waiting, an orange smudge in the pale dark. Lucrece doesn't say anything more. When he opens his eyes again, the crow is gone. Her insistent beak has left a small dent in the hood, a flake of paint missing and the gray primer showing through. Jared bites his tongue against the pain and drags himself off the car.

Lucrece is sitting alone at the kitchen table when she hears footsteps somewhere in the apartment. She's been clutching a single black feather for almost two hours now, a feather she found on the bedspread after she came back from the Eye of Horus. She's still surprised that it worked, that the bridge between the crow and Jared was strong enough, that *she* was strong enough to make an actual telepathic connection. If it even *was* anything as simple as telepathy. All Lucrece is really certain of right now is the terrible vertigo and disarming emptiness that the effort left coiled inside her. That, and her relief at hearing Jared's voice again.

"I'm in here," she calls out, pushing her chair back from the table. There are more footsteps and the flutter of wings, so she tries to stand, has to steady herself against one corner of the table.

Christ, maybe I broke something in my brain, she thinks, fighting back a sudden wave of nausea. From the bedroom, there's the sound of breaking glass and Jared cursing.

"C'mon, you pussy," she tells herself. This time she manages to make it all the way to the living room doorway before she has to stop and brace herself against a wall to keep from falling on her ass.

"We gotta get you a goddamn cell phone, Jared Poe," she says, and laughs, but it's a hollow, anxious sort of laugh. "I don't think I want to try that particular trick again."

Another ten feet and she's made it all the way into the bedroom. Jared is lying facedown on the canopy bed with the crow standing over him, faithful as a television watchdog. The bird glances up at Lucrece and caws once.

Jesus, so much fucking blood, she thinks, flashing back on the first time she walked into the room after Benny's death—it's not *that* bad, but it's bad enough. Bad enough to trigger a lingering déjà vu that leaves her feeling even more queasy and disoriented.

"I'm not dead," Jared croaks, the way someone with a really bad hangover whispers, as if he's afraid even his voice will break the world. "I'm still not dead."

"Shhh . . . don't talk, Jared." She tries not to sound as frightened as she is, tries not to look away. But there's a hole in the back of his head that she could put her fist into, a shattered rim of white bone matted with drying blood and hair and clinging bits of gray matter.

Lucrece sits down on the bed beside him. She reaches for his hand and he clutches hers, squeezes so hard that it hurts, but she doesn't say anything. She just squeezes back as hard as she can, and the crow looks at her approvingly.

"It's not as bad as it looks," Jared says, tries to laugh and starts coughing instead.

"You weren't supposed to go after them," Lucrece says. She only realizes that she's crying when she tastes a drop of salty water at one corner of her mouth. "The crow is here to protect you, Jared. But she can't, not if you—"

"But they're *dead*," Jared says, interrupting her. Then he

163

rolls slightly to one side so that Lucrece can see the carnival mask still strapped around his face and the place where the bullet went in—a small black hole, no bigger than a dime. The blood vessels in his eyes have hemorrhaged, the scleral whites turned red, and his pupils are huge and dilated. Those terrible, hurting eyes and the mask, but there's nothing left that she can recognize as Jared. Only his voice, and even that seems somehow changed, older and some of the anger drained away, and whatever's left behind is much darker. Much more dangerous.

"And I can't be sorry for that. I don't give a fuck *what* I was supposed to do . . . I can't be sorry for that."

"You don't have to be sorry, Jared," she says, wishes she weren't crying, wishes he didn't have to see her cry. "But the person who killed Benny is still *out* there, and *that's* why you've come back. Not to get your fool head blown off trying to settle all these old scores with the whole goddamn world."

"The bird hasn't exactly been much help with the main matter," he says, and closes his eyes, and she's glad not to have to look into them, ashamed of her relief but relieved anyway.

"It's not her fault," Lucrece says. "I think there's something *wrong* about the killer. Something that's getting in the way."

"You said that already," Jared mumbles. "Last night."

"The police found another one this morning. A body in the fountain in Audubon Park. The news didn't have a lot of details, but it's him, Jared. I know it's him."

"I'm not a goddamn detective, Lucrece. I don't know how to track down a serial killer. I was just a photographer . . ."

"Then you have to find someone who *is* a detective. The cop who's handling this new murder, maybe him . . ."

Jared's grip on her hand relaxes suddenly, unexpectedly, and his eyelids flutter.

"Jared? What's happening?"

"Maybe I'm dying," he says, so quietly that she barely catches his voice over the wind howling down Ursulines Street. "Maybe I screwed up, and that's the only chance I get."

The crow caws again and Lucrece moves closer to Jared. She brushes his hair back from his face, and when she begins to remove the mask he flinches, tenses, but doesn't stop her from doing it.

"I'm not going to hurt you, Jared."

Underneath the mask Jared's face is streaked with gore and dirt and there are livid bruises around both his eyes. His nose has been bleeding and there's a crust of dried blood caked around his nostrils.

"I'm going to clean you up a little, that's all." Lucrece looks past Jared to the crow. She can still hear its thoughts. She follows its instructions exactly, moving slowly, and Jared lets her. The cutting on her back tingles, the scars in the shape of a crow, as they did when they were fresh and just beginning to heal.

"We're going to help you, both of us. And you'll find the son of a bitch who killed Benny."

"One way or another," Jared whispers.

"One way or another," Lucrece replies, and drops the ruined mask to the bedroom floor.

eight

THE BAD SCENE IN AUDUBON PARK WAS THE PERFECTLY
shitty start to a perfectly shitty day. It's past three in the afternoon now and the hangover has found Frank again, even though
he's already slipped into the bathroom twice for hits off the bottle of Jack Daniel's he always keeps tucked safe inside his locker.
Otherwise he's just been sitting at his desk since he and Wallace
got back from Metairie, pretending to make some sort of progress with the day's paperwork, the report on the murder in
Audubon Park and stuff he should have finished days ago. His
head feels like an overripe melon, ready to burst from its own
weight.

"So you really gonna skip out on the party at the chamber
of horrors this evening?" Wallace asks. Frank opens one eye,
glares past his typewriter and the clutter of unfinished reports
and carbon paper. By comparison, Wallace's desk is an exercise
in obsessive neatness, more like some spinster librarian's desk
than a cop's. Just the sight of those pathologically neat stacks
and the freshly sharpened pencils in a souvenir Saints mug
makes Frank want to punch his partner in the face.

"I think you and Tierney can probably handle the fucking
autopsy without me," he says. Wallace shrugs.

"Shit, I don't even know what's left to autopsy, Frank. I
mean, how's she gonna cut that mess up any more?"

167

Frank shakes three cherry Maalox tablets from a plastic bottle, four Bayer extra-strength from another, and pops all seven at once, chews them dry.

"That's disgusting, Frank," Wallace says, and starts typing again. Every time a key strikes paper Frank thinks that's the final straw and his head's going to pop.

"Jesus, Wally. Can't that wait?"

"I ain't gettin' behind with all this shit just 'cause you have a hangover, Frank."

"You're a damned considerate fuck, Wally," Frank says around the powdery mouthful of aspirin and antacid. He closes his eyes again and swallows the mess.

"Anyway," Wallace says, "if the evac orders come through, nobody'll be doing anything but wadin' outta here."

That morning the National Hurricane Center had posted a hurricane warning for most of southeastern Louisiana, from the coast as far inland as Baton Rouge. Michael was due to make landfall sometime between midnight and one A.M., unless they got lucky and the storm decided to kick the shit out of east Texas instead.

"One can always hope," Frank mutters. His mouth feels like he's just eaten a handful of bitter cherry-flavored chalk. He decides it's been long enough since the last drink for him to deserve another.

"I'm gonna go puke," he says, standing up, and Wallace just nods and keeps pecking away on his old Royal manual.

"Thanks for caring."

"Sure thing, Franklin," Wallace says and hits the return lever. The Royal's carriage pings and slams violently to the left.

"One day that piece of shit's gonna take off all your fingers, Wally," he says, and staggers toward the toilet.

The cloying smells of stale piss and bright green deodorant cakes burn Frank's sinuses. For a few precarious moments he thinks maybe he really will puke. He leans against the sink and stares at the face in the mirror. Frank hasn't shaved since the day before, and his skin is the color of raw oysters. There are little beads of sweat on his forehead and upper lip, bags under his eyes that could pass for bruises.

"You're not lookin' so great, Frankie," he says, and turns the hot-water knob. The faucet whistles and then makes an ugly coughing noise before it starts spitting icy, rust-stained water. Frank dips his hands into the sink, splashes his face with the stuff. It smells like mud but it feels good. When he looks back up at the mirror, though, he can't say that he looks any better—just wetter.

"You're a fucking slob," he tells himself. "*That's* what you are."

Frank takes the half-pint of bourbon from the inside pocket of his blazer and unscrews the cap. "Cheers," he says, offering a mercy toast to the sick-looking guy in the mirror. That's when he sees the bird perched on top of one of the stalls, watching him. A huge black crow like something from an old Hammer horror film. Frank almost drops the bottle.

"I need to talk to you, Frank Gray." For just a second Frank thinks the bird said that, the long second that it takes him to turn around and see the man in the black latex coat sitting beneath the room's single small window.

The man's wearing a leather hood, open zippers where the eyes and mouth should be, a slit for the nose. Frank thinks he saw something like it in a bondage magazine once.

"Who the fuck are you?" Frank reaches for his gun, stops halfway when the man pulls the shotgun out from under his coat and pumps it once.

"Please," the man says. "I've had enough of that shit today. All I want to do is talk to you. I swear."

"Jesus," Frank whispers, glancing at the door, at least five yards away. There's no way he could make it without getting his head blown off. "Someone else could walk through that door at any second. What are you gonna do then?"

"Deal with it when it happens," the man replies.

"I just don't want to get shot because somebody has to take a dump, you know?"

"Then we better get this over with quickly, Detective."

"Jesus," Frank says again. "Would you believe this is the second time in the past twenty-four hours someone's pulled a gun on me in the john?"

"You're investigating the murder in Audubon Park this morning, aren't you?" The man gets up slowly, keeping the barrel of the gun pointed at Frank's chest. The crow caws loudly and flaps its wings.

"I guess the bird's yours, huh?" Frank asks, sparing another glance at the crow.

"Something like that. Now answer the question."

"Yeah, me and my partner got that one. Sure. Now will you please point that fucking cannon somewhere else?"

The gun doesn't move an inch, and Frank tries to concentrate on being a cop, not just some scared asshole with a shotgun aimed at him. He notes the man isn't wearing a shirt under the jacket. No shoes either. He's wearing ragged black pants that might have been nice once. There's a pool of water at his feet, dripping off his body.

"You think it's the Bourbon Street Ripper, don't you?" the man says, but Frank's looking at the little window. Too small and too far off the ground for someone to climb through. And besides, it's locked from the inside. The rain beats on the dirty, fly-blown glass.

"What do you think?" Frank asks the man.

"I think you're stalling."

"No, I'm just trying to figure out how the fuck you got in here without someone seeing you. You and that bird aren't really what I'd call inconspicuous."

"It's a long story, and believe me, you wouldn't buy it if I did tell you. Now answer the question, Detective. Do you think the body in the park this morning was a victim of the Ripper or not?"

Frank nods slowly. "Maybe. I'm waiting to see what the autopsy turns up."

"So you think the Ripper's still out there? That Jared Poe wasn't the killer after all?" Frank catches a glint of anger in the man's voice now, like sunlight off the blade of a knife.

"That's not exactly what I said."

"But is it what you *think?*" the man growls, and the crow caws again.

Frank sighs and looks at the bottle of Jack Daniel's in his shaking left hand.

"You mind if I have a drink of this first?" he asks, and the man says no, so Frank takes a drink. Courage in a bottle. Right now that's precisely what he needs, because he's pretty goddamn sure there's no way this freak's just going to let him walk away no matter how many questions he answers.

Frank sets the bottle on the edge of the sink and wipes his mouth with the back of one hand.

"We thought it was just a copycat," he says. "It still might be a copycat. I didn't work the Poe case or any of the Ripper murders. So I'm a little new to this shit."

And then he notices the drops of blood that have started falling from underneath the man's long coat, a crimson trickle mixing with the rainwater on the filthy tile floor.

"You're bleeding." Frank points at the drops. "Why don't you just tell me who the hell you are and maybe I can help you."

"We're both looking for the same killer, Frank Gray," the man in the leather hood says. "And I don't really give a shit which of us finds him first. But I want you to know this—Jared Poe didn't kill *anyone*. Not Benjamin DuBois or anybody else."

"Is that a fact?" Frank replies, looking toward the door again, trying to think of some way to buy a little more time. "You need a doctor," he says.

"No, Detective. I need a goddamn undertaker."

The door to the rest room opens and the crow cries out, leaps into the air, and seems somehow to fill the whole room with the sound of its wings. Frank ducks for cover, dives for one of the stalls, reaching back for his pistol as he moves. The stall door slams wide open and he bangs his knee against the porcelain edge of the toilet bowl. He crouches, waiting for the freak in the mask to pull the trigger, waiting for the killing thunder of the shotgun.

"What the fuck are you doing in here, Frank?" Wallace asks, peering cautiously into the stall. "Who were you talking to?"

Frank's heart sounds like a kettledrum in his ears and every cell in his body is drowning in adrenaline. He feels more sober than he has in weeks. He shakes his head and returns his gun to his shoulder holster.

"If you didn't see him I think I'd better just keep my mouth shut, Wally," he says.

"You better not be gettin' the fuckin' DTs on me, Franklin. We got entirely too much crazy shit goin' down already without you seein' ghosts in the little boys' room." Wallace reaches down to help Frank up from the floor. "The orders just came in to evacuate the whole goddamn parish. *Everyone*."

"Wonderful," Frank mutters. There's something greasy on his hands from the floor and he pulls a wad of toilet paper from the roll to wipe them.

"That ain't all. And you ain't gonna even believe this other shit. They just found the DA over on St. Ann, sittin' in his car with his head blown off. Somebody used both barrels on him."

Frank has to sit down fast or he knows that he's going to fall. So he just sits on the toilet, still holding the wadded paper, and stares up at his partner.

The shotgun, he thinks, and then, like tic-tac-toe: *Vince Norris and then Jim Unger. And now John Harrod* . . .

We're both looking for the same killer, the man in the black hood said, the man with a crow. The man who must have walked out through the fucking wall.

"It's gonna be a long night, Franklin," Wallace says. "You might want to get some coffee in you while there's time. I just made a fresh pot."

"Yeah," Frank says. He can still hear the sound of the crow's wings, the velvet flutter loud as the storm. "That sounds like a good idea, Wally."

Jared stands on the roof and stares toward the river, toward the place where the river hides behind cold and colorless sheets of rain. His body parts the hurricane like the bow of a ship; there's something inside him that's even bigger, wilder than the whirling demon of water and wind. He holds the crow close to his body, sheltering it from the gales.

"Nobody got killed," he says. Lucrece is there somewhere, approving, but he doesn't need an answer. There's nothing left to do now but wait and hope the detective eventually leads him to the man who killed Benny.

The wind screams. Jared strokes the bird's smooth feathers with his gauze-swaddled hands.

Frank is filling a Styrofoam cup from Wallace's scalding pot of coffee when the telephone on his desk rings. He lets it ring two more times, and a fourth, taking a tentative sip of the bitter brew, before he picks up the receiver.

"Yeah," he says. For a second there is nothing but silence from the other end.

"Hello?"

"Gray?" a voice asks. "Detective *Frank* Gray?" The voice is male—Frank's pretty sure of that—but high, soft, almost androgynous. He wonders if it's being electronically disguised. Frank sets the cup down on the edge of his desk. The coffee tastes almost as bad as he expected.

"Yeah," he says. "You got him. What can I do for you?"

Frank hears something dry, like paper being slowly crumbled between callused palms. The caller inhales loudly, draws a sharp, uneven breath.

"The homosexual police officer who was at the fountain this morning?"

The man drawls the word—"homo-*sex*-shul"—and Frank feels the sweat popping out all over his body, the cold, creeping sensation like icy spider feet up his spine.

"What do you *want*, buddy?"

"To talk." The dry crackling sound comes through the receiver again.

"Yeah, well, I'm real short of conversation right now, so unless you fuckin' get to the point in the next five seconds I'm hanging up."

"You wouldn't want to do that," the man says.

"Why is that, buddy?" Frank asks. The sweat is starting to make him cold.

Another pause, and then, "'On the morrow *he* will leave me as my Hopes have flown before,'" the man says softly.

"Jesus," Frank whispers. "Who the fuck are you?"

There's the dry sound again, and the voice continues.

"'Startled at the stillness broken by reply so aptly spoken, *Doubtless*, said I, *"What it utters is its only stock and store . . ."*'"

"Look, freako. Tell me who you are or I'm hanging up right this fucking *minute*."

"No," the man says, and Frank can hear him smiling. "No, you won't. Because I'm the man, aren't I, Frank Gray? Not poor Jared Poe. Me. *I'm the man*."

"You're the fucker in the mask, aren't you?"

"I don't wear masks. Only They need masks. I have nothing left to conceal."

"I'm hanging up now," Frank says.

"I don't think so. I'd listen if I were you. Unless you want the photographs to go to the media."

"Excuse me?" Frank sits down in his chair. There's no sign of Wallace, who was going down the hall for an update on the storm.

"Don't make me get sordid, Detective. I don't like to have to talk like that. To *say* those things aloud. But there are pictures. There have been plenty of opportunities . . ."

"Listen, fucker—"

"My name is Lethe," the man says. "Joseph Lethe. The body you found this morning, that was my work, Frank Gray."

Frank holds the phone away from his face as if he's just discovered it's crawling with some contagion or filth, holds it a foot from his face and stares across the disorderly assembly of desks and typewriters. This phone isn't wired, even if there were time for a trace.

There have been plenty of opportunities, the man said.

"Jesus H. fucking," Frank whispers, and hesitantly puts the phone to his ear again. "What do you want?"

"Good boy," the man says. "You want to know the truth, don't you, Frank?"

"You're saying you put the body in the fountain?"

"Oh, I'm saying a lot more than that, Detective. But not yet. Not over the phone."

And then the man named Joseph Lethe gives Frank an address and a time, and Frank scribbles it quickly on an old deli napkin.

"I don't have to tell you to come alone, Frank. Or not to talk to anyone else about our little conversation."

"Yeah," Frank says. "There's a goddamn hurricane coming, you know?"

"It doesn't matter. I can't wait any longer," the man says. "But cheer up. You're going to be a hero. How many faggot cops get to be heroes? You should be happy."

"Why?" Frank asks. A fat drop of sweat falls from his forehead to the top of the desk.

"Because I'm tired. That's all. It's been a long time and I'm tired. I want to stop now. They know who I am anyway, don't They? So what's the point in going on?"

"But why me?"

"Because you're such a good boy, Frank. Because . . ." The voice trails off, is quiet for the time it takes Frank's heart to beat eight times and skip once.

"Mr. Lethe? Are you still there?"

"There was lightning here. Did you hear it?" The man sounds different now. The glee and smug self-assurance in his voice has been replaced by a distance, a sad uncertainty. "When I was a child, I was struck by lightning," he says. "I was struck . . ."

"I don't understand. Is that important?" Frank asks him. He sees Wallace coming back through the doorway from the hall, looking straight at Frank and shaking his head.

"Isn't it?" Joseph Lethe asks back, asks as though he really needs the answer. Then the line goes dead and Frank hangs up the telephone.

"You don't even want to know," Wallace says, sitting down at his own desk across from Frank. "If those eggheads at the weather bureau are right, we're gonna be lookin' for a new job soon, 'cause there might not even *be* a New Orleans when Michael gets done with us."

"Yeah, look," Frank says, standing up, not sure his legs will hold him, but he's standing up anyway. "That was my sister on the phone, Wally. There's a family emergency and I have to go. I'll meet you back here later."

Frank takes his raincoat off the coat rack near the radiator, where it's been drying since they got back from Metairie.

"You never told me you had a sister, Frank."

"We're not really very close," Frank replies, already halfway to the door.

"You don't tell me shit, Franklin. You don't tell me anything unless I ask . . ."

But then Frank's in the hallway and there are other voices, people getting ready for the storm, and he can't hear Wallace anymore. On his way to the car he remembers why the name Joseph Lethe sounded familiar. Something he had to read for high school, a book on Greek mythology, and it named the five rivers that divide the underworld from the world of the living. One of them was the River Lethe, the river of forgetfulness.

Joseph Lethe pulls off the tissue paper cover he put over the receiver to protect him from germs and nanites. He hangs up the pay phone, wads the paper, and lets it fall toward the wet asphalt of the parking lot. The wind grabs it and whisks it off before it can hit the ground. He watches it flying away, sailing high over the roofs of the few cars parked outside the K&B, into the low, uneasy sky.

"I was struck," he says again, wondering how long until there will be more lightning. "I was struck."

And it's true. When he was a boy, barely eight years old and living with his family in Houma. *Don't stand under a tree when it storms*, his grandfather had said. His grandfather had told him that lots of times. But once there had been a thunderstorm and he forgot and hid beneath an old oak for shelter. The white fire came down and split the tree in two, cleaved it open and flowed through the earth into him. He can still remember that instant when he was full of fire. He came to some time later, lying in the rain, and someone had been standing over him, asking him his name over and over. *Do you know your name, boy? Can you tell me your name?*

But the lightning had left something inside him, something small and hard inside his head, and he *couldn't* remember his name. He knew other things, though. New things the lightning had wanted him to know. But not his name. That was part of the cost, his name. And he could never wear a watch after that, and compass needles acted funny when he was around. He didn't tell his parents, made the man asking his name promise not to tell, because he was okay and there was no need to tell them, was there? But they knew he was different after that day. They looked at him differently and spoke to him differently.

An old black woman—Julianna, who sold his mother tomatoes—said he wasn't right after that. She told his mother there was something bad inside him and that she knew a voodoo man in the bayou who could make him right again. That was the last time his mother bought Julianna's big red tomatoes or green frying tomatoes. But his mother looked at him differently, like she knew that everything the old woman had said was true.

The faggot cop will come, he thinks. *Not because he really cares who I am, but because he's afraid of what I know and what I might do with that knowledge. The same reason They're all afraid of me. Because I'm the man . . .*

A red Volkswagen sputters noisily past the pay phone, spraying muddy water from the flooded parking lot all over Joseph Lethe's shoes. He watches it go, stands there expressionless, water soaking right through his socks to his feet. Then he wipes his hands on his raincoat, and, safe in his knowledge and resolve, safe from the black wings spread above the drowning city, he crosses Napoleon Avenue to his car.

Lucrece is sitting on the couch in the living room paging through one of Benny's old *Sandman* comic books. There's nothing else she can do and so she's been sitting here for almost an hour pretending to read her dead brother's comics. But she's having trouble making any sense of the story, something about the King of Dreams and his crazy little sister looking for their lost brother. And there's a raven named Matthew. But she's having trouble following the plot from one issue to the next, her head too full of Jared, too full of waiting.

The radio was on earlier but they weren't playing any music, just going on and on about the storm, so she finally turned it off. There's nothing she really needs to know about the hurricane that she can't hear through the plaster-and-stucco walls of the apartment. It's not as if she can run from it, can join the exodus that's already begun from the Quarter. So she'd rather not know the latest facts and figures, thank you very much, wind speed and expected landfall, tidal surge. She puts on a CD instead, Black Tape for a Blue Girl's *Remnants of a Deeper Purity*. The strings and keyboards haven't helped her relax as she hoped they might, but they are a better backdrop for the sound of the storm than the anxious voices on the radio. The music makes her drowsy and she thinks about trying to sleep. It's been almost two days now since she's slept or eaten or bathed.

But Jared's out there somewhere, so there's no way she can sleep. She has to stop herself from trying to send her mind out to find him every five minutes. Her nose has been bleeding off and on, and her head still hurts from the last time.

There's a hard knock at the door. Lucrece jumps, almost cries out. But it's probably just the cops, she thinks, or the Red Cross or someone like that, someone to tell her she has to leave, and she isn't sure how she's going to convince them that she can't. That she has to stay, has to be here for Jared, never mind the goddamn storm.

She lays the comic book on the coffee table and gets up off the couch, smooths the wrinkles from her black dress without thinking. Whoever's out there knocks again, impatient, and Lucrece shouts at the door, "Just a minute."

While I nodded, nearly napping, suddenly there came a tapping . . .

"Jesus, girl. Give that tired old shit a rest, okay?" she mutters to herself, and crosses the room to the door.

. . .

It takes Frank almost half an hour to reach the address on Tchoupitoulas Street that Joseph Lethe gave him. The streets are flooding and already there are fatigue-green National Guard trucks and soldiers at roadblocks. His badge gets him through, but the wind buffets his car like a toy. Driving against the storm is like running in a nightmare, racing something huge and terrible that's right behind you and gaining, and your feet weigh at *least* three hundred pounds each. Only in this dream there are fallen trees and downed power lines, stalled cars and accidents, that have to be circumnavigated.

So instead of the fifteen minutes the man on the phone gave him, it takes Frank half an hour. And then there's nothing at the address but a vacant, weedy lot with one withered chinaberry tree separating it from the street. Frank parks against the curb and sits staring out at the tree, cursing the fucking storm and his fucking luck. Then there's a brilliant flash of lightning and he sees something silvery nailed to the trunk of the tree, flapping furiously in the wind.

I was struck . . .

Frank gets out of the car. The storm drags at him, claws at his clothes and hair with invisible, windy fingers, as if it would rather he not see whatever's stuck to the tree. But it's only a deflated Mylar balloon; it was once shaped like a heart and he can still read FOREVER in big red letters. The balloon has been ripped open, flattened, and there's a plastic sandwich bag stapled to it.

Frank tears the bag free. The Mylar comes off too and is swallowed instantly by the storm. The hurricane tugs hungrily at the plastic bag in his hand as he heads back to the car, already drenched straight through his raincoat.

Inside his car the howling wind is muffled. *Muzzled*, Frank thinks, locking the door.

Inside the sandwich bag there's a folded page torn from a yellow legal pad. Frank removes it, unfolds it, smooths the page flat against the car seat. The paper is wet but the writing on it is in pencil, so that doesn't really matter. And it's only another address and another time, someplace on Millaudon Street on the other side of Audubon Park.

"Shit," he hisses and slaps his hand loudly against the sun-cracked dashboard. He remembers that day years ago in the Iberville projects when Linda Getty nearly bled to death while he shouted "Ten-thirteen!" repeatedly into the handset of his patrol car's radio. He remembers no one answering him, all because Linda was a dyke and they wanted her off the force. What if all of it, the phone call and that weirdo fucker in the crapper, *all* of it, is just a goddamn practical joke? Or worse. What if they *know*?

A branch comes off the chinaberry tree and crashes down onto the windshield, leaving a crack three or four inches long in the glass before the wind snatches it away again. Frank turns the key in the ignition, starts the car again, and pulls quickly away from the vacant lot before the storm brings the whole damn tree down on top of him.

You're gettin' paranoid, Frank.

"Maybe so," he says, and makes a wide U-turn on Tchoupitoulas, heading west toward the park. "And maybe not." His voice *sounds* brave, sounds certain, as confident as all the television cops of his childhood. But the fear filling up his belly and the prickling sensation on the back of his neck say otherwise. And a small but strident voice deep inside is telling him to get the hell out while the getting's good, that there's a fucking *hurricane* coming, for Christ's sake, and it's not like anyone would really blame him if he just let this one go for now.

Unless you want the photographs to go to the papers, the voice on the phone said. Frank doesn't think there *are* any pictures, but he can't be *sure*. He knows that he has no choice after all, that his apprehension is useless because it is irrelevant. That he's going to do whatever Joseph Lethe tells him because he has made secrets of his life, secrets that can maim, and now they're being held against his throat. He squints through the windshield as the useless wipers flail, and follows the unsteady beams of the headlights.

"Please tell me what you want," Lucrece whispers, hating that she sounds so scared. The hand in the latex glove slaps her again, slaps her so hard her mouth is full of blood. She lets it run down her chin rather than swallow it. The taste of her own blood has always made her sick.

"*I* ask *you* the questions," the man says. "That's the *rule*." The man with eyes the color of stone is kneeling over her, checking the knots he's made with the white nylon rope, the knots that bind her wrists and ankles tight. He has a pistol pressed hard against the soft spot just below her breastbone.

"I know who you are," she says. He pauses and looks back at her from beneath the greasy, dangling hair that keeps falling across his face. He brushes his bangs out of the way again, exposing his thin, hatchet-sharp face. He looks excited and expectant, and his hands are shaking.

"You're the sick son of a bitch who killed my brother," Lucrece says.

"I'm so much more than that," the man replies, and a nervous, shy smile creeps slowly across his face. "But you already know that *too*, don't you? I'm sure They've told you everything about me."

"Jared died because of you," she whispers, flinching, expecting the hand again. But the man only smiles a little wider and hides his mouth with the latex-covered fingers of his free hand, as if he's suddenly realized that he's smiling and he doesn't want her to see, doesn't want her to know his excitement or the pleasure he's taking in this scene.

He moves his hand, slowly, and he isn't smiling anymore.

"Did They also tell you that it wasn't supposed to be your brother? Did They tell you it was *supposed* to be you and I sort of fucked things up?"

Lucrece shuts her eyes, not wanting to believe what he's saying, but she knows that he's telling her the truth. So many times she's wished that it could have been her instead of Benny, knows that if it had been her then at least Benny still would have had Jared. And now this crazy man is telling her that was his intention all along.

"But that's what we get second chances for, right, *Lucas?*" he asks her, and the way he says that name it's almost as good as another slap, almost as painful.

"You're already dead," she says. The words feel good coming out of her mouth, crossing her torn and swelling lips. "You have no idea what you've started or where it will end."

The man bends over her. She doesn't open her eyes but she can feel him just inches from her face, can smell his breath like mouthwash and bad teeth.

"Is that what They told you, Lucas DuBois? Did They tell you I was just some psycho serial killer with a hard-on for trans-sexuals and little boys in women's underwear?"

When she doesn't answer or even open her eyes, he slaps her again, hits her so hard that her ears ring.

"Answer me, you dickless bastard!"

"A dead man," she says, and he hits her.

"No, no, *no!*" He rages above her like the storm, as though all the wild fury of the hurricane has been distilled and poured into this skinny, insane man. She ignores the pain in her head and reaches into him, tries to reach into him the way she reached out to Jared and the crow.

When her mind brushes against his, she screams. There's something coiled deep inside his skull, a serpent made of living fire, a writhing bolt of pure white heat that strikes out at her and sears its way back across her thoughts. Lucrece's body goes taut as a board, seizing, and she bites a ragged slash across her tongue.

"I'm the place where it *all* stops, Lucas! I'm the foil that stands for order against Their chaos. Against *your* chaos, Lucas DuBois."

But now his words flow around and away from her, repelled by the charge from the white-hot crucible of his brain. The memory of a blazing power that can split trees like cordwood and incinerate bone, something more than a memory. Something hotter than a star that snakes its way inside her, between each and every cell in her body, that squeezes itself between her

182

molecules, between the subatomic particles of her, until there's no telling what is Lucrece and what is the thing pouring out of the man's mind.

Her eyelids flutter open. He towers above her, fire and steam pouring from every orifice in his skull. It drips like molten slag from his lips, flows like lava from his ears, and falls sizzling to her skin. There's no pulling back, no breaking her link with this scalding mind. Her back arches and she can hear her vertebrae grinding against one another.

"I am the river," he says, and those fiery eyes are so terribly close now. But the last thought before Lucrece loses consciousness is not of this monster, this man infected by electricity and madness. Her last thought is of Jared, and she makes a tiny hole, a pinprick, in the fire and forces the thought away from herself, boosting it with the borrowed force of the lunatic's rage. Then there is nothing but the sound of static and merciful darkness.

Joseph Lethe backs quickly away from the thing that calls itself Lucrece DuBois, the thing that They've constructed so skillfully of male flesh to mimic a woman's. He's breathless and frightened; there's no denying that he felt it reach inside him, felt its unclean mind pressed squirming against his own before it screamed and began to buck about on the floor and foam at the mouth. It had been reading his very thoughts, his soul.

But there was something there it hadn't expected, something that shielded and protected him from its prying, alien attention. Something that struck back and left it helpless, unconscious, maybe even dead. He grips the stainless-steel butt of the gun tighter and jabs the snubby barrel between the thing's artificial breasts.

"You bit off more than you could chew, didn't you?" he says, gasping out the words. "You're not even *half* as fucking smart as you think you are."

It's gone now, that part of it that laid his mind open like a gray Gulf oyster, but he can still *feel* it. Like some sticky, sugary residue left to ferment inside his head, and he itches in places he knows he can never reach to scratch. Joseph Lethe feels something cold and undeniable that he hasn't felt in a long time, something he is only supposed to inflict, not suffer himself. He feels violated.

So he sheds the name Joseph Lethe and becomes Jordan again, hoping the change will leave him cleaner, but it doesn't. Cautiously Jordan touches the transsexual's throat, presses two reluctant fingers against its throat. There's a pulse, a very weak, erratic pulse, but it's still alive.

"What were you trying to do to me, fucker? You *touched* me," and his finger tightens the slightest bit on the trigger of the pistol. "You've contaminated me." He wants to empty the clip into its poisonous black heart. Maybe then he would feel even. Revenge isn't much, but he knows that he'll never be free of whatever wriggling, inhuman essence it has planted inside him, so maybe revenge will have to do.

"I am the river," he whispers, like a prayer, and the barrel of the gun moves slowly from the space between its breasts to a spot just beneath its chin. "I am the conduit for all that is pure, and you have polluted me."

But he can't kill it, not yet, not here. There's still too much it has to tell him about the nightmares and the black-winged creature chasing him across the sky. And it still has an important role to play in the trap he's set for the faggot police detective. It *will* die, but it has to die later, slowly, somewhere else. For the moment something else will have to do.

Something more subtle, he thinks. "Something more poetic," he says aloud.

Jordan uses the barrel of the gun to push aside its skirt. His gloved hands expose its clever, deceiving sex. His penis stirs awake inside his pants and he bites down on the tip of his tongue. He's never done this, not even once. He's never allowed himself to be fooled by Their masquerade and so there's never been any danger of that sort of contact, that sort of weakness. He's known from the very beginning that it was part of Their game, like the spiny jaws of a Venus flytrap spread wide, waiting for the flies.

But this is different, Jordan tells himself. It has nothing to do with desire, nothing to do with anything as base as lust. This will be a message to Them that he will not be violated again, that to violate him is to invite the rape of Their own. It's ingenious, really. And he will take proper precautions to protect himself from anything inside it that might be meant for him, from any viruses or nanites that might have been installed during the final stages of its reassignment.

"I am the river," he says again, and his trigger finger begins to relax.

Jordan unzips his pants and checks the clock on the mantle to be sure that there's time, that he won't miss the detective, and then he lays the gun on the floor of Jared Poe's apartment.

Jared and the crow are watching Frank Gray from the front porch of an abandoned house on Millaudon Street. Across the street from them the detective curses and rips a second patch of Mylar from the bole of a pecan tree. Then he struggles against the storm and climbs back inside his car.

"The killer's playing with him, isn't he?" Jared asks, and the crow answers him softly. Only her head is poking out of the front of Benny's frock coat.

"Keeping him busy. Baiting him . . ."

And then Jared hears Lucrece, hears her so loud and strong that the force of her knocks him backward a few steps until he collides with the boarded-up front door of the old house. A voice without sound that rushes straight through him; not even words, just a crippling flash of Lucrece, Lucrece hurting and afraid for him, *warning* him. Then she's gone again. Jared slumps, trembling, against the weathered boards at his back, shaken and sweating beneath the leather hood she placed over his bullet-shattered skull.

"Lucrece," he whispers. Then the crow caws loudly, shifts impatiently inside the rubber coat. Jared looks up and sees that Frank Gray's car is pulling away, heading north up Millaudon Street.

"If I lose him now, I might not get another chance," Jared

says. The crow makes a sound that seems like confirmation. Already the detective's car is just a dim pair of taillights in rain.

"Jesus, Lucrece, be careful," he says. "And thanks." He steps off the porch into the waiting storm.

The second note has led Frank to a convenience store on a run-down stretch of Magazine Street. All the windows have been covered with fresh yellow-brown sheets of plywood and the place appears to be deserted, the owners and employees having long since fled the hurricane.

Smarter motherfuckers than me, he thinks, and spies a third patch of Mylar nailed to the plywood. He can see that there's a small brown paper bag stuck up there as well. The wind knocks him off his feet twice on his way to and back from the front of the store, sends him sprawling into the flooded street. There's almost a foot of frothy slate gray water flowing down Magazine Street now, and by the time he gets back into the car he's so wet he might as well have swum as tried to walk.

He sits behind the wheel holding another swatch of Mylar from another ruined balloon. This one says CONGRATS! in eager cursive. Frank tosses it into the backseat and takes a deep breath before he opens the paper bag.

This is the last one, he swears to himself. *Unless there's something really goddamn convincing in here, this is the last stop on this wild-goose chase.*

Inside there's another plastic bag, and this one doesn't have just a note. There's an index finger as well, severed cleanly at the knuckle, a smooth bit of white bone showing on one end and a nail painted black at the other.

"Shit on me," Frank groans as he opens the bag and fishes out the carefully folded note. There's dried and not-so-dried blood on the yellow legal paper, crimson still tacky to the touch, and it comes off on his hands as he unfolds the page. There's the next address in the same handwriting. "Just in case you're doubting me," it says at the top.

Frank refolds the letter and drops it back into the bag with the finger, puts them both back into the paper bag and shoves the bag under his seat.

Out of sight, out of mind.

"Yeah, right," he mumbles, shifting out of park into reverse and backing away from the convenience store. "Whoever said that wasn't sitting on top of a goddamn severed human finger."

Frank puts the car in drive and rolls back along the makeshift tributary of the Mississippi that Magazine Street has become.

Lucrece wakes up very slowly, drifts by almost imperceptible degrees from a dream about Aaron Marsh and the Eye of Horus, a dream about the stuffed dodo in its glass case. Only in the dream the dodo bird was the one from *Alice in Wonderland*, the one from John Tenniel's drawings, with hands and a walking stick. And it had been not inside the case but standing next to her and Aaron, watching the rain fall through the shop's display windows.

"The race is over," Aaron said, and Lucrece said, "As wet as ever. It doesn't seem to dry me at all."

And the dodo said very solemnly as it tapped its cane against the floor, "*Everybody* has won, and *all* must have prizes."

Lucrece is just about to ask the dodo if the thimble from the pocket of her dress will do, if it's a decent enough prize, when she smells ammonia and begins to cough herself awake.

She opens her eyes and there's a bright light somewhere close, so close that she can feel the warmth of its scalding bulb. The heat makes her remember what it was like to touch the man's mind, the man who forced his way inside the apartment, the man who killed Benny. She forgets the dream and remembers that sizzling flood of power from his mind, remembers his hands on her, the perfect *wrongness* of his soul. She coughs again, her throat dry and rough as sandpaper. Then a plastic straw is thrust between her lips.

"Drink," the man says. He's standing very close. The straw bumps insistently against her teeth, stabs at her gums. "Drink," he says again.

187

She sucks on the straw and her mouth fills with lukewarm water. She swallows and it helps a little, so she sucks another mouthful from the straw.

"That's enough," he says, and takes the straw away. It trails a string of thick saliva from her lips, down her chin.

Her wrists are still bound together, tied to something overhead, and she's hanging naked in the glare of the light. Both of her arms have gone completely numb from the weight of her body. She stretches her legs and the tips of her bare toes brush a hard, cold floor, like gritty concrete or sandstone.

"I was just saying it's a shame there's not time to do this properly," the man remarks. The light seems to move, plays across her body. "I was just saying that you're a prize."

The air smells like dust and distant rain, mildew and oily rags. The ammonia is still burning her sinuses. She can hear the storm outside, but now it sounds very far away.

"Where am I?" she asks him. Her voice sounds almost as bad as her throat feels.

"Where I need you to be, Lucas. At the nexus, at the heart of the snare."

"That isn't my name," she croaks, but he ignores her.

"I could learn things from you if there were more time. If I had time to do the whole procedure. But he'll be here soon and I've hardly even started."

It doesn't matter that she has no idea what he's talking about. Whatever it is, it means he's going to kill her. He's a predator and she is his chosen prey, stripped and hung up for the slaughter like a hog waiting for the blade across its throat. There's nothing else she needs to know.

"None of this is what you think," she says. "You don't have to do this again."

"Oh, it's *exactly* what I think," he says. She can almost see him standing in the shadows behind the light, a darker patch in the rough shape of a man. "It's much too late now for any more lies. I saw your back when I was . . . I saw your back. The scar."

"Nosy little fuck, aren't you?" Lucrece realizes that it's hard to get her breath, that she's slowly suffocating, as in a crucifixion. She might have been hanging here for hours.

188

"Tell me about the bird, Lucas. I *dream* about the black bird, and there's its mark on your back."

"You want to know about the black bird?" she replies, gasping for the air she needs to make the words, to remain conscious. "I can tell you about the black bird. Get me down from here and I'll tell you about the fucking black bird."

"I can't do that," he says sternly, reproachfully. "You know that, Lucas. I can't risk that. There's not time."

"Then I can't help you," she gasps. "Sorry. You'll just have to find out about the bird on your own." She sucks in another stinging breath and adds, "He's coming, very soon."

"I'm not afraid of you or any of Them," the man sneers, but she can tell that he is. That he's very much afraid. "You can't trick me into letting you go by trying to scare me."

She can taste his fear now. Because it is so fucking delicious, so sweet and ripe and maybe all she'll ever know of justice, Lucrece says simply, "The crow is *his* vengeance, motherfucker, and you're *her* victim."

She expects immediate retribution, swift punishment served in exchange for the truth he didn't really want to hear, a knife or a needle for her honesty. But the man just stands very still on the other side of the light. She can hear him breathing.

"Things fall from the sky," he says. "Shining, bleeding *things* fall from the sky and the fabric of humanity itself is altered. And They expect me to watch and do nothing? Did They really think that not a single man would stand against Them?"

"You're insane," Lucrece whispers, and knows that if he doesn't finish it soon, she'll begin to cry. There's simply too much pain and she's too scared of dying alone in this stinking dark place. And she doesn't want the son of a bitch who killed Benny to see her cry.

"Don't tell me about vengeance, Lucas DuBois. I am the whole world's vengeance against Their atrocities."

"No," she croaks, and swallows, shaking her head, wishing she had the strength to laugh, the strength to show him how ludicrous he is. "No. You're just a sad, crazy asshole who likes to kill people. And that's all you are. That's all you'll ever be."

And then there's the sound of metal against metal, the

sound of small sharp things, and Lucrece closes her eyes because she doesn't want to see.

By the time Michael's outer rain bands have crossed the ribbonlike barrier of the Chandeleur Islands the storm has become a monster even by the monstrous standards of hurricanes. Its swirling cyclone bulk blankets the coast from the mouth of the Pascagoula River all the way across the southeastern corner of Louisiana. Born somewhere off the west coast of Africa, it has grown from an embryonic disturbance, a disorganized fetus of showers and thunderstorms, and has traveled the trade winds almost six thousand miles to the Gulf of Mexico.

Now it is ready to spend its fury against the Mississippi delta. By late afternoon there are maximum sustained winds of more than 195 miles an hour, and Michael is upgraded to a category-five hurricane.

At its calm, unblinking eye Michael has lifted a mound of seawater a foot and a half high and almost fifty miles across, a storm surge pulled up by its violently low pressure and aimed at the already rain-glutted bayous, at cypress swamps and small towns barely above sea level to begin with. And at New Orleans, the red bull's-eye at the end of its long odyssey across the Atlantic.

At 4:35 P.M. a tiny shrimp boat named *Eloise*, caught deep inside the storm, radios for assistance from its location somewhere in Breton Sound near Fort St. Philip. The captain reports that his ship's barometer is reading 26.10 inches; three days later he and his two-man crew will be found floating in the Gulf, but his report will be cautiously noted by meteorologists as the lowest pressure ever recorded in the Western Hemisphere.

At 4:57 P.M. a reconnaissance plane tracking the storm, dumping its load of instrument-laden dropsonde canisters into the eye of the hurricane, nervously reports a gigantic shadow, "like a huge black bird," falling across the relatively calm waters of the fifty-mile-wide center of the storm. The pilot and crew will later dismiss the incident as a mistake, as nothing more than the shadow of their own plane or a trick of the clouds.

At 5:03 P.M. a weather satellite in geostationary orbit twenty-two thousand miles above the Gulf sends back color images of another shadow, an India-ink-black smudge that will eventually be described in an internal NHC report as "the crow anomaly." Less than thirty seconds later the satellite's computer vomits a frantic, senseless stream of data and shuts itself down.

Michael turns, dispassionate as cancer, unstoppable as fate, its silver-white back turned to heaven and its bruise-dark belly laid across the face of an angry, impotent world. And a terrible, raging night comes to the living and the dead of the city of New Orleans.

nine

THE SIXTH NOTE PROMISED FRANK THAT IT WOULD BE THE last. It has led him to this derelict hulk of a factory near the river, a towering edifice of stones laid before the turn of the century and abandoned now to rats and the homeless, to furry brown bats and the elements. He parks on a vast expanse of weed-fractured concrete, flooded now like everything else, a submerged forest of dandelions, thistles, and polk salad on the edge of the factory ruins.

Frank has to fight to get the door of the car open, wrestling against the zealous wind, and then he has to wrestle it closed again. For a moment the storm holds him at bay, pressed helplessly against the car, just another bit of debris at the mercy of the hurricane. He shades his eyes from the stinging rain and all the shit being hurled through the air and stares up at the corpse of industry sprawled out before him, its crumbling masonry and towering brick smokestacks silhouetted against the Erector-set framework of the Greater New Orleans Bridge and, farther on, the blue-black wall of the storm's turbulent heart. The sight of such a terrible majesty bearing down upon the city is almost enough to make him forget himself and whatever's waiting for him inside the old factory. Almost. A man could go mad, he thinks, staring into the faceless countenance of such a thing, forced to acknowledge such a power. Something sails through

193

the air and grazes his left cheek, slices a deep furrow and is gone, and the wind is lapping greedily at Frank's bleeding face.

He pulls himself along the rain-slick side of the car. Tiny wavelets crash against his pants legs. A sheet of corrugated tin whirls past overhead, a rusty guillotine spinning end over razor-sharp end, and Frank gets the message: *Stay out here a little longer and you're a dead man*. So he grits his teeth like a good cop and keeps going.

It's less than twenty yards to the closest door into the factory, but the storm knocks him down again and again, and once he gashes the palm of his right hand on a broken wine bottle hiding like shark teeth just beneath the water. Finally he reaches the building, solid brick and mortar to support him. A peeling metal door hangs crooked on its hinges, ready to be torn loose at any moment and sucked into the maelstrom. Frank manages to pull it open a crack and immediately the wind rips the handle from his hands, slams the door back against the wall. He crosses the threshold and the storm lets him go, confident that the shelter of the factory can last only so long.

Frank stops just inside, faced with a darkness so absolute that the premature twilight framed in the doorway behind him seems brilliant by comparison. He's still standing in several inches of cold water, but at least he's protected from the wind and driving rain, and the noise of the storm is muffled by the thick walls to a dull and constant roar.

He reaches into his dripping jacket and draws his Beretta 92-F from its shoulder holster. The gash in his hand hurts bad and is bleeding like a son of a bitch, but there's nothing to be done for it now. Of course it *had* to be his fucking right hand, no way he could have fallen on his left. He takes a Kel-light flashlight from one back pocket, not expecting it to work, expecting it to be full of water and the batteries drowned. But when he switches it on, a weak beam shines across the vast dark puddle of the floor. He aims it a little higher and there's a brick archway only a few feet to one side where the floor slants upward to drier ground.

"You better be here somewhere, motherfucker," he says. His voice sounds very small in the vast tomb of the building.

He steps through the arch. There is more light on the other side, velvet-soft shades of gray only a few degrees from actual black, but it's an improvement. There are tall rows of windows along the southern side of the building, the side facing the river and the oncoming storm, the last dregs of daylight filtering down to the floor through air thickened by its time inside the factory. Frank shines the Kel-light along the wall near the arch and sees a rickety-looking iron staircase bolted into the brick, leading up into the gloom, toward the second story of the building.

"Hey!" he shouts. There is a sudden, riotous flutter of wings from high above him; only pigeons or maybe swallows nesting in the rafters, but he can't help remembering the big black crow the guy in the mask had with him. A couple of charcoal feathers spiral lazily down, passing through the beam of his flashlight on their way to the concrete floor. When the birds are quiet again, Frank listens for any indication that he's not alone, that Joseph Lethe is waiting for him in the gloom.

"Listen, asshole! I'm tired of playing hide-and-go-seek with your dumb ass!"

But there's no response, no human response, only the incessant whistling drone of the storm outside and the subtler noises of the old factory.

"Jesus," he whispers. Keeping the flashlight aimed just in front of his feet and the Beretta's rubber grip squeezed tightly in his aching, bloody right hand, Frank Gray begins to climb the stairs.

There's a small landing at the top, a square platform of plate steel and cement that sags alarmingly to one side, and guardrails that have all but rusted away. As he steps onto it Frank realizes he is standing at least fifty or sixty feet above the factory floor. The tall windows waver on the opposite side of what seems like a bottomless void. Through the filthy, broken panes, he can see the roofs of lower buildings along the northern shore of the Mississippi and the swollen river itself like some impossibly giant cottonmouth moccasin, the rough white-capped water for scales. But he looks away; there's already enough shit to deal with without worrying about what's going to happen when the river comes across the levee.

There's a steel fire door set into the wall. When he pushes against it the door creaks loudly and swings open. What he sees through the doorway almost sends him screaming back down the precarious stairs: a floodlight clamped to a sawhorse, its glare revealing a mutilated body suspended by its wrists from a steel hook. The corpse's bloodless legs are spread out in a wide inverted V, each ankle bound with white nylon cord that has been tied securely through iron eyes in the floor. The body has been completely eviscerated, slit from the genitals all the way up to the chin, and the blood-drenched floor beneath it is scattered with discarded organs and entrails, bluish loops of intestine and darker, meaty lumps he can't identify. The abdominal cavity is empty, a hollowed-out shell of muscle and cartilage and bone. There are literally buckets of clotting blood on the floor, plastic mop pails filled almost to overflowing, and, behind the floodlight, a small table covered with surgical instruments and stray strips of skin and meat. Where the body isn't smeared with blood and gore, its skin is the powdery color of chalk dust. But at least he can't see the face. Its head has lolled back, away from him, and the dead eyes, if they've even been left in its skull, stare toward the ceiling somewhere high overhead. It's impossible for him to tell if the corpse is male or female.

Frank swallows hard and wipes his sweating forehead on the back of the hand holding his flashlight. He didn't puke at the mess in the fountain in Audubon Park and he sure as hell isn't going to puke now.

"Lethe?" he asks. When there's no reply, he says, "I know you're still here."

There's movement to his left, then something fast he only barely glimpses from the corner of one eye. Frank doesn't take time to check his target or aim. He's acting purely on fear and adrenaline as he squeezes off three rounds from the Beretta. The nine-millimeter shells hit nothing but solid brick and the gunshots leave his ears ringing.

"*Fuck*," he mutters, and there are footsteps coming up fast behind him and hard, cold metal pressed to his temple before he can turn around.

"It's over, Detective. I win." Frank recognizes the voice from the phone call. "Drop your gun and take one step backward."

"If I drop my gun I'm dead."

"You're already dead, Detective, just as soon I want you that way. Now drop your fucking gun *and* the flashlight and do exactly what I said. One step back."

Frank lets the Beretta slip from his bleeding hand and it clatters noisily to the floor, drops the Kel-light and its lens shatters. He takes one step backward. The pistol muzzle pressed to his skull moves with him.

"Now turn and look at it," the voice says.

"What is the fucking point of this?" Franks asks. "Do you just want to see me scared? Is that it? 'Cause if that's all you want, you already got it, okay?"

"I want to see you *dead*, faggot," the voice says, the purring, effeminate voice speaking directly into his ear now. "I want to see you dead and condemned for your crimes against your own masculinity. Turn and look at it, Frank Gray."

So Frank turns, slowly, to face the madman's butchery.

"This doesn't even make *sense*, Lethe," he says, trying not let the fear show in his voice. There might still be a chance to get out of this alive if he can stay calm, if he can stay cool.

"I'm Jordan now," the man says, and he steps around to stand in front of Frank but the barrel of his gun doesn't move an inch. There's nothing remarkable about him, a man younger than Frank expected and almost handsome in a gaunt, heroin-addled sort of way. Probably not the perfect match for an FBI serial-killer profile.

"But you are the same man I spoke with on the phone, the one who left the messages leading me here, right? The man who said he was tired and wanted this to stop?"

"Yes," the man says softly.

"So, what? Were you just lying to get me out here?"

"There's nothing here that you need to understand, Detective. Nothing at all. You are not an innocent."

And the man who has become Jordan pulls the trigger and for Frank Gray the world ends quickly in the cracking sound of thunder.

• • •

Jordan kneels beside the detective's still body and presses two gloved fingers to the throat, feeling for a pulse that he already knows isn't there. Then he examines the dark powder burns at the temple, lifts a loose flap of scalp and hair already matted with blood, and stares at the bullet hole a moment. He's never before killed anyone who didn't exhibit at least the behavioral symptoms of gender transgression.

And I still haven't, he thinks after a moment of quiet deliberation. *This man had sex with other men, and isn't that a violation of gender?*

Jordan nods, reassured. He places his gun in Frank Gray's right hand, folds the detective's palm around the butt of the pistol and carefully threads an index finger through the trigger guard. He uses the dead man's left hand to add a few additional fingerprints to the stainless steel barrel, and then he picks up the Beretta and steps away from the body. He glances from the gutted transsexual to the prostrate form of the cop like a sculptor admiring a finished piece. And it really isn't so different, he tells himself, the painstaking orchestration of matter into an arrangement that better suits his needs.

What the police will find here will suit his needs too, as perfectly as the body of Benjamin DuBois once did, as perfectly as the evidence he left in Jared Poe's apartment a year ago: a fingerprint lifted from a spoon with a strip of Scotch tape, a couple of pages of poetry. And this is so much more damning, so much more elaborate. He feels a staggering pride that he has actually managed to pull it off.

But it isn't truly finished, not yet. There's one small touch left to add for consistency's sake.

Jordan sits down in the space between the soles of the detective's shoes and the sticky, wet patch beneath the remains of the second DuBois twin and takes a black Sharpie marker from one shirt pocket. He's committed the whole poem to memory by now, all 108 lines of it, and that's something else to be proud of as he leans over the spot on the floor that he swept clean with a whiskbroom earlier in the day. He prints the lines as neatly as he can.

Stern Despair returned, instead of the sweet hope he dared abjure—That sad answer, "Nevermore!"

When he's finished, Jordan goes back to Frank Gray's body and places the pen in his left hand, folds those fingers tightly closed around it.

Two birds with one stone, he thinks, and the thought makes him smile. It's good to be such a clever man. They'll all lose his trail now. Even if the cops believe that Jared Poe was guilty, he knows that they've begun looking for a second killer to explain the murders fitting the Ripper MO since Poe's one-way trip up to Angola. And a dead faggot cop is the perfect fall guy. Shortly before he reached the apartment on Ursulines, Jordan dropped a letter to the *Times-Picayune* into a mailbox, Frank Gray's confession to sodomy and the killings.

And the assassin bird sent into his dreams and visions by the others—it will lose him as well now that its link to this world has been severed. He saw the scar clearly enough on the transsexual's bare back. Without a living conduit the creature will lose his scent and be forced to return to Them empty-handed. But, just to be safe, he'll move on. There's a road map of the Southeast in his glove compartment, and he's circled Memphis and Dallas, Atlanta and Birmingham. All his calculations aren't complete, but at least one of these cities will be right for his work. By the time They realize what's happened, just how badly They've underestimated again, he'll be miles and miles away, hidden by the walls of a different city and the syllables of a different name.

Jordan looks back at the gutted corpse again and remembers what he told the thing before he killed it. It truly was a pity that he did not have more time. There was so much it might have revealed to him if only there had been the time to employ more subtle techniques. But then he thinks of those other cities again, those other cities on other rivers. He lets his eyes wander higher, up above the body and the white-hot nimbus of the floodlight. High above the abattoir this room has become, there are windows that have been painted over, windows painted black decades ago.

I have all the time I need, he thinks. *And the world, when I am done, will be as simple and solid as those panes, as perfectly, rationally opaque.*

But then the shadow of something immense and winged stretches itself across the row of windows, the shadow of something a hundred times darker than any shade of paint, darker than the eye of man can even see. *The color of absence*, Jordan thinks as the windows explode and the ebony shards rain down over him.

Even as he falls toward the floor and the cowering man caught in the single pool of light, Jared knows he's too late, that the storm and his injuries have slowed him down enough that some crucial chance has been missed, that something has gone horribly and completely wrong. And then he sees her face, Lucrece's pale face staring up at him through the razor torrent of falling glass, and her eyes are as dead as any eyes that ever looked out blindly from the head of a corpse. In the instant it takes him to reach the ground he sees the rest of it, exactly what has been done to her and the body of the dead detective and the words printed neatly across the floor.

He lands as smoothly as a cat, dropping to all fours as the last of the broken windows smashes to powder against the concrete around him. The skinny, frightened man has fallen, cut and bleeding from a hundred different wounds, and is scrambling frantically away from Jared across the factory floor. The crow flaps past Jared, a living missile of sleek black feathers, and dives for the fleeing killer.

"*No!*" the man screams as Jared stands. "No, I stopped you!" The crow has reached the man and is pecking viciously at arms and hands raised protectively over his head.

Jared looks back once at Lucrece and he knows that if anything but sour rage remained in him, even a faint speck of light, that the sight of her hanging there has burned it from him forever.

"I can't kill you slowly enough," he says, turning toward the man who murdered Benny, the man who killed Lucrece, the man he still has no name for. "Not to pay for half of what you've done to me and the people I loved."

The man swats wildly at the crow and scrambles another foot toward the open door.

"But I'm making you a promise, motherfucker. You can be sure that I'm going to try."

And then Jared sees the stainless-steel semiautomatic pistol clutched in the man's scratched and bleeding hands, sees the man's finger wrapped around the trigger. Before he can even shout a warning, the gun goes off and the crow falls in a heap of broken bones and blood-soaked feathers. She shudders once and the gun fires again, blowing off her head.

It is as if whatever life-substitute has animated Jared's cells, whatever dragged him from the grave and kept him moving for two days, is abruptly taken away, the strings on the marionette severed in one clean snip. Jared falls, breathless, to his knees.

"*No*, I said!" and now the man is screaming at the top of his lungs and there are flecks of spittle flying from his thin lips. "I *beat* you! I *beat* you," and then the pistol goes off a third time, splattering what's left of the crow in two or three different directions.

Jared's vision blurs and begins to fade out around the edges. He struggles desperately with the zipper on the back of the leather hood but it sticks. Finally the fabric rips, tears free open along a weak seam, and he pulls the mask off and collapses, curls himself into a fetal ball on the glass-littered concrete, a pathetic, hurting thing made of dead flesh unable to die.

The man with the gun is laughing, an awful, hysterical laugh that says everything there is to be said about insanity without using a single word. He turns away from the crow, apparently satisfied that she's truly, irretrievably dead, and he points the gun at Jared.

"What am I going to have to *do* before you start to take me seriously?" he yells. "Before you figure out that you can't win? That I'm never going to fucking stop?" Then he gets a look at Jared's ruined face and recognition washes slowly across his deranged features.

201

"Oh," he says, all the laughter draining out of his voice, and he takes a step away from Jared. "No. You're not him. He's dead."

Jared opens his mouth to tell the man to fuck off, to ram the gun up his ass, but all he manages is a dry, strangling sound.

"There are *rules*," the man says incredulously, unbelieving. "There are rules that even They cannot violate, rules that bind even Their hands. Jared Poe is dead and the dead stay that way.

"I have no idea what kind of trick this is, my friend. But it isn't going to work. I know better," and he pulls the trigger and puts a bullet in Jared's chest. Ribs disintegrate, become shrapnel, puncturing his heart and lungs. Jared rolls over onto his back, coughing up gouts of arterial blood.

"I *know* the rules."

The next shot tears into Jared's belly and the bullet shatters his spine.

"No matter *how* much They twist and bend them, no matter how They try to cheat the natural order . . . I am pure of mind and body and I know the goddamn rules!"

Jared vomits another mouthful of blood and stares helplessly up at the thin and raving man. He opens his mouth and the words come slowly, slogging their way out of him in a sticky red trickle.

"Then kill me," he croaks. "If you . . . if you know the rules . . . then kill me."

The man chews uncertainly at his lower lip. Jared can see his Adam's apple bob up and down as he swallows. He leans over and puts the gun to Jared's forehead, presses its barrel an inch above the hole Harrod's pistol has already made in Jared's face.

"No," he says a moment later. "That's not why you're here. You're here to kill me, but you couldn't." The gun moves away as he stands up straight again. "Whatever you really are, I need to know the things you know. I need to know about the bird and the visions They've made me see."

The man's eyes almost seem to glimmer, like a child gazing deep into a bag filled with Halloween candy or someone poised on the brink of an abyss who has just grasped the concept of bottomlessness. He thumbs the safety switch on the gun and stuffs it into the band of his trousers.

And then there's the taut, staccato sound of ropes snapping and the man looks up, past Jared, and begins to scream.

Lucrece has no way of knowing how long she's been drifting in the gray places, minutes or weeks, floating weightless through mists the color of papier-mâché, cold mists that smell faintly of brine and pressed flowers. There is no up or down here, and only the vaguest sense of her body. Occasionally she remembers herself, or recalls the memory of herself, and hesitantly touches fingertips to her face to be sure that she's still there.

There's a faint tugging sensation at her feet, and that's all that might pass for direction. When she stares off that way, squints hard to try to see something through the insubstantial tendrils of the mist, she thinks that maybe there's a light there, far away. It seems warm, a soft, faintly pulsating point in a place where all other points are the same. And it would be so easy, she knows, to go to it, to fall through millennia and distances past perceiving, to let it swallow her the way it's meant to swallow everything in the end. To give up the pain and the weight of being in exchange for a brilliant, flickering moment of peace before oblivion.

Lucrece folds her arms about her chest, pulls her knees up close to her body, and looks away from it.

"This is a bunch of hippie bullshit," she says, and her voice seems to fill the entire universe, all the empty space eager to be filled, the sulking mist jealous of the light and its hoarding appetite.

For an instant or an hour the light flares, bathes her in a wash of its comfort, a gentle cascade of heat filled with promises. Lucrece closes her eyes, or only remembers what it's like to close her eyes, remembering Benny and Jared, remembering the man and his sharp and cutting tools, and she shakes her head.

"No," she says. "You can keep it. I don't want it now."

The warmth is taken away and there's a sudden rustling, like a rain of autumn leaves. Something rubs itself brusquely across her face, something musty and dry that tickles and makes her flinch, and when Lucrece opens her eyes again she's standing in a grove of dead and withered trees. The mist presses in close on every side, roils like alien storm clouds, as if this is only the most tenuous oasis and might be reclaimed at any moment. But at least there's solid ground beneath her feet, even if it's only cracked and barren earth that's never known rain. A breeze blows through the limbs and sets them to rattling, sweeps up an ashy dust that settles around Lucrece like a shroud.

And the trees are filled with crows.

A hundred or a thousand pairs of golden eyes, eyes like amber beads, watching her, patient as time.

"Send me back," she says, not asking, demanding, not caring if they can hear the anger in her voice, the acid contempt. "Send me back to help Jared."

They turn as one, releasing her from their glare, and look together into the highest branches of the tallest of the trees. Lucrece looks with them and sees the one they've turned to face, perched above them all: a crow so black, so impossibly enormous that he might have been the very first, the incarnation of age clothed in ragged black feathers. His eyes burn with a hundred million years of collected sunlight and starlight. And he knows her name.

"I have the right to ask," she says.

The great bird spreads his wings and a raucous cry rises up from the others, a cry that Lucrece understands is laughter, bitter, wicked laughter at her temerity, that she would dare to demand what is theirs alone to give. She looks away, unable to bear the sound or the glare of those ancient, piercing eyes. She glances down at her bare, dusty feet. Now there is something on the ground just in front of her, a barely recognizable smear of drying blood and feathers, and she knows that it's the corpse of Jared's crow.

The great bird folds his wings again, quieting the others, and she can hear him speaking inside her head.

One of us has already died for your brother, he says. *A single sacrifice is sufficient for his soul.*

She doesn't reply, can only stare at the dead crow at her feet, trying to recall what Aaron Marsh read from the old German manuscript, afraid to even wonder what has happened to Jared if his crow has been killed.

We will not give another.

"For those who have the symbol," Lucrece says, "the passage is easy." She forces herself to look up, to face those judging eyes and again the court of crows caws and croaks its scorn for her.

"For those who have the symbol, the passage is easy," she repeats, and turns to show them the scar across her back.

They're screaming now, furious, insulted bird voices raised in confusion and outrage, anger to match even her own. Lucrece knows better than to turn toward them again. She imagines them descending on her, their stabbing beaks and battering wings punishing her impudence. But she's been torn apart before and there are things she's more afraid of.

Then I'll take you myself, woman, and we'll be done with this. But if you fail . . .

"I *won't* fail," she says.

Without warning, this small wasted patch of ground is split silently apart. Lucrece is plunging, ferried on strong black wings that have made this trip too many times to count. They pass through fire and chilling cold places that have never known light, soar above nameless starving atrocities that snatch at them with claws of iron and ivory. And in the end Lucrece has no time to regret or be afraid for herself, only enough time to prepare for whatever's waiting at the end of the journey.

Lucrece raises her head and opens her eyes, and the man who calls himself by the names of rivers fills his lungs and screams again and again. The knots he tied so carefully are unraveling and the ropes are ripping loose, snapping like sewing thread. In another moment her hands and ankles are free and she drops to the floor.

Jared has managed to roll over and he too can see her and the crow, as big as a raven, bigger, big as a fucking vulture, perched on her shoulder. The man tries to move but his legs are paralyzed and useless and all he can do is watch as the organs heaped at her feet begin to twitch and slide toward Lucrece. The blood itself flows backward, pours over the rims of the buckets and flows like a retreating red tide across the floor. It all rises as if suspended on invisible wires, a puppet show for ghouls. Everything the man has taken from her, every bit of flesh and every drop of spilled blood, becomes a swirling, living cloud, rushing to refill the empty cavity of Lucrece's body.

She throws back her head and the sound that pours from her mouth makes the killer's screams seem as insignificant as a whisper. When the air is clean of her, when Lucrece is once again whole, the slash that his scalpels and bone saws have made closes itself up, knits itself shut with flesh that has become as fluid and impervious as water. She sinks to her knees, gasping, and the killer draws the Beretta and flips off the safety.

"Lucrece!" Jared shouts, but the gun goes off before she can move, blowing a hole in her left shoulder. The huge crow leaps into the air and flaps safely away into the shadows, and Jared watches as the bullet hole heals before his eyes.

Lucrece stands up then, and her lips are curled back from her white teeth in a terrible inhuman snarl, an animal smile for the man still pointing his useless gun at her.

"You're going to have to do better than that, Jordan," she says. "You're going to have to do a whole hell of a lot better than that."

He pulls the trigger again and the right side of her face dissolves in a spray of blood and splintered bone, a gaping wound that vanishes almost as quickly as it appeared. Lucrece shakes her head and takes a deep breath; the smile never leaves her lips.

"That's a pretty goddamn cool trick, isn't it, Jordan?" She takes a step toward the man.

"*Stop!*" he screams. "Stop right this fucking minute." Now he is pointing the gun at Jared.

"Oh, fuck this," Jared says. "Finish this tired bullshit, Lucrece. Get it over with."

206

"You can't kill him, Jordan. And you can't kill me." Before the man can move she takes the gun from his hand and flings it away into the darkness beyond the glare of the floodlight. "You're never going to kill anyone ever again."

Lucrece grips the man by the front of his shirt and lifts him into the air. She holds him almost a foot off the floor, his feet kicking uselessly at nothing.

"How does it feel?" she asks. "How does it feel to dangle with your life in someone else's hands?"

"I am the river . . ." he wheezes. She slaps him so hard that his upper lip splits and his front teeth snap off at the gum line.

"No, you're not, Jordan," she says. "But we've already been through all this once and I don't feel like saying it again. It really doesn't make any difference anymore what you think."

She drops him, but before the man can run she catches him by the back of his collar and shoves him to the floor next to Jared. He moans and tries to scramble away, but Lucrece holds him still.

"I think we have to do this together, Jared," she says. "Or one of us is screwed."

From somewhere in the shadows the crow caws a coarse affirmation. And all around them the storm howls and bellows. Cold rain is blowing in through the broken windows overhead and the walls of the old factory have begun to buckle and groan from the force of the wind.

"Thanks for coming back for me, Lucrece," Jared says as she begins to grind Jordan flat against the concrete. "You didn't have to . . ."

"Yes, I did, Jared," she replies. "Yes, I did."

As the factory that has stood for more than a hundred years beneath the baking delta sun begins to come apart around them, as the floor drops away beneath them and the walls are broken by the hurricane's fury, they crush the life from the man that has robbed each of them of the thing that they loved above all else. Satisfied, the crow rises into the storm-maddened night and the circle closes in the shriek of twisting metal and the crash of falling bricks.

ten

THROUGH THE CYCLOPS EYE OF THE HURRICANE LUCRECE CAR-
ries Jared's body away from the ruin and rubble of the fallen
factory. She follows the crow as it flies high above the devas-
tated city, wades past overturned cars and the unclaimed
corpses of the freshly drowned. When they reach Prytania
Street, Benny is waiting for them just outside the gates of
Lafayette No. 1. He smiles gently for them, the same gentle
smile that Lucrece has kept inside her for so long, preserved in
the imperfect scrapbook of her memories.

Benny bends and kisses Jared, presses his lips to his lover's.
Jared's eyes flutter open and tears roll down his grateful cheeks.

"Is it over?" he asks.

Benny nods. "It's over."

And then Benjamin DuBois kisses his sister's cheek and the
three of them walk together past the other monuments, all the
other names engraved in weathered marble and granite, stone
worn smooth by time and sorrow.

Outside the crumbling cemetery walls, as the backside of
Michael's spinning eye wall reaches the city, the lull in the
storm passes, and for the unfortunate living, the long night of
rain and anguish begins.

epilogue

Aaron Marsh nibbles on a space cake as he leafs through an ornithological tome in Dutch, which he is teaching himself from the inside out. He has a little flat high above Prinsengracht with a nice view of the canal if he leans out and cranes his neck a little. The afternoon sky is like damp gray wool. An intermittent autumn rain spits against the thick glass of his window. He has come to love it here.

Aaron got out of New Orleans the night before Hurricane Michael hit, packing only the dodo in its oversized velvet traveling case and catching a Greyhound bus, the one form of transport that never seemed to stop running. At first he'd only gone as far as Birmingham, Alabama, where he stayed with friends and watched the destruction of his adopted home from afar. He felt very little emotion, even when he learned that the Eye of Horus was a total loss. The water had taken nearly everything and destroyed whatever it left behind. But he'd kept the place well insured, and the payoff might last him the rest of his life, provided he didn't live too long. The only things he really regretted losing were the books.

He found that he had no desire to return. This only intensified a week later, when he saw a news item from New Orleans

211

about two bodies discovered in a warehouse near the river. They'd been on an upper floor and hadn't gotten washed away. Bodies were everywhere, of course, but these attracted media attention when one of them was identified as the cop who'd supposedly confessed to the new Ripper slayings.

There was some doubt about the cop's confession anyway. Several of his colleagues testified that he was a good solid detective, that they could alibi him for the dates of the murders, that the letter wasn't even in his handwriting. Suspicion fell on the other corpse, who turned out to own a Riverside mansion full of the flooded remains of some very sick shit. The cop was given a hero's funeral. The other fellow was still being looked into.

Thanks to a couple of persistent queer activist groups and a sympathetic reporter from the *Times-Picayune*, Jared Poe was finally and publically declared innocent of the Bourbon Street Ripper killings. When he heard of this, Aaron thought for a moment of beautiful, sad Lucrece DuBois and her strange predawn visit to his shop. He wondered what had become of her in the midst of all this hoopla. Mostly, though, he acted like the selfish old man he was, traveling where he liked, pleasing only himself, putting the pieces of his life in order. He has fetched up here in Amsterdam and believes he will stay.

Tap. Tap. Tap. The rain must be getting harder. Aaron glances at the window, and his hand freezes in the act of turning a page.

It is only a small crow, but it's peering in at him as if it has urgent business here—and perhaps it does. Even from this distance Aaron can see that it's carrying a tiny scroll of paper in its beak.

He stands up slowly, crosses to the window and hesitates only a moment before turning the latch. The window swings out and the bird hops in, glancing up at him almost apologetically, as if to say, *I know I'm dripping all over the place, I'll only stay a minute . . .*

"Make yourself at home," he says, holding out his hand. The crow drops the scroll into Aaron's wrinkled palm as if relieved to be done with it, stretches its wings and shakes out its feathers, glances around the room. It is just beginning to look comfortable when its eye lights upon the stuffed dodo in its gleaming glass case.

The crow gives a single strangled caw of horror, hops backward and disappears through the open window in a black fluster.

"Ah, well," says Aaron and unrolls the paper.

He recognizes the flowing hand at once; Lucrece DuBois came to him with plenty of shopping lists. There are five words only and room for no more, in ink the color of dried blood. But they are five words that will stay with him as long as he lives:

Sometimes fairy tales come true.

Watch out for other books in *The Crow* series
published by *Voyager*

The Crow:
Clash by Night

Chet Williamson

Based on the characters by James O'Barr

The Eternal One.

A crazed militia has planted a bomb in a daycare centre
and a dedicated teacher discovers it just in time to get
herself and the children to safety.

Almost. For we are in the dark universe of The Crow,
where the innocent must die so that justice can triumph.
Where a woman devoted to peace must don camouflage
as she prowls with her black-winged familiar through
the tangled underworld of hate on a search-and-destroy
mission that leads her from gun shows to the rubble of the
disaster.

A rubble that is stirring with new and hideous life . . .

ISBN 0 00 648366 6